THE GARDEN OF ADONIS

The GARDEN *of* ADONIS

By

CAROLINE GORDON

NEW YORK

COOPER SQUARE PUBLISHERS, INC.

1971

Originally Published 1937
Copyright © 1937 by Caroline Tate
Reprinted by Permission of Charles Scribner's Sons
Published 1971 by Cooper Square Publishers, Inc.
59 Fourth Avenue, New York, N. Y. 10003
International Standard Book No. 0-8154-0399-2
Library of Congress Catalog Card No. 70-164530

Printed in the United States of America, by
Noble Offset Printers, Inc. New York, N.Y. 10003

To

MARGARET and PAUL CAMPBELL

These [the gardens of Adonis] were baskets or pots filled with earth in which wheat, barley, lettuces, fennel, and various kinds of flowers were sown and tended for eight days, chiefly or exclusively by women. Fostered by the sun's heat, the plants shot up rapidly, but having no root they withered as rapidly away, and at the end of eight days were carried out with the images of the dead Adonis and flung with them into the sea or into springs. . . .

SIR JAMES G. FRAZER: *The Golden Bough.*

THE GARDEN OF ADONIS

CHAPTER ONE

THE DOOR was gray with age and streaked with green mold. Unlatched and sagging on its hinges, it swung towards them a little in the wind. Ote kicked it back against the wall and held it there with his foot while his mother and father passed before him with their burdens. Joe Mortimer was carrying the parts of a bedstead and Nora, his wife, had pressed against her bosom the bushel basket that held all their kitchen utensils. Their figures, the man's and the woman's, hung black for a moment in the bright square of the doorway, then they moved on into the half light of the room. Ote set the heavy box of fruit jars down so that it propped the door open, and followed them into the house.

The great room was lit only by one window but little patches of light came down through the chinks in the chimney and spattered on to the cold hearthstone. Ote strode across the room and flung the window open. Taking out his pocket knife he slashed off the boughs of a little poplar tree that pushed up breast high against the sill.

"Need all the light you can get in here," he said.

Joe Mortimer had set the bedstead up and was standing now looking through the open doorway in mild disapproval. "Folks going away they ought to fasten up," he said. "Don't look right to leave a house standin open to anybody comes along the road."

Ote gave a short laugh. "Ain't nothin in this house anybody could steal." He walked over and stirred with the tip of his brogue a heap of rags that lay darkly in one corner of the room. "Naw," he said, "they ain't left nothin here anybody'd trouble to take."

His mother, on her knees, unpacking the fruit jars, turned around and gestured towards some shelves that were fitted into the embrasure between the chimney and the fireplace. "I'm glad them Sheelers didn't tear them shelves down," she said. "Hit's the only place in this house whar a person can set fruit and the dogs not git at it."

Her husband gazed at the black, worn boards. "Them shelves was in thar when we first come here to live," he said; "them very shelves. Hit's a wonder now nobody ain't torn them down."

Mrs. Mortimer crushed the newspaper wrappings of the fruit jars together and threw the ball into the fireplace. "Them Sheelers was nasty," she said, "nasty about everything they done."

Ote walked out on to the porch. The flooring rattled under his feet. He stepped aside to avoid a great hole in one of the broad planks. "An old house," he thought, "rotten everywhere and 'bout to fall down. Worse'n the other one. Seems a pity now to be moving into a house worse'n the one you left. But the Old Man he couldn't expect to do no better. Seventy years old if he was a day. No, he couldn't expect to do no better. . . ."

He went down the path to where the mules stood, docile before the high-loaded wagon. He unfastened the trace chains and threw them over the mules' backs, then with two deft movements gathered all the gear together and pitched it to one side of the road. The mules took a step forward, then fell to eating the red clover that thrust through the crazy paling of the fence. A fine team, in good order, their winter coats still heavy on them. The furry side of one, the younger, was as yet ungalled by the trace chain. He remembered how as children he and his brother, Joe, had watched the young mules being broken to work, had watched how in the spring the heavy hair sank closer and closer to the side under the sliding of the trace chain until finally it was all gone and there was only the sleek hide, shining like oiled leather. They were grown then, Joe said. A mule was old, time he done that much work.

He patted the young mule on the neck. She put her ears back and lowered her head. He stepped aside expertly, laughing. "You would, would you?" It occurred to him that this was the first time he'd had his hands on a mule for—how long was it?—three years now. He looked down at his blunt, grease-stained fingers that were still sunk in the mule's coat. When he had first gone into the automobile factory his shoulders, his back, even his legs had ached more from inaction than ever they had ached from a long day in the field. It seemed to him that it was only his hands that were alive. And once he had a terrible dream. Dead he was and lying in his coffin, only the coffin was the same board that he lay on during his working hours. But even though he was dead the chassis kept moving on over him just the same and as each chassis arrived his living hands reached up out of his dead body to screw on the bolt. The same bolt he had screwed on for eight hours a day for nearly a year. He would be screwing it on now if they hadn't laid him off. He had been one of the first to go, of course. But in the end they had laid the good mechanics off just as fast as the others. That Pendleton who ate at Mrs. Farris' and hadn't brought his wife and children up from Alabama yet. He remembered that man's face across the table, the dark eyes that stared at their own news, the hands that like the spinning belt of an engine wove something continually in the air.

Ote had spoken out while the man was still talking. "Well, I ain't goin to wait for them to lay me off. I'm goin back to the farm."

The man laughed. "Hell! If you got a farm to go to."

Ote didn't have a farm but he knew one to go to. He had thought at first that it would be the Proctor place. The Old Man had lived at Proctor's for five years. He had made one or two good tobacco crops there. Ote remembered one letter in which he said his share of the crop was five hundred dollars. But that must have been the first year he went there. He hadn't paid out now for two or three years. Mr. Proctor had carried him as long as he could before he told him he'd better find another home. It was hard for a man past seventy to find a home any time, but it was harder than usual this year. Some people weren't even making any trades. Let the land lay, they said. Warn't getting anything for their tobacco, anyhow, and it cost money to put a crop in. Luckily Mr. Proctors' new tenants had moved in late. Ote and his father and his mother had been able to stay in the cabin at Proctor's 'way past Christmas. New Year's had come and gone, Ground Hog Day, even, and Joe Mortimer hadn't made a trade. Mammy had fretted about not getting the ground broke for her garden and then somebody had told her there was a patch of mustard greens going to waste over at Hanging Tree. She had sent Ote over in the buggy to pick some. Mr. Ben Allard was down at the patch that morning. He sent Joe Mortimer word that he could have the old house by the spring if he wanted it.

4

The Garden of Adonis

The Old Man and Mister Ben hadn't traded yet. They didn't even know, Ote and his father, how much land they were going to work. There would be enough land to go around, though—only four other families—and the place was four hundred acres in all. But the Old Man wanted that field next to the house. He liked that field better than any other field on this side of the farm. The gum sink field was cold, he always maintained, and the new ground—the piece of land that had been cleared when Ote was eleven years old—was the poorest of all. It was funny: Joe Mortimer, no matter where he was living, always harked back in memory to this place. If he were cropping anywhere in the neighborhood he would ride over some time during the summer to look at the crops and, back at home, would compare the yields of the various fields, saying he could have told them not to put watermelons down by the branch if they'd only taken the trouble to ask his advice. But Old Man Mortimer had been born on this place. Perhaps a man always thought a lot of the first land he ever worked. It settled into his mind, somehow, so that no matter where he lived or what land he was working he was always comparing it to those fields he had known first as a boy.

He looked up. His father was standing in the doorway, shouting at him.

"You done lost all the sense you ever had, in town? Going to stand thar and let them mules cut the oats all to pieces?"

Ote started. He had not even seen the narrow strip of green that edged the field. He ran towards it now, shouting. "Hey, Hey! You git out of thar!"

The old mule backed off slowly, then broke and ran for the gate. The young mule followed. Ote wiped the perspiration from his face and started back towards the house. Joe

5

Mortimer had come down the path and was trying to corral the mules in a corner of the fence. Ote watched his father's bent figure dodging clumsily back and forth between the two mules. The Old Man was showing his age, showing it more this year than he ever had before. He was old, for a fact, to be still working in the field. But he had to, now all his boys were gone. Ote smiled a little, remembering how peremptorily his father's voice had rung out only the moment before. He could still get his dander up quick but he warn't nothing compared to what he used to be. Was a time when Joe Mortimer had four grown boys in the field: Joe, Ed, Albert and Berry. Five, counting him, Ote. Worked 'em, too, the Old Man did from kin to can't. Ote could remember Ed stumbling over him up there in the loft in what seemed the middle of the night. It was Ed's job to ring the farm bell. At four o'clock, sometimes three. The hands at Hanging Tree slept later these days. He had heard that Mister Ben had a shiftless crew.

The Old Man had driven the mules into the little rickety stable that stood a stone's throw from the house and yet under the shadow of the great spreading silver poplar tree. He propped the door shut with a forked stick and came over to the wagon. "Gimme a hand," he said; "we got to git these things in the house."

Ote lifted the body of the stove from out of the pile of household goods. With Joe's aid he balanced it on his shoulders and stuck a stovepipe under his arm. Joe followed with two rocking chairs.

Mrs. Mortimer saw them coming and hurried out to meet them. "Take it round," she cried shrilly. "Take it round to the back. Ain't no use in tracking up the house with soot."

In the lean-to Ote let one end of the stove down slowly on

to the battered square of zinc. Joe had bent over and was inserting the legs into the sockets. Ote set one length of pipe over the stub that protruded from the body of the stove, fitted the joint on to that and swung the whole neatly into place in the flue. Mrs. Mortimer, behind him, heaved a sigh of relief.

"*Well!* I never seen a stove go up as quick as that. Usually, takes everybody on the place and soot all over everything. But Ote, he always did have a knack."

Ote watched his mother ranging her pots and pans on the deal table. "Be nice now, Mammy, if you had a square of oilcloth to put on that," he said. "That lady I lived with in *D*etroit she had oilcloth on all her tables, blue, with figures on 'em." He paused. "She had oilcloth on the floor," he said; "Linoleum she called it."

Nora, fitting a small skillet into a larger one, spoke absently. "Oilcloth on the floor! Never heard of such a thing."

She left the kitchen and went into the larger room. Joe had gone back to the wagon and was coming up the path with the footboard of a bed under one arm, a little red rocking chair under the other. Nora laughed as he began setting the lounge bed up in the far corner of the room.

"I believe you done lost your mind, Pappy. Thar you go settin the chillun's bed up in that corner like the chillun was all still here."

Joe looked at her bewilderedly, then his face broke into a smile. "That bed, hit always set right thar," he said, "and thar's whar I was settin it."

"Ote can have a room to himself," Nora said. "Be a shame now, only three of us, for him to have to sleep in the room with the old folks."

Ote approached and taking the bed down leaned the pieces

up against the wall. "I'll set it up after dinner," he said. Sitting down on the window sill he regarded the picture his mother was hanging over the mantel shelf. A heavy picture in a tarnished gold frame. A young woman, a madonna they called her, sitting very straight in a big, carved chair. She had on a flowing robe and a kind of veil thing over her head. There was a year-old baby on her knee. The child was half turned around towards his mother but the woman looked straight over his head. Her eyes in the shadow of the veil were dark and mysterious. He remembered now that wherever you went they followed you. When he was a child they had looked straight across the room to where the little bed stood in this corner—the boy's bed. Mammy never let the girls and boys sleep in the same bed. May and Pearl slept in the other room and Joe and Albert upstairs but he and Berry, when he was little, had slept in the lounge bed here in this corner, at least in the winter time. But he could not ever remember going to sleep in this bed. He had been afraid of it. The carved wooden ball that surmounted the footboard had always seemed to him the grinning face of a devil, the fluting that ran from the end of the ball a lolling tongue, a worm hole in the center an evil eye just closing in a wink. He was uneasily conscious too that on the headboard there was another, larger devil's head. Doubtless they grinned back and forth at each other over his sleeping body. As a small child he had gone to sleep every night on the hearth rug or in somebody's lap but sooner or later they picked him up and put him into this bed. He waked then no matter how sleepy he was, and he stayed awake or slept only in snatches until the warm body of Berry falling into bed beside him took away the fear of devils.

He walked out on the porch. Joe Mortimer had dragged

a rocking chair up and was sitting there now smoking a pipe. He smiled placidly at Ote. "Ain't no use gittin in a swivet," he said. "Always takes two or three days to git settled."

Ote nodded. He watched his father's hand fumbling with the pipe. It was gnarled and the blue veins stood up in cords as if the flesh were shrinking away from them. "He can't do much in the crop," he thought, and then feeling the strength in his own body, "well, one thing, I'm strong. Strong enough for two. . . ."

He jerked a sack of Bull Durham from out of his shirt pocket. While his hands swiftly rolled the cigarette his eyes travelled the road that ran from the old house back into the farm. An offshoot of the big road it was now but the older of the two: the old post road he had heard people call it. It ran along one whole side of the sixty-acre field, then turning sharply to the right, dipped down into a wooded hollow. That hollow was on the outskirts of the small stretch of woodland that lay between this house and the Big House. In the old days they put the house in the middle of the farm, no matter how far you had to go to get to it. Must be mighty inconvenient now when people rode in cars. That little stretch of road was wet even in summer. And there was one place where even a buggy could get stuck.

Miss Fanny's buggy had got stuck that day and he and Ed and Frank Allard had had to push her out. The storm had come up suddenly and was over as suddenly. A cloudburst. It had swollen the branch and had started little streams of water down all the gullies. He and Ed had stood there in the doorway watching the rain beat down. The minute it stopped they lit out for the branch. Frank Allard and Letty were already there. They didn't have so far to come. They had forgotten that Miss Fanny had started off for Mr. Rufus Crenfew's right after dinner. The four of them had gone to work building a dam. Suddenly there was the sound of wheels and Miss Fanny was looking down at them from the high buggy seat, the little nigger beside her grinning as if he knew what was to come.

"Get in," she said, "get in here this minute"; and when Letty protested that they were wet and would get her wet she said: "Well, stand up behind then. Letty Allard, you want to get a good whipping?"

Letty had stood up behind and Frank had squeezed in beside the little nigger. Old Eagle pulled the buggy through the branch, all right, but he couldn't make it through that clayey stretch on the other side. Miss Fanny had had to get out and stand in the mud while the three boys and the little nigger pushed the buggy with Letty still in it up on to high ground.

Miss Fanny got in then and hustled Frank in. The buggy disappeared quickly around the bend in the road but their voices had drifted back:

". . . No, I don't want 'em coming to the house and I don't want you going down there. . . . You want to catch the itch?"

But the next day she had walked down to the mail and had sat right here on this porch to eat a fried pie that Mammy had just taken out of the skillet. He and his brothers and sisters had never played with Frank and Letty after that. They didn't have to. There was enough of *them* to play 'mongst themselves. It was Frank and Letty that was lonesome. They would have run off to play with the Mortimer children. Time and again they tried it. But Ed wouldn't let them. Just stood in the middle of the road and looked at them. "You better

go home. . . . Your mammy might be calling you. . . ."
And they would turn around and walk back to the house.

He shoved the sack of tobacco into his pocket and lit his
cigarette. His father was leaning forward in his rocking chair
to peer down the road.

"They's somebody comin. Somebody from the House."

Ote watched a car detach itself from the dark of the woods.
It came up over the rise and halted. A man was descending
from it.

"It's Mister Ben," Ote said, "it's Mister Ben Allard."

CHAPTER TWO

THE OLD Negress put her head in at the door. "Mister Ben, you goin for Miss Letty, you better git started."

The man at the desk looked up from the calculations he was making on a torn slip of paper. His eyes rested on her vaguely for a moment, then they cleared. "Letty?" he said. "Goin right this minute. Git my hat."

She had brought his wide Panama with the frayed brim and was looking disapprovingly at his wrinkled cotton trousers and corduroy coat. "Ain't you goin to dress up, Mister Ben? You goin to town, ain't you goin to dress up?"

Allard had turned back to the desk and was regarding two pieces of machinery which lay on its surface, parts of a mower. He moved one of them nearer to the other, made a rotary motion with his hand. "Get that thing in there fixed and she'd cut all right," he said. "Dress up, Pansy? Well, maybe so. Miss Letty's mighty particular."

He disappeared into a dressing room that adjoined the enormous, cluttered bedroom and came out in a few minutes wearing a tweed golfing suit. The tweeds, originally of sturdy costly material, were weathered to a rusty brown, torn in one or two places and discolored by stains. They had evidently been cut to a larger frame than his and hung on him loosely. He seemed dubious about the fit. Before leaving the room he advanced to a mirror and inspected himself.

"This suit don't fit as well as the last one," he remarked.

The old Negress in the doorway considered. "I was to tighten them pants up in the waistband maybe they wouldn't hang so long in the laig."

Allard, knotting his tie, shook his head. "Ain't no use in doing that. I like 'em loose."

He took the hat which she extended, clapped it on his head and went out the back way. A small roadster, its fenders and wheels plastered with drying mud, was drawn up at the back steps. A few yards away a Negro boy was turning a grindstone. Allard looked at him, seemed about to call him over, then shook his head. "Naw," he said, "I better drive myself."

He climbed in and, frowning, began to manipulate the gears. The smell of burning carbon rose and hung in the air. After a few false starts the car lurched forward. Allard with a sigh settled himself behind the wheel. For a few minutes he drove carefully with the nervous concentration of a man who is more used to handling horses than machinery. After a little he relapsed into his abstracted mood. As he drove along, his thoughts emerged in mutterings, snatches of a conversation he seemed to be having with some imaginary person.

"I know that, Mr. Woodward. I know all about that. . . . Naw, I don't want you to do any more'n you can do. I don't want any man to do more'n he feels he can do. . . . Last August? You bet I remember. But God, man, I ain't a weather bureau. How'd I know it was going to hail in August? On a farm you got to keep taking chances. . . ." The mutterings merged into humming, then broke out again: *"Well, say you sell me out next spring. You ain't going to get*

your money back. All you've done is broke me and you ain't helped yourself any, far as I can see. . . ." There was a pause then a sigh. "Six hundred dollars is running it close but yes, I can get my crop out, with six hundred dollars. . . ."

Approaching a gate he broke off. The car under his nervous manipulation veered to the left, then came to an abrupt halt. Allard looked down, saw that the left fender rested against the heavy oak king post. He backed the car, halted again, then climbed out. He spoke aloud: "Trouble with these damn things, you got to keep your eye on 'em every minute."

When he had driven the car through and had closed the gate he pulled his watch out, stood irresolute a second, then turned off into a path that led along the side of the field. He pursued the path until he reached the end at the fence corner. The fence corner was littered with shavings and here and there cigarette butts had been trampled into the grass. Allard stopped and turned one over with his foot. It had been dropped here three days ago when he had been here with the two men from town. It did not seem that long ago or perhaps it seemed longer, a lifetime or a minute, a period, anyhow, not to be measured as time is ordinarily measured. He sat down on the top rail. From here one had a good view of the patch of oats and the rolling ground beyond it. But he was not looking at the oats or at the ground which would be re-broken soon for tobacco. He was frowning as he tried to recall the scene exactly. He had been sitting here, whittling on a sassafras bough, when he saw the two men come up over the rise, the fat banker, Woodward, puffing a little, Simpson, the bank's "farm manager" he called himself—it had got to the point nowadays where they felt that if they lent you money they had a right to tell you how to run your farm—Simpson, getting over the ground with more ease than Woodward and looking about knowingly as he came. They had been passing by, they said, and Simpson wanted to take a look at the sheep. That, he supposed, was permissible. The flock, mortgaged to half its value, was as much the bank's property as his own.

Well, they had looked at the sheep and Simpson had wanted to know if he wasn't late in shearing them. He didn't bother with Simpson much, just looked him in the eye once, saying: "Mr. Simpson, any fool knows that you don't shear sheep before the fourteenth of May unless you want them all to lie down and die on you." Simpson had had a lot to say after that but he, Ben, had paid no attention. He had been thinking all the time of his note, overdue a month now at the bank. He had been wondering why Woodward had come out to see him about it. It would have been more businesslike, surely, to sit there in his bank until he, Ben Allard, came in to beg him to renew the note. He would have done it, all right. He had just put it off day after day in the way now that he was getting older he constantly put off disagreeable things. He had intended to do it next week and he hadn't really visualized the possibility that Woodward would refuse him.

The idea came to him, suddenly, in the midst of some remark of Simpson's. As if a voice, the voice of a fourth person, had spoken out there in the field: *"To sell you out. That's what they've come for. To sell you out."*

He had, of course, expected that always, or at least for the last ten years. But it had never been now, this spring. It had always been the next spring or the next. One crop away, anyhow. He had been so dazed by the thought that the thing so long expected was at last upon him that he hadn't been able to follow what Simpson was saying. He had just sat there whittling—his hands had moved mechanically all that time—and in those few minutes, whittling on the sassafras stick, he had known what it was to lose the farm. Yes, he had seen it, felt it drop away from him acre by acre until he stood up, a naked, landless man. A curious thing. As if the man in the light gray overcoat had waved his hand and a sea had crept up. He had watched it spread. The north field first, the meadow adjoining, then the woods and last of all this south field in which they sat. He had, he supposed, been clean out of his head, for a few seconds. At any rate he had been strangely occupied in wondering what would become of himself and Woodward and Simpson when the land was gone out from under them. Yes, he had pictured them retreating before the devouring tide, climbing the fence, setting foot on Bill Browder's land, moving on, on. It was then that he reached out and, touching the cedar bough beside him, was surprised to find it as solid as ever under his hand, as prickly, as brittle.

In the silence that there must have been, Woodward's voice had sounded—self-contained, equable, the voice of a man about to make a concession.

"Well, Ben, you expecting a good year?"

His revulsion had been so great that for a moment he had been afraid he would vomit. He heard himself speak irritably:

"God, man! I ain't a weather bureau."

There had been some talk after that, Simpson keeping discreetly silent. What it came down to was that if he got out a good crop, forty acres of tobacco at least, Woodward would let him have six hundred dollars. He hadn't cavilled at any of the arrangements. He could hear himself now, speaking reasonably, a tinge, perhaps, of fawning in his tones. "Yes, that's running it close but I can do it. I've got a pretty good force. Yes, I can get my crop out, on six hundred dollars."

They had left soon after that. He had sat there watching them plough their way over the muddy field. When the two heads had bobbed below the rim of the slope he had slid from his fence rail. He had stood up, flung his arms wide above his head. He had wanted to shout, to sing. He had actually checked an impulse to stoop down and touch the earth. Instead he went down to the barn and gave old Jim hell about letting a cow and calf get together. His voice must have given him away. The old Negro, while he protested his innocence, had slewed about on his stool to turn shrewd, smoky eyes on his master's face, and then had suddenly set off on a dogtrot for his cabin. The news that Mister Ben had staved off the mortgage again must have been all over the place that night. He remembered waking the next morning and hearing a Negro singing in the field, the first time in months.

He got down off the fence and took the path back along the field. He walked slowly, his eyes now roving the field, now bent absently on the path that was dappled with shade from the young trees growing beside the fence. Once where the shadows of two gigantic flower petals interlaced he stopped and looked up, surprised to find the boughs over his head white. Dogwood in bloom already! Letty would be sorry to miss it. She came down every spring and got branches of blossoms to put in the house.

As he walked along, faster now, his thoughts were on his daughter. She had been in Countsville three, no, four months now. Longer than she had ever been away from home before in her life. He wondered how anybody could bear to stay in a town that long, especially in the spring when there was so much coming on, so much to do. But a young girl, of course, didn't want to bury herself in the country. It was fortunate that she had pleasant places to visit.

He was back at the car. He got in and, not putting his mind on the operations this time, succeeded in starting the engine almost immediately. He settled back in his seat, feeling an agreeable sense of power as the car spun along the rutted road. He surmounted a little rise. The smoking chimneys of the Old House were before him. Involuntarily he slowed down. Always when he passed this place he had the feeling that he should be living here instead of in the other house at the end of the farm. It was, of course, because he had been born in that house and had spent his boyhood and his brief married life there. His married life? It had not lasted long. Eight years they had lived in the old house by the spring. . . . Then Rose had died.

In March it had been, when Frank was seven years old. They said that all young should be born in May. Letty would have been born then if things had gone right. He had been out in the field when the Negro girl came running. He had found Aunt Siny already at the house doing everything she could and somebody had had the sense to send a nigger boy on a horse for the doctor. It was Aunt Siny who had told him to go get Miss Fanny. Rose must have been dying then. . . .

He had run every step of the way to the new house. His mother was sitting on the porch, a chair drawn up in front of her, her workbasket on her knee. She must have known that something was wrong when she saw him running across the yard. And in those few seconds she had had time to decide what it was. He could swear that when he spoke there had been across her face a swift flash of something—not as strong as joy, rather, relief. It was as if while sorrowing—properly—for Rose's death, which in that instant must have been for her accomplished, she had leaped swiftly ahead in her mind to foresee what life would be like for her without Rose. . . . But when she got up she was shaking. He had had to give her an arm up out of her chair. "Seven months," she said as they went hurriedly across the lawn. "Seven months, that's the dangerous time," and then sharply: "Run in my room and get all those white rags out of the wardrobe drawer. . . ."

But Rose was dead when they got back to the old house. Dead, and the little red-faced baby filling the whole place with its squallings. The old lady had stepped over and had taken it from Aunt Siny's arms before she turned her attention to the woman on the bed. He had made her take it out of the room. He had made them all get out while he dropped down beside the bed. But her face on the pillow was white, her hand cold. He had not even felt she was in the room. After a while, he got up and went out on the porch. He remembered now how the white hot sunshine had blinded him . . . as if he had been coming up from the bottom of the sea. . . .

Three weeks later he had moved up to the big house. The baby was already there, of course, with her bottles and diapers and things. His mother had made him send away a hound dog that howled at the moon, because the baby was hard enough to get to sleep at night anyhow.

He could remember lying awake night after night in his old room upstairs, staring at the moon that rose up always at that window, and in the back of the house the baby's thin wailing going on and on until near daybreak a change would come over the whole house and you knew that everybody slept the brief sleep of exhaustion. After a while he had taken to hiding a bottle in an old stump there at the edge of the woods. He would walk down to it every night just before bedtime. His mother had got on to it, of course. "Never knew you to take such an interest in walking before, Ben," and once when the baby had left her less exhausted than usual in the evening she had said with a sardonic twinkle in her eye: " 'Bout time for your evening walk. Want me to go with you?"

It was funny. He had no real recollection of Letty as a baby but one memory—it might almost have been his first sight of her—was very vivid. He had been sitting in a chair under the sugar tree reading. They had left the baby sitting on a spread-out sheet, her play things all about her. His mother had cautioned him not to let her get anything in her mouth, so he had put down his book and had sat watching her. He had been watching her when she set out crawling slowly towards the edge of the sheet. He had intended to let her get to the edge before he hauled her back but she stopped at the chair, stopped and taking firm hold of it pulled herself to her full height. He could see her eyes now, dark and intent under the shadow of her high forehead, coming slowly up over the chair seat. They had stayed there a moment staring at each other before her grip gave way and she plopped back on her little bottom. He had recognized the achievement by picking her up and tossing her high above his head the way old Uncle Jim used to do to them when they were children. She crowed with delight but Miss Fanny and Aunt Siny had caught sight of him simultaneously and had both come running to take the child away from him. . . .

Letty had not been a particularly pretty child. Her features were indefinite, her coloring subdued except for the hazel eyes which had always seemed too large for a child's face.

But she had grown up to those eyes, had bloomed out considerably in the last few years until now, he supposed, she was considered a beauty. No—he suddenly made a distinction—Letty was not beautiful. She was pretty. Her mother now had been a beauty, would be still if she were living, for beauty such as hers is not dependent on youthful bloom but inheres in the structure of the face. Her hair that waved softly over her head and was knotted at the nape of her neck—no, she had worn it higher than that, a Psyche knot they called it—her rather large blue eyes with dark lashes, her high-bridged, perfect little nose. Those features alone would have made a beauty out of any woman. And she was sweet, sweet and winsome. A winsomeness that his mother, his sisters, none of the women of his family had had. He thought sometimes that he detected traces of it in Letty but it was fleeting as if the spirit of her mother had flashed through her a moment and was gone.

Letty did not resemble either her mother or her father. She looked, as a matter of fact, more like his own old sweetheart, Maggie Carew, than anybody in the family. His mother when she was living had made enough of that. He remembered the day she had made the discovery, a few years before her death, when Letty was only ten years old. Watching the child coming up the walk she had said suddenly, "Good Lord, that child looks like Maggie Carew." He had not looked at her but he had known that her shrewd old eyes were fixed on him. He had said calmly, "Nothing strange in that, is there?" There was nothing strange in it. Rose and Maggie Carew were own first cousins. The resemblance had bothered his mother more than it ever had him. She had always thought that it was the Maggie Carew affair that had kept him a bachelor for ten years, so that he had been a man of thirty-five when he married Rose, still in her twenties.

His mind went back to that old sorrowful time when he had been in love with Maggie Carew, then veered away quickly as it had done often these forty years. The things a man could live through, could live down in this life! . . . Well, he could never have done it if it hadn't been for Rose. . . .

He had arrived at the back door of the tenant house. There was nobody in sight, but the sound of measured rocking came from the front. He walked around the house and stepped up on the porch. Mrs. Mortimer looked up from the black-eyed peas she was shelling and fixed him with near-sighted very blue eyes. The furrows in her forehead relaxed. She smiled warmly: "Mist' Ben! I declar I didn't know who you was for a minute."

She rose clumsily, still clutching the newspaper that held the pea pods, and pushed a chair towards him with her foot. A large woman whose black hair was already going gray. And fatter than she had been last time she lived here. The waistband of her checkered apron cut like a cord into the roll of flesh about her middle. Nora O'Donnell she had been, the great-granddaughter of the old miller, Bracy. Good folks, the Bracys and the O'Donnells too.

He smiled at her cordially. Waving the chair aside he sat down on the floor with his back against a post. "I thought y'all'd be just about moving in today," he said.

Mrs. Mortimer rocked gently, her lips still creased in a smile. "Yas sir. I said to 'em if you goin might as well go now. 'T'ain't no use settin around a place once you make up your mind to leave. And I'm one that likes to get my garden in early. . . . Got the ground broke yet for your garden?"

Allard shook his head. He took his pipe out. Sitting up straight he swung his legs down on to the ground. "I'm not much on these early gyardens," he said. "Half the time the seed rots in the ground. There's a good growing spell comes along in April. If you get your gyarden in then it'll grow right off and if you don't get it in then you ain't goin to have much of a gyarden no matter what you do."

Mrs. Mortimer compressed her lips. "That's right," she said, "for ever'thing but peas. Now I get my English peas in first warm spell in February. Come early or late I get 'em in then and I have the name of raisin right good peas. . . . Mister Ben, the prettiest pea patch I ever seen was right back of the house, here. It was when the twins were babies. I mind what a time we had keepin 'em from pickin the bloom. . . . But that was a long time ago. . . ."

Allard turned about so that he faced her. Nora, he thought, had always had more sense than her husband, more *judgment*. And she never made trouble with the other tenants. A good woman to have on the place. "Well, I'm glad to see y'all back," he said heartily. "You didn't like it so well, over there, eh?"

She pursed her lips. "I liked and I didn't like," she said, "but it's like I tell 'em, Mist' Ben. It takes all kinds to make a world."

"You know these folks we got here on the place now?" he asked. "Named Sheeler. They're Stewart County folks."

Mrs. Mortimer shook her head. "I don't what you might call know any Stewart County folks," she said. "I never stepped my foot into Stewart County in my life, Mist' Ben, and that's a fact."

"That so?" he said absently. "Well, they raise mighty good tobacco over there. Looks like it's better'n ours. Poor as the land is, looks like they can raise better tobacco." He smiled at the woman. "They work it harder, I reckon."

"Joe, he says you couldn't hire him to make a tobacco crop in Stewart County," Mrs. Mortimer said. "Could give him the whole of Stewart County and he'd ne'er put a plow in it. Says if I got to work gi'me good land. And Ote, he's the same way. Looks like you been raised to work good land you can't bear to fool with no other. Now this land here it suits Joe. Looks like wherever he's alivin he's always tellin me 'bout what he raised at Hangintree. I said to him when we moved here, I said . . ." She raised her voice as her husband and son came around the corner of the house, "Joe, I was just sayin to Mist' Ben, now you done got back to Hangintree I hope you going to stay satisfied. . . ."

Allard got up as the two men approached. If Nora had taken on flesh Joe Mortimer had lost it. He was thinner than Allard had ever seen him before and more stooped. Well, he was getting along in years and he had worked hard in the field all his life. Ote was an upstanding young fellow, built more like his mother than his father. He had her Irish blue eyes and the same broad, comely face. The O'Donnells were probably better stock than the Mortimers. Joe looked much more like a poor white man than Ote did. Mortimer . . . He wondered how poor white folks came to have such a fine name. You saw it in Shakespeare . . . and what was it in English history about Mortimers?

"Well, Joe," he said, "I'm glad to see you. . . . This your youngest boy, ain't it?" The men shook hands. Allard resumed his seat on the floor. Young Mortimer sat facing him, leaning against the other post. Joe Mortimer stood beside them a moment, then stepped down off the porch and picked up a stick from under one of the trees. He came back and took the vacant chair and drawing his knife out fell to whittling. Looking at Allard he addressed his wife:

"And who was it wanted to move away from Proctor's?" Nora tossed her head. "And who is it wouldn't be wantin to move off from a place like that?" she asked.

Allard thought she looked very Irish, her chin suddenly firm where her neck was uplifted and her beautiful blue eyes gleaming. All the Mortimers, the O'Donnells, rather, had Irish turns of speech. But it was not long since they had come over from the old country. Nora's father, Jerry O'Donnell, had landed in this country just in time for the Civil War and had fought all the way through it, with old Cousin John Llewellyn. He had come home from the war with Cousin John and had lived at Penhally till he died. It was at Penhally that he had married Nora's mother, Cordy Bracy. A strong friendship had lasted all their lives between the two men. He had heard Cousin Lucy speak of it laughingly: "Of course John has a good many friends but his *dearest* friend is Jerry O'Donnell. . . ."

". . . and the water runnin right into the kitchen whenever it rained," Nora said, "Mist' Ben, I wisht you could a seen it."

He was irritated as he always was by talk of repairs. He smiled shortly. "Ain't many folks fixin up their houses these days," he said. "Ain't got the money. This old house hasn't had a nail driven in it for Lord knows how long."

"You take a house built like this, built in the old times to last, hit don't need so much fixin," Nora said. "But these here ramshackle little houses built out of sidin you got to keep nailin 'em up or they'll come down on you. . . ."

Allard turned to the men. "We due to have a good year," he said. "Had a drouth now for two years running. 'Fore we fix up any houses here, though, we got to build a new barn. If things look good I might start it this fall. Put it right there on the line between those three fields. That's a heap better place than the old barn was. . . ." He took his pipe out of his mouth and held it suspended in air while his eyes sought the spot, marked for him by two tall cedar trees. "A heap better place," he said, "facing this way and I'll build it into the side of that hill. I saw one built like that once. Jim dandy. Keeps an even temperature, all over the barn. . . ."

He became aware that Joe Mortimer was looking up, craftily, from his whittling. "Mist' Ben, you going to let me have this here field?"

"I wasn't thinkin you'd want to work that much land," Allard said, "but now you got Ote you ought to make five acres of tobacco. . . . How'd you like to put in some Burley?"

Joe let the stick he was whittling fall across his knee. "I ain't never what you might call raised any Burley," he said. "Now dark-fired tobacco I understand. I was raised you might say between the rows." He turned his mild gaze first on his son and then on Allard. "Hit's a fact now," he said, "you put me in a tobacco patch and they's something tells me what to do and when to do it. I don't never have to study about what to do. They's something *tells* me. One time I was livin over here on the aidge of Montgomery and I had fifteen acres of tobacco on the place of a man named Sinton. Elbert Sinton his name was and raised good tobacco too. Me and him was walkin over the patch one morning. The twenty-fifth of August it was. He looks up at the sun and he says, "These here heavy dews is shore puttin the weight on this tobacco. Thar's some folks cuttin now but it'll be money in our pockets if we let this here tobacco stand, another week anyhow. . . ." That man he started off for town and I was going back to the house and as I walked back down them rows something spoke in my year plain as I'm speaking now to you; 'Joe,' hit said, *'Joe Mortimer!* You turn in now and cut your tobacco!' I went on walkin. 'I be dawg if I do,' I says, 'I ain't goin to get in no trouble with that man.' Hotheaded fellow he was. Moved to Montgomery because he killed a nigger over in Christian County. "Naw, suh,' I says, 'I ain't going to git in no trouble.' But hit kept right on and first thing I knew I was up at the barn huntin up the knives! We went over and got Ed Stevens and his gang to help us and 'fore night we had fifteen acres of that tobacco cut. They come a black frost that night and mighty nigh all the rest was ruined. Lawd, you ought to heard that man cuss when he come out in the field next morning. 'You son of a gun,' he says, 'whyn't you tell me you smelled frost?' And ever after that that man was after me to tell him what it was going to do. 'Joe, is it goin to rain? . . . Joe, when we going to git a season? Joe . . .' "

Ote interrupted him impatiently: "I've seen a sight of Burley raised. That time I was workin in Louisville I used to go out to Potters' every Sat'day night with Ernest. Old Man Potter didn't raise nothin but Burley, him nor his boys. Said they wouldn't fool with no other kind of tobacco. Ain't no manner of comparison, they said. Don't have to work it much as dark-fired, don't have to fire it, sun cuoyhs it for you. . . ."

"The question is can you git anything for hit?" Joe asked.

"Oh, yes," Allard said quickly. "Burley's bringing a good price now. Only trouble is they ain't a Burley market at Gloversville. But we could truck it to Staton. It's light, you see, don't weigh like dark tobacco. Wouldn't cost much to truck it over. . . ." He looked at Ote. "There's another thing," he said; " 'd'you ever see any of this new kind of clover, Lespedeza they call it? Beats alfalfa all hollow."

"This land'll bring clover," Joe said, "I ain't never seen the time e'er field on this place wouldn't bring clover."

He spoke without looking up, sitting hunched up in his chair his fingers moving steadily in their slow whittling. Allard's eyes rested for a moment on the seamed, weathered face whose every line drooped downward, on the stubby, gnarled fingers that no matter what the man said kept on with their slow whittling. He knew exactly the expression that would be in Joe's eyes if he looked up, a veiled, suspicious, somehow stubborn look. An immense weariness descended upon him. Since he had begun farming, at the age of sixteen, it seemed to him that he had looked into thousands of just such eyes, had opposed himself for years now, always unavailingly, to that same veiled stubbornness. They *were* like dumb, driven cattle, only they were so mortally afraid of being driven. They had the deep-seated conviction that anything that was good for you was necessarily bad for them, so they always opposed you, never directly, but with that residue of stubbornness that made them forget some orders, carry out others a day late, anything, *anything* to bring your efforts to naught so that every year more and more effort was demanded from you—you had to put more and more of yourself into it, to get the simplest thing done—until finally, he supposed, you became so weary that you didn't really care whether the thing were done or not. You would just lie down, then, not giving a damn and Joe Mortimer, or Ote if Joe was not living, would lend a hand to shovel you under the sod and that would be an end of that. . . . But the boy, Ote, was looking at him, a frank, interested look. He looked back at Ote, his blue eyes that had been shadowed a moment before by the thought of death glowing as they always glowed when he was carried away with some new plan. . . .

"It ain't so much for bringing the land up," he said. "Lots of people around here raising it for the seed. You know what that seed brought last year? Thirty cents a pound. Providin it don't have dodder in it. . . . Thirty cents a pound."

"Thirty cents . . ." Ote said, "now what'll that stuff make to the acre, Mist' Ben?"

"Chance Llewellyn, he put in twenty acres over at Penhally last year," Allard told him. "It made six thousand pounds of seed. He saved a good deal for seed but he could a sold every bit of it. Got thirty cents for most of it, twenty for some. He's saving four hundred pounds of seed for me, at the old price. . . . I was thinkin I'd put some in this field. . . ."

Ote stood up. Unconsciously he squared his shoulders. He turned as Allard had done and looked out over the field. "Say twenty acres," he said, "You put in twenty acres. There's money in it if it stays at the same price."

Joe spoke up. "Hit's something I don't know nothin about, in no way nor manner. You understand it, Mist' Ben?"

"I never have raised any," Allard said, "but they's two or three crops around here I been watching and Chance Llewellyn he's had good success with it and he'll advise us. . . ." He recalled himself. "Well, I better be gettin back. You and Ote goin to start breakin your ground tomorrow?"

"We'll start in first thing in the morning," Joe said.

Allard nodded. "Well, I better be goin. Have to go to town to meet Miss Letty."

He strode off down the path. The Mortimers sat silent, watching his lean figure disappear into the sassafras bushes

29

that bordered the field. Joe spoke first: "Mist' Ben, he's done broke a lot last few years."

Nora was smiling. "But he don't change none," she said. "He's been that same way ever since I can remember him. Always thinking next year hit's going to be a big one. Hit's amazing now, ain't it, the way a man can keep his spirits up . . . from year to year. . . ?"

Their eyes still on the striding, lean figure, she and her husband exchanged glances, mysterious, shadowed as if by the same inner knowledge. Ote was still standing looking off across the field. His eyes narrowed as he measured where the half-way division would come. "I'd just as soon put thirty acres in that new clover," he said. "It stands to reason that that thar seed ain't goin to keep on selling high time everybody gits a stand of it. Hit ain't goin to keep on sellin high and we'd ought to make while the makin's good."

His father reached over and knocked the ashes out of his pipe against the post. "You and Mist' Ben kin have your lesbeder," he said, "and I don't mind givin you a hand in the field. . . . But I'm goin to put my crop in, same as always. Dark tobacco. I growed up raisin it and I ain't ready to give it up for ever' new fangled thing comes along."

CHAPTER THREE

Ben Allard drove the car up to the front door of the ugly, gray house. He and his daughter got out. The girl started up the steps. Mr. Allard stood still, shouting, "Jimmy! Jimmy!"

A little Negro boy appeared from around the corner of the house. A smaller girl was running beside him. Ben Allard waved her back. "Run 'long. Run 'long, now! Jimmy, you get these bags upstairs for Miss Letty."

The little boy lifted one of the suitcases and began toiling up the steps with it. Ben Allard held the door open for Letty, then stood holding it until the little Negro had got both the bags inside the house. Letty walked on through the darkened hall and mounted the stairs into the upper hall. She walked swiftly, her high heels clicking on the bare boards. She opened the door of her own room. It was dark in here, too, the blinds all drawn precisely to the level of the window sill. The hazy, glimmering light fell on dark red roses in a silver bowl on a little bedside table. The bed was covered with an obviously new counterpane.

Ben Allard had followed Letty into the room. He went over and jerked up a shade. "Aunt Pansy got everything right?"

The girl was standing in the middle of the floor. Her eyes were on the counterpane. It was made of some artificial silk; pink and yellow flowers sprawled on the green latticework which formed the background.

Allard moved nearer the bed. He, too, regarded the counterpane. "I came in here the other day and seemed to me things looked sort of shabby. I told Aunt Pansy to buy you a new spread when she went to town Saturday." He frowned, still contemplating the counterpane. "It looks kind of bright, don't it?"

"Oh, you can't have things too bright these days," the girl said cheerfully. "I don't like it as well as that little old fashioned quilt I had on the bed but it'll do for a change." She suddenly threw her arms about his neck and kissed his weathered cheek. "You mustn't go buying me new counterpanes," she said.

"Well, looks like we ought to do something," he said, "you been away so long. I believe Pansy's got fried chicken for supper. Hope you haven't got too high falutin to eat fried chicken."

"It's forty cents a pound," she said absently.

The little Negro had brought in the last suitcase and was setting it down. She opened her purse, found a dime and gave it to him, then turned back to her father. "I reckon I'll unpack now," she said.

He nodded, gave some direction to the little Negro, who scuttled off down the hall then lingered a moment in the doorway. "You better lie down now and get a nap," he said. "You've got plenty of time before dinner."

The door closed behind him. The girl waited until the sound of his footsteps had died away in the hall. Then she walked over and sitting down in front of the dressing table, regarded her image in the mirror: a slim girl of twenty-four in a black coatlike dress with a small black hat pulled down over her bright hair. She lifted her hat off and flung it from her on to the bed and then sat a moment staring into her own eyes. They were long eyes of the shape that is usually called "almond," pale brown in color, but fringed with dark, upcurling lashes. She had always wished her eyes were darker but she liked her long lashes and now she slowly closed her eyes once or twice so that she might approve their play on her pale cheek. She thought that she looked paler than usual today and opened her bag and took out lipstick—she never used rouge. When she had finished outlining her lips she looked at herself again, then rose from the mirror and walked about the room. She paused beside her bags, bent down and unfastened one strap, then let it drop and resumed her walking about the room. She came to the window and looked down. The sugar trees made a rampart all about this side of the house. The broad new leaves shone in the afternoon sun, depth on depth, a sea of green, with a curved black branch showing here and there like the crest of a billow. She knew suddenly that standing here looking down from these east windows the same thought had come to her every summer— would come for as many summers as she lived in this house.

She turned from the window. Her hand went to her heart. "It's happened . . ." she thought, "I'm home . . . back at home. . . ."

She had an hysterical desire to repeat the words aloud to some one. There should be some one to say them to, some one who had said all along that it could not happen. But she had known all along that it would. For weeks the knowledge had been in the back of her mind. And all day yesterday she had reminded herself at intervals that sooner or later it would come, this moment when she would stand and say to herself: "It is over. You won't see him again."

She flung herself face down on the bed. Lying there with the knuckles of her thumbs pressed into her closed eyes, she thought about the man she loved. His name was Jim Carter. He was married to a woman named Sara. She had seen him, had talked with him seven times in her life. No, eight if she counted the first time she saw him. She sat up on the bed, her lips drew back; she made a little hysterical sound as she thought of their first meeting. The brother and sister-in-law whom she was visiting had been dining with somebody or other. She had gone to a dance with Bob Prentwell. But she had a frightful headache, so they came home early. She made Bob leave her on the doorstep—she really couldn't stand any more of him that evening. She had her own key and let herself in. The house was quite dark. She went through the hall and into the living room and was feeling about on the table for a lamp when a voice spoke out of the dark: "You want more light in here?"

The sound of the voice *had* frightened her but not for more than a second. She had realized almost in the moment of hearing it that the tone was one of reassurance. And then a light came on and the man, saying that he was a friend of the family, ran over and put his arms about her as if she were a child.

It had been a ridiculous action, so ridiculous that as soon as she got over her fright she had laughed in his face. He had seemed relieved at that and had gone off and sat down in a corner while she flung herself into the nearest chair. They had gone on sitting there, paying no attention to each other beyond a casual question asked or answered for the sake of politeness until Frank and Elise came in and found them like that.

A few nights later she had been dancing at the Mountain Club and had looked over to see a square-set, sunburned man, obviously older than the others, standing in the doorway with

34

arms folded, frowning out over the crowd. She had thought him attractive, with his dark blue eyes and his very brown face, and had given him the second glance that one gives an attractive man. Then she recognized him as her brother's friend and when she caught his eye she smiled at him. He came straight over to ask her to dance. But they had not got around the floor once before he said it was too hot in here and they would sit this one out. He had surprised her that night by telling her that he wanted to give a dinner party for her. He had surprised her still more the night of the dinner party by asking her to drive out into the country with him the next afternoon to look at a dog he was having trained.

She had known then that he was a little smitten with her but she had not thought anything of that; older men often were smitten with her.

He had seemed so old then; thirty-seven he said he was, to her twenty-four. Why, she still went with college boys! Bill Fauntleroy who had been in love with her for five years now was only twenty-three. Jim Carter would think of Bill as a child. . . . He had tried thinking of her, treating her as a child too, but it hadn't worked. "No," she thought, firming her chin suddenly, "*that* hadn't worked. He'd have to try something else."

Her thoughts went back to that afternoon in the country. They got out to the place about four o'clock. The man who was training the dog for Jim was away from home but his wife called the dog and it came running. A little Llewellyn setter, no better-looking, really, than Old Sue at home but Jim said she had as much bird sense as any dog he'd ever had. They walked off over the fields, the dog tagging them at first and then going off about her own business. "Quartering the field," Jim called it. She saw that he was keen about dogs, so

35

she began asking him questions, the way you did with any man. He said that a long time ago, when he was a kid, he had some good dogs and he told her a lot about one called Tribulation "that had won a championship." She asked him if this one was likely to win a championship and he laughed and said, "hardly." He hadn't had any dogs for years and he had got this one mostly by accident. Ed Rollow was going to St. Louis to live and couldn't take his dog. Jim said she was a good little bitch. He hated to see her fall into the wrong hands, so he had bought her from Ed. He hadn't done any hunting for years but he thought he might come out and shoot a few birds over her this fall. She was staunch as they made 'em, he said.

They came to the foot of the slope. A stream ran here, bisecting the meadow. Tall grasses bordered it on each side. Jim found some steps that had been cut into the bank. They went down to the spring which was enclosed in a concrete box. Jim took up a tin cup which was chained to an iron ring, lifted the concrete lid and dipped her up a drink of water and showed her the pipe which connected with the hydraulic ram. "Elkins gets his whole water supply from here," he said. "Ram pumps four or five hundred gallons a day. He uses it to water stock and everything."

The familiar words about watering stock reminded her of her father. She looked at Jim Carter with curiosity. She had thought of him as a city man but for the first time she imagined him in the country and saw that he would be at home there.

She sat down on the concrete slab and he took a place beside her. His eyes roved over the meadow, to the field beyond where a man was plowing. "I'd like to have a little place like this," he said suddenly. "Run it with just one 'hand' and do a lot of it myself."

"Would you know how?" she asked, amused.

"You bet I would," he said promptly. "Girl, I was raised in the country. You never have seen our old place out on the edge of town?"

She said that she hadn't, and followed her instinct to please by adding that she had heard that it was very attractive.

He laughed. "I don't know about that. House hasn't been repaired in years and all the outbuildings have rotted down. There's nobody living there now except my mother and an old cousin and you know how old ladies are. I did put a coat of paint on it two or three years ago but it turned out that it wasn't the color my mother wanted. She's been riding me about it ever since."

"It sounds like our place at home," she said, allowing a faint bitterness to creep into her tone.

"Is your father hard run?" he asked. "Most farmers are, these days."

"Oh, I reckon he's hard run," she said, "but I don't know whether it'd be any different if he weren't. Every year something falls down. He never even thinks of replacing it. He's so busy with his crops."

"Tobacco?" he asked.

She nodded. "He raises other things but that's all we ever sell."

"Doesn't he raise any beef cattle?" he asked.

"I don't know," she said vaguely. "I see a lot of cattle around. I don't know what becomes of them."

He laughed. "Women are funny," he said frankly. "Now

a man couldn't live on a place without at least knowing what's going on. But you're like my sisters. Helen lived out there in the country all her life and one day when she was eighteen we discovered that she thought a cow gave milk all the year round, whether she had a calf or not."

She laughed back at him. "I never really have understood about that."

"What do you do to amuse yourself?" he asked. "It must be pretty dull for you out there."

"It's dreadful," she said frankly. "Of course I want to be with Daddy as much as I can but I have to have a change sometimes. When he sells his tobacco in the winter I take all the money he gives me and put it in clothes and go off on a visit."

"But it must be nice in the summer," he persisted. "Don't you ever ride horseback?"

"I have a horse," she said, "but I get tired of riding by myself. Of course it's different in the summer when Bill's at home. We ride a lot together."

"Who's Bill?"

"He lives in Gloversville. He's off at college in the winter."

He laughed. "So you go visiting?"

She nodded.

"Why don't you raise something? You could raise dogs. I'll get you a good bitch and get you started."

She shrugged her shoulders and as she looked at him she realized that he was admiring the play of her long lashes. "I hate doggy women," she said. "Horses are bad enough. Heavens! We had a fine stallion once. The whole place was in an uproar. I couldn't even ride to the mail box alone."

He nodded. "Yes," he said reflectively, "a woman really

can't raise horses, unless she has a lot of experienced help.
And dogs are troublesome too, the breeding and all."

She did not answer. She was looking down at her hands,
linked together in her lap. They were narrow, with slim
fingers and beautifully tapered nails. She had always admired her own hands, so much so that she had never been
able to yield to the vogue for highly colored nail polish. Her
hands, she had thought fastidiously, should not look like Mrs.
Vanderbilt's and everybody else's.

She became aware that the man beside her was breathing
heavily. She turned and gave him a brief, provocative smile.

Now in her half-darkened room at home she remembered
that moment and flung herself down on the bed again,
knuckles pressed into her eyes. That smile, given almost automatically, seemed to her now the unluckiest action of her life.
For she did not know and now perhaps she never would
know whether he had interpreted her smile as a challenge
or whether what happened would have happened anyhow.
She sat up on the bed, her crumpled handkerchief rolled
into a ball. That, she thought passionately, was what she
wanted. She wanted it to have happened anyhow, without
any invitation, any manœuvring from her. She looked around
the room with hot, dazed eyes. She muttered: "I might have
that. I might at least have that."

She closed her eyes so that she might re-create the moment.
They were sitting there on the concrete slab and when she
looked at him over her shoulder he put his arm about her,
drew her to him and kissed her. He had done it not hurriedly
but firmly and possessively—as if they were accustomed always to greet each other like that but had not met for a long

time. She had kissed him back as she had never kissed any man, leaning towards him, thrusting her body against his, parting her lips for his deep kiss.

He let her go, gave a little sigh, then leaned forward. His hands drummed once or twice on the concrete wall, then were still. Finally he looked up. "Sorry," he said and smiled.

It was the kind of smile, she realized, that got him out of scrapes, scrapes, probably with women. It made her angry, to think of his smiling at other women like that. She averted her gaze, staring at the very bright, green grasses that thrust up about the wall. Then she was aware of his hand on her arm. "Don't be hard on me," he said. "I know I oughtn't to have done that."

She managed a smile. She told him that it did not matter. She said—and believed it at the time—that she would never think of it again. He patted her arm. "You're a nice kid," he said.

They sat there a few minutes longer. The dog came down to the stream to drink, then went back up into the meadow. They saw her break through the grasses, then stop, with lifted forefoot and stiffened tail. Jim put his hand on the gun that he had stood up beside him. "If I was any good I'd go up there," he said.

"Why?"

"She's on a point. You ought to shoot over them when they're on a point."

She did not answer. She was watching the evening sky with the birds flying through it. A chimney stood up out of a grove of trees. They would circle about it and then with one straight motion dart in. Swift as a swallow, she thought. That's what people mean when they say "swift as a swallow!" . . . She wondered whether he really did consider her a child, or if he were just saying that because he thought it was a bad idea to make love to Frank's little sister. Little? I'm twenty-four. Almost an old maid.

He stood up. "You reckon we better be going?" She nodded and put her hand on the arm he offered. They started up the steep, wet steps. Taking them at the same time as they did their bodies were close together. They went up one step, up two. Her hand rested as lightly as she could rest it on his arm. She did not incline her body ever so slightly towards his but he kissed her again just before they emerged into the meadow, kissed her and then looked down at her, smiling that smile she did not like. "This is getting to be a habit," he said.

"A bad habit?" she said. He laughed and did not speak again until they reached the car, parked in Elkins' wood lot.

They talked of anything and everything going back to town. When he left her at the front door of Frank's house he made no reference to what had happened and he did not mention any future engagement. She was too excited at the moment to think about that. But she lay awake that night wondering whether he would call in the morning. He did not call that day or the day after. But she thought she would see him Saturday night at the Mountain Club dance. She was going with Joe Mercer. She worried herself to death all afternoon planning how she would get rid of him, for she had made up her mind that she would see Jim Carter that night and talk to him.

But he didn't come. All that week he didn't turn up at any of the places you'd have expected him to. And then the next Saturday he appeared at the club. It was nearly midnight. She was dancing with Joe Mercer. She got away from Joe and went to the ladies' room and stayed what seemed a long while. When she came out she saw Jim Carter standing, talking with some men. The group of men broke up. It looked as though he would move off with them. But he didn't. He just stood there watching her as she came walking towards him. She said, "How are you, Mr. Carter?" and he said, "I'm fine, Miss Letty," and as she came abreast of him put the tips of his fingers under her elbow and steered her towards the nearest door.

They walked out on the porch and then down the steps into the shrubbery. The pool had just been filled and there were chairs sitting all about. He pulled out two of these chairs and they sat down. There was a big lilac bush behind them. Its leaves made shadows on the water which was bluish from the fresh-painted walls. They did not sit there long. She could remember every word that they said:

"Do you like to swim?"

"I like to very much. But I can't dive."

"It's easy. If you were going to stay here longer I'd teach you."

A pause. "That's nice of you."

His laughter. "You're a funny kid."

"I shall be twenty-four my next birthday."

"I suppose that seems awfully old to you."

"It's pretty old, for a girl."

"I guess it's pretty tiresome, being a girl and just sitting around waiting for things to happen."

"It's not as much fun as you'd think."

"You ought to get married. . . ."

"I'm engaged to be married now."

A pause. "Does that mean anything?"

"I don't know. I've been engaged twice before."

"I see. It doesn't take, eh?"

"Doesn't seem to. I must be peculiar."

His hearty tones. "Well, when you do marry, you be sure to marry the right man."

"I certainly will. . . . Anything else I can do for you?"

"No," he said, "no. There isn't anything you can do for me or I for you. And I think we'd better go back in the house."

He stood up. She stood up too. They went back along the path but at the fork she took the right hand so that they were going the long way to the house. He did not speak but once. "When are you going home?" "Next Wednesday," she said and stopped. "Next Wednesday," she repeated. "Do you want me to go like this?"

She was whispering but he answered out loud. "I sure do. I want you to go—and I want you to go just like this."

She laughed for she could tell that a smile had come on his face. "You needn't worry about me," she said.

He shook his head, like a man pursued by gnats. "I don't want to *have* to worry about you," he said. He said that but he still stood there as if he no longer wanted to go back to the house. She put her hand on his arm and made him look down at her.

"I'm in love with you," she said.

"I know it," he said.

She moved closer to him. "Let's go down that path," she said and pointed.

But he stood motionless, even when she pressed herself against him, put her arms about his neck. He stood there, shaking his head. "I'll be damned if I will," he said.

She sat up, opening her eyes wide. But they had been closed too long and yellow and green specks floated before her, obscuring her vision. She walked to the window and as her vision cleared stood looking out over the fields. The dying sun was framed—had been framed ever since she could remember—by the worn, white sash. The landscape in which the sun declined was like something pictured: the smooth sweep of the meadow off from the house, the woods that closed in a little on either side and in the center of the picture a cabin, half hidden by a grove of trees. The Davenports lived there —or was it the Sheelers? She had been away from home so long that she didn't even know the names of the people on the place. She turned her head.

A buggy was coming down the road. It was full of people: two young men and two girls on the seat, a child at their feet, another child standing up at the back. The girls were sitting in the boys' laps, all talking and laughing shrilly with not even a glance for this lonely old gray house. They were on their way to the cabin in the grove. Saturday night, of course. She had heard Aunt Pansy say that the Sheelers had more company than any white folks she had ever seen. They were supposed to stop work on Friday afternoon in order to devote the whole week end to jollification. She tried to imagine what poor white people's parties were like. They danced, no doubt—only they danced old-fashioned square dances—and they drank. One of the Sheeler boys was suspected of being a bootlegger. And they made love. A great deal of that. You never heard of a poor white girl's being an old maid, or very rarely. It was only girls like herself or Cousin Elizabeth over at Sycamore who turned out old maids.

Jimmy was standing beneath the window. "Miss Letty, here's the mail."

The girl looked down, recognized the handwriting on an envelope. "Try throwing it, Jimmy," she said. The little

Negro flipped the letter into the air. It fell to the ground. He tried again. This time it reached Letty's downstretched hand. She opened it and read it. It was from her *fiancé*, Bill Fauntleroy. He said that he was leaving Charlottesville Saturday night and expected to be with her by three o'clock on Monday afternoon.

CHAPTER FOUR

Towards nightfall May and her husband, Ed Trivers, came driving up in a one-horse wagon with their two children. Hearing the approach of a vehicle, Ote went out and stood on the porch, not knowing who it was until his sister's voice came to him out of the half-dark: "Well, Ote, ain't you goin to speak to us?"

She handed the larger child over the wheel to her brother and leaning forward presented a cold cheek for his kiss. "This here one's Joe," she said, "and yon's Freeman, for Ed's pappy."

Ote shook hands with his brother-in-law. "Want I should help you unhook?" he asked.

"Naw," Ed said, "I'll just stake this here old nag out before you can say Jack Robinson." He led the horse off towards the stable. Ote strode up the path before his sister, carrying the squirming child in his arms. Inside he scrutinized the rosy, tow-haired little boy before the light of the oil lamp. "Kind of coon-faced," he said. "Durned if he ain't the coon-facedest boy ever I seen but I reckon he'll grow out of it." He raised the child up to the length of his arms, then dropped him shrieking with laughter into the middle of Nora's high feathered bed. "Granny," he called, "come here and git your baby."

Nora came hurrying from the kitchen, where she had been

frying meat, and, kneeling, caught the boy to her bosom. "Granny's 'ittle darlin," she cooed. "At's what 'twas, Granny's little darlin. . . . She turned to her son. "You, Ote," she said sharply, "step out and git some wood. Best have a fire on this hearth. Can't you see May's most froze to death . . . and these chillun too?"

The little boy flopped, released himself from her embrace and crawling off the bed caught hold of Ote's leg and held to it tightly. Ote shook him off roughly. "You better lemme alone, you better lemme alone now. One thing I fancy hit's coon meat. You better look out now, I'll have me a good coon steak for supper."

Mrs. Mortimer unfastened the child's hands from Ote's leg. "G'wan now. . . . I got to git back to my supper." From her chimney corner May spoke wearily: "Don't git him started. Onct you git him started you cain't shake him off."

Ed had finished unhooking his horse and had staked him on the edge of the field when Ote went out in the yard. Together they searched over the ground until they found a broken poplar bough. Ote cut it into lengths while Ed scooped chips into an old basket. When Ote entered the house Ed had a light blaze going in the great fireplace. Having completed his labors he was standing now, his back to the fire, one arm resting on the mantel shelf. A small man, sparely built, with a thatch of auburn hair and a sparse auburn beard, he moved with a certain quiet dignity and when he spoke his very bright, very blue eyes seemed to return from a distance to rest on the listener.

Ote threw two or three of his little logs upon the fire, then dropped the rest down at the side of the hearth. Dragging up a chair he got out his sack of Bull Durham and began to roll a cigarette. He proffered the sack to Ed, who shook his head with an absent, benevolent smile. "I don't use it," he said.

May tittered. "Didn't you know Ed was saved and sanctified?" She had taken a seat near the fire and unwrapping the blanket that served the infant as a coat was exposing its feet to the flames. As Ote watched her she unfastened her dress and gave the baby the breast. A slight color rose in her sallow cheek as she met Ote's eyes. "I gave him some on the road," she said, "but looks like hit didn't do him no good. His feet so cold look like nothin didn't do him no good."

The child pushed at her breast with his tiny, almost transparent hands and emitted fretful wails. A small, rather pallid baby with vague, staring blue eyes under a domelike forehead. Not as healthy-looking as the little boy, but maybe that was because it was so little. Mrs. Mortimer, hurrying from big room to kitchen, stopped once to look over May's shoulder. "Maybe you ain't got enough for him," she said. "Don't look like to me you got much in there for him."

"I reckon he gits enough," May said wearily. "I reckon he just ain't got a good start yit." Her eyes sought Ote's as if he were a stranger whose acquaintance she half-heartedly wished to make. "How'd you like in *De*troit?" she asked.

"It was all right," Ote said; "all right while it lasted. You take anybody making seven dollars a day hit's bound to seem all right to 'em. Seven dollars. That's what I was makin when I was laid off. But I was down at the bottom. Some of those fellers, it wasn't nothin for 'em to make ten and twelve dollars a day. . . ."

"But didn't it cost a heap to live?" May asked shrewdly. "Didn't you have to spend all you made, just livin? That's what all of 'em tell me."

Ote waved a hand largely about the room. "Well, yes," he

said, "they was lots of things a man could spend his money for. . . . But then he was havin a good time. You got to figure on that. Spendin your money but spendin it *for* something. . . ."

Nora, passing again, spoke tartly: "Not just settin around the fire with a lot of old folks. Ote's done got mighy high ideas since he's been to *De*troit."

Ed shook his head. "Them cities," he said, "they ain't a thing to 'em. Ain't a thing but wickedness." He ran his hand over his auburn thatch of hair. "I was in Nashville onct," he said, "to the fair. 'Bout ten year ago it was. A whole day I spent in that town just walking around and looking at sights. I wish now I hadn't went. They ain't a thing to it."

Ote smiled maliciously. "You stay with me one night," he said. "You stay right along with me and I'll take you places and show you sights. . . . Course hit'll cost you money but ain't no use in livin in a city if you ain't got money to spend. . . ."

There was a gentle condescension in Ed's smile. "Naw, Ote," he said, "when I was a young man I was like you, always studyin meanness, but now I found my Saviour I don't study about nothin but salvation. . . ."

The door behind them opened. Joe was standing in the doorway. "Who that studyin salvation?" he asked. "I'm bound it warn't Ote."

Ote shook his head. "Naw," he said. "Ote, he's studyin how to make a livin. That's enough for one man to study about these days."

Joe advanced and picked the little boy up from where he sat in the middle of the floor." Come on," he said. "Come on, y'all, and git your supper."

In the kitchen Nora had laid the plates on the checkered

red-and-white cloth. The platter of fried meat and a bowl of
gravy were at one end before Joe, the dish of black-eyed peas
before her own plate. While they were sitting down she went
into the big room and got a jar of fruit down from the
shelves. Holding it up to the light of the oil lamp she scrutinized it. "Is it jam or preserves?" she asked. "It's hard to tell."
Ote seized the jar from her and making Ed hold it for him,
opened it with one turn of his wrist. "Hit's jam," he said,
"and I'm going to open it before you take it away from us."

Nora handed the heavy, sallow biscuits around. "This stove,
hit ain't settled," she apologized. "Looks like hit don't never
bake good for a week or two after a movin."

She broke the biscuits into little bits, covered them with
gravy and fed the morsels to the child whom she held on her
lap. May tiptoed in from the big room, shutting the door
noiselessly behind her. "He's sleepin' now," she said, "and his
stomach's full. Maybe I can eat my supper in peace."

They ate in silence except for the small, cooing sounds that
Mrs. Mortimer made from time to time to the little boy. Ote
helped himself liberally to fried meat and gravy and jam but
refused the dish of black-eyed peas that Nora twice pushed
towards him.

"That place I boarded at in Detroit," he said, "we had
fresh meat ever' day and onct that woman give us tomatoes,
in the dead of winter."

"Hunh!" Nora said. "No wonder all your money went.
Right down your throat. I'd be ashamed, Otho Mortimer!
Hit's a fact now, he come home with two dollars to his name.
. . . Two dollars and him working away from home for
three years."

Ote laughed awkwardly. "I'd a had twenty-two dollars,"
he said, "if I hadn't a loant some of it. Forty-two dollars I

had on me the day I was laid off and twelve of it was borrowed off me 'fore I left the boarding house. The rest it taken to get home. . . . Want I should a walked?"

He pushed his chair back and rose from the table. Joe and Ed followed him into the big room.

Joe threw another log on the fire and the three men sat down in the rockers that were ranged about the hearth. Joe took a twist of tobacco out of his pocket and bit off a chew. Ote drew out his sack of tobacco, but finding it was almost empty put it back into his pocket. "I reckon I'll chew tonight," he said. "Seems like I just got to have a cigarette mornins."

Joe shook his head. "I raised five boys," he said, "and Ote's the first of e'er one of 'em to smoke cigarettes."

"What's the matter with smokin cigarettes?" Ote asked truculently. "Ain't no worse 'n chawin any day."

"They ain't a thing the matter with it," Joe said. "Ain't e'er thing I could name the matter with it. Just don't look right to me. "He chuckled. "I declar," he said, "old as I am it jest don't look right to me to see a great big grown man a-settin up thar puffin on them little papers." He stared at the fire. "I mind the time," he said reminiscently, "when a whole passel of us went from here to the Hopkinsville fair. We got thar at sun up and we stayed till 'way in the night but of all the sights I saw that day they's only one stays in my mind. Paid two bits I did to see it. I reckon that's why it stays so in my mind. . . ."

"What was it?" Ote asked. "Must a been something pretty good for you to pay out two bits to look at."

"Hit war a boy," Joe said, "hit war a boy about your age a layin on some straw and a-puffin on a cigarette. The sign outside hit said 'Cigarette Fiend' and had a lot of pictures of devils a flyin' round in the air but when you got in thar warn't a thing but this boy a layin thar and a-puffin on his cigarette. He looked sickly, like he might have a tech of the jaundice. I mind how going home some of 'em argued about how long that boy'd last smokin them cigarettes the way he did. Your mammy thought he war marked for death right soon, a-smokin them pizen things, but thar was some said that boy might go on that same way for years like Mister Robert Allard that took morphine till the longest day he lived but he took sech a little at a time that his system got accustomed to it and t'warn't no more to him than turnip sallet." He laughed and slapped his knee. "But to think," he said, "of me payin a quarter to see that ar boy smokin a cigarette and here I can set up any night and look at Ote free."

"You ain't goin to be lookin at me long," Ote said. "Done got down where I can't afford store tobacco. Reckon I'll have to smoke it out of the barn."

"It won't hurt you none," Joe said. "Always seemed a piece of foolishness to me, a man goin and payin out good money for tobacco when all he's got to do is reach up and git it out of the barn. . . ."

Ed turned his serious blue eyes on them. "You don't have to pay out money for hit," he said gently, "and you don't have to reach up and git it out the barn. Hit's all a notion, usin tobacco, jest a notion folks got and cain't git rid of."

"How'd you quit?" Ote asked. "Seems to me you used tobacco like anybody else when you first come a-courtin May."

"I started in chawin when I was eight years old," Ed said, "and from that day forward I war hardly you might say without a chaw in my mouth. My mammy used to whup me to git me to lay my cud on the mantel shelf meal times. She did, for a fact. Said it would pizen me shore to have all that tobacco goin down my stommick long with my victuals."

"What made you quit?" Ote asked.

"He got religion," Joe answered. "They's lots of people quit usin tobacco on account of gettin religion."

"It was ten year ago," Ed said, "ten year ago when I was twenty-six years old. I was out in the field by myself a-pizenin plants. I had the gun goin and a handkercher tied over my face to keep the Paris Green from gettin in my nose. I had a big chaw of tobacco in my cheek and I says to myself: 'Ed, it's a good thing now you don't use a pipe or it'd be full of this here pizen shore.' And then I spit that ar cud out of my mouth and I says, 'From this day forward I don't use tobacco in no shape or form. In no shape or form,' I says. Ten year ago it was, when I was twenty-six. And I ain't teched tobacco from that day to this."

"Don't no cravin ever come over you?" Ote asked. "Don't sometimes you feel you jest got to have a chaw?"

Ed shook his head. "Hit's all a notion," he said, "jest one of them notions afflicts us poor mortals."

"Ed, you shore can talk like a book," Joe said admiringly. "Hit comes from goin to preachin so reg'lar, don't it?"

"I dunno," Ed said. "They's words come to me. Words come sometimes I ain't no idea whar they come from." He looked up at his wife, who entered the room just then with her mother and the little boy. "May, what's the word I used to you the other day and you said you never hearn the like of it before?"

She shook her head. "I dunno," she said, "they don't stay in my mind." She took the chair nearest the fire that Ote vacated for her. In a moment she turned and laid her hand on her father's knee. "Pappy, you got e'er chaw of tobacco?" she asked.

Joe pulled the twist out of his pocket and she bit a chew off and returned it to him. Ote laughed. "You ain't got May to stop usin tobacco yit," he said.

Ed smiled benevolently on his wife. "May ain't had time to go to meetin much," he said. "Let her git to goin to meetin reg'lar onct and let her git saved and sanctified and she'll quit usin tobacco and not think no more about it. . . ."

Nora stared musingly into the fire. "I've knowed a heap of sanctified folks in my time," she said, "and they was certainly good folks. But it's something I can't understand. I've studied about hit, lots of times, and yet they's something about it I cain't make out somehow."

Ed looked at her. His eyes were bright, his expression solemn yet eager. "Hit's jest like the Book says," he told her. "Hit's a mystery. Poor mortal man, he ain't expected to onderstand it."

Ote looked at his brother-in-law curiously. It occurred to him that Ed at that moment looked like the pictures of Jesus. He did, for a fact. With that raggedy beard and the burning look in his eyes. Certainly a change had come over him since he had become sanctified. He remembered Ed very well when he first came a-courtin May, a fumbling, awkward kind of fellow. People laughed at him. "Ed's all right," they said, "honest as the day is long," and that was the best word anybody could give him. He didn't suppose they thought any more of him now. Ed worked hard and he had the name of making a good crop but it seemed hard for him to get a home. He had just had to move this year, to a poor farm on Pea Ridge. No, he didn't suppose folks thought any more of Ed than they ever did, but it seemed like Ed didn't care. He

54

would speak to you, smiling, and then look away as if he didn't have time to listen to your answers, as if what you said couldn't make any difference to him. It was like he was studying something important all the time and didn't have time to fool with other folks whereas before he had been always at you with soft words, in those days leading the talk to May as much as he could: "Your sister, Pearl, she's a pretty girl, she shore is, but May's my favorite. . . ." And he had pretended to see a vast difference in the twins, whereas to Ote they had always seemed as like as two peas. Pearl had been a little the better dispositioned, perhaps. As a girl May had been high-tempered, but getting married and having children was taking that out of her. Well, it was time she got settled. She was thirty-one years old, seven years older than he himself was. . . .

May was asking her father if he had traded with Mister Ben yet. Ote spoke up. "Course he's traded," he said sharply. "What you think we'd be here for if we hadn't traded?"

"I dunno," May said vaguely: "thought maybe Mist' Ben jest told Pap he could stay here till he got some other place to go." She looked at her brother, fire leaping in her faded eyes. " 'Tain't so easy as you think gittin a place these days," she said. "They's some folks over at Mister Harrel's, man and a woman and five chillun, livin' in a corner of a tobacco barn. Got paper nailed up in one of the stalls to make 'em a room. But they's lots of cold weather comin yit, and hit's draughty. Draughty for that little baby. It ain't two months old yit."

Nora shook her head. "It's bad when folks ain't got a place to go and it's hard on little chillun. Looks like folks that have got ought to all git together and he'p those that ain't. Looks like if they'd do that they wouldn't be so much sufferin."

55

"Half the time they ain't got themselves," May said, "and they's some folks that are ornery. You lay yo'se'f out to he'p 'em and they'll turn right around and do you all the meanness they kin. Mist' Harrel, he had some folks like that on his place year before last. Mist' Harrel, he said he didn't want that man workin on his place if he never had another plough stuck in the ground. Said he warn't no manner of use nohow and he warn't. He was mean. Mean as garbroth, him and all his chillun. But they was a new baby in that family too and Mist' Harrel, he told 'em they could stay in that house till they could make 'em a trade somewhar else. That man he jest set down thar on the front porch. Anybody said anything to him he'd laugh: 'Well, he said I could stay here till I made a trade, didn't he?' and thar he set. Sheriff had to come put 'em off fi'n'lly. . . ." She stirred and sank back in her chair, her brief moment of animation over. "They was cousins to the folks livin' on this place," she said, "Sheeler they name was. . . ."

"Mist' Ben he was askin me about them Sheelers today," Nora said, "askin me, but I put him off. Tole him I didn't what you might call know any Stewart County folks. I don't believe in speakin ill of anybody, let 'em be as ornery as you please. It's like what they say: 'Give a dog a bad name. . . .'"

"You couldn't give them folks a bad name," Joe said. "I been knowin Sheelers all my life now and I ain't knowed e'er one was any count, not to say right down mean. . . ." He spat into the fire. "I'm right satisfied to be where I'm at," he said. "Mist' Ben Allard he's got his ways like everybody else but I onderstand him and he onderstands me. I ain't never had words with Mist' Ben in my life. . . ."

"Mister Ben's broke," Nora said; "seems like he's more broken'n what he ought to be at his age." She laughed. "I was livin on this place when Mist' Ben first started in farming, right after Mister Tom died. He was cocky as they make 'em then. Remember them folks named Grove that moved down here from Muhlenberg County? And after they got here they didn't like and they wouldn't work and yit they wouldn't move off the place neither. . . .

Joe threw back his head and guffawed. "I can see 'em now, he said, "them two boys and the ole man, on mules they was and a ole, broken-down horse they had. I was a settin right here on this porch when they come through the gate. Passed this house they did like a streak of lightning. And in a few minutes here come Mister Ben lickety split across the field on that little sorrel horse of his'n a shootin as hard as he could tear. He'd look at them people and then he'd throw that gun up in the ar and shoot hard as he could at the woods but that gun hit'd keep sinkin like it was all he could do to keep from pluggin 'em. Nora, she fell to cryin. Some of you chillun was out on the road berryin. 'Lawd God,' she says, 'he's a-killin my chillun. He's a-shootin 'em down dead. Joe, you go out thar and see how many of 'em is layin dead in the road this minute.' Well, I went out I did and I hollered at Mister Ben just as he went through the gate. 'For God's sake,' I said, 'don't shoot no Mortimers.' I hollered after him I did: 'Shoot all the Groves you want to,' I hollered, 'but *don't —shoot—no—Mortimers!*'"

"Did he pay any attention to you?" Ed asked. "Did he pay you any attention?"

Joe shook his head. "He shot 'em all the way to Price's Station. Shot 'em ever' step of the way and when he turned around and come home thar was ole Miz Grove and her married daughter and all the chillun a-settin out here on the side of the road cryin. He made 'em take their foot in their hand and walk after the men folks. And he sent two niggers down to the cabin to load up their stuff and haul it off. Said he warn't goin to have no Grove step they foot on his place again, man or woman."

May laughed from her corner. "What was Miss Fanny doin? I lay Miss Fanny was in it somehow."

"Naw," Joe said, "that was one time Miss Fanny didn't have nothin to say. She jest sot thar a-tremblin and cryin. 'Ben's goin to git killed, Ben's goin to git killed. Them mean white folks'll kill Ben shore. . . .'" Ote laughed. He looked down at the little boy who had worked his way around the circle and was clinging now to his uncle's knee. "You know what I'm goin to do?" he said and caught the child up in his arms. "I'm goin to grease your head and pin your years back and swallow you whole." He made passes with his hands over the child's forhead. The little boy squealed with delight. Ote stood up and tossed him towards the ceiling.

"You quit that, Ote," Nora protested. "You'll bump that baby's brains out."

"You take him, then," Ote said. "I don't want him. You take him." He dumped the protesting child into his mother's lap and took his hat from the peg behind the door. "Well," he said, "I reckon I'll go out and take a look at the crops."

Their laughter pursued him down the path. He heard his mother's voice rising above the others. "Ote, he's done stayed in town so long I reckin he don't hardly know one crop from another," and Ed's bass, surprisingly deep for a little man: "Naw, you take a boy raised in the country and hit don't never leave him. He can go 'way and live the half of his life and you take and put him back on the farm and he'll know how to do same as if he'd never been off the land. . . ."

The oblong of yellow light had vanished from the path.

Somebody had risen and shut the door that he had left open. The voices were muted suddenly, like a fiddle tune dying away under the hand.

He went down the little rise and stood in the middle of the road that led back into the farm. A fair night, cool but still and with a million stars shining, so bright they made the little moon look pale. He threw his head back to look at them. It occurred to him that it had been a long time since he had seen any stars, seen them, that is, for what they were. In town you hardly ever looked up at the sky because the lights were always around you so bright, brighter than stars, really. . . .

He saw suddenly the long table at the boarding house, with the hard, electric light beating down on the glass bowl of artificial fruit that stood in the center of the table. It had struck with a glitter on the eye-glasses of Simpson, the paint superintendent who read in his room at night and never went out with the boys. Next to him had sat Bill Turner. Bill was the first friend Ote had made at the boarding house. It was Bill who had got him his job at the factory, Bill who had taken him the first time to that house down by the water works, Bill who had made him acquainted with Lottie. . . .

He grinned to himself at the thought of his mother's words: "Right down your throat. . . . I'd be ashamed, Otho Mortimer. . . ." Lottie, he thought, had got more of his money than he had ever spent at Miss Jeanie's. That watch he had bought her Christmas and the lavaliere and just before he was laid off, the bracelet. . . . He wondered if Lottie was out with Bill tonight. Be just like her. No, she probably had a new fellow by this time. . . .

He had arrived at the edge of the little woodland. Even here the road was bright. The moon hung right over the woods now. He could see it through the branches when he looked up. Bad luck, they said, to look at the new moon through trees—no, that was through the leaves. Didn't matter, probably, if the trees had no leaves on them. "Anyway," he said to himself, "I couldn't have much worse luck than what I got now. . . ." He crossed the cold, brightly glancing stream and took the same path that Ben Allard had walked along earlier in the day. A lonesome walk, through these woods. He felt sorry for the people who lived at the far end of the place. Back in the brush for sure. It was better to be there on the side of the road as the old house was. At least you could look out and see somebody going along once in a while. He tried to remember the names of the people that were living on the place this year. Sheeler, that was one family and the others were Lightwoods or Shutts, he couldn't remember which. He had a sudden desire to see somebody not of his own family. He told himself that if there was a light burning in either of the houses he might go in and pass the time of day. Not sit long, just enough to be neighborly. . . .

He emerged from the woods. The house loomed before him, a big, ugly gray house set in a wide yard with sugar trees all about. He passed down the lane and entered the stable lot. The house had looked dark from the side but he saw now that there was a light in one of the side rooms. The drawn shade was brightly illuminated. A man's shadow was black against it: Mister Ben sitting beside the table that held the lamp. As he watched, the shadow wavered, shot suddenly to the height of the window and disappeared. Mister Ben was getting up to put a stick of stovewood on the fire. He wondered what Mister Ben did with himself evenings. No company ever, not even a fiddle tune to cheer him up. He just sat there, one side of that table with a book in his hands. It was a wonder how anybody could endure to sit reading a book a whole long evening. But he was old. There was no place for him to go, anyhow—no place for anybody to go here in the deep country, the nearest picture show ten miles away.

It came to him how different living in the country was from living in town. In town there was the feeling all the time of the people about you. Even if you didn't know them to speak to they were there all the time. You couldn't take three steps along the street without meeting somebody, but here you were by yourself most of the time, with nobody, that is, but your own folks. Here on this big farm, besides his own folks, there were no white people except the Sheelers and Shutts and Miss Letty and Mister Ben. He could walk around here in these fields all night and not meet a living soul but a nigger, maybe, taking the short cut home from Penhally.

"It's being by yourself," he thought. "It's being by yourself all the time. That's what it is. . . ."

He had a sick longing for the boarding house, the smell of hot supper cooking, the close, warm atmosphere of the dining room, the men's voices and laughter, the brushing of one body against another as they crowded into the dining room. If he was there tonight he and Bill would eat their dinner in a hurry and go somewhere. It might be to see a girl, maybe just to a picture show. It wouldn't matter so they went *somewhere.*

"I wisht I was back," he said aloud, "I wish to God I was back in that town. . . ."

He left the stable lot and set off on a path that wound through a field towards the woods. A mock orange hedge divided this field from the road. It was broken or burned down in some places. Through the gaps in the hedge he caught glimpses of the road below, a deep, rutted road impassable except for buggies. All the new tenant houses on the place were along this road. The first house was dark, nobody living in it or else all gone to bed, but lights shone from the double log cabin in the grove. It was here, probably, that the Sheelers lived. He had heard his mother or some of them say that there was a big family. A big family or they had lots of company. There were figures passing and repassing the windows and from one of the rooms came the sound of a fiddle being tuned.

A dog about the cabin had got wind of Ote's approach and was baying, a hound's deep, menacing bay. It drowned the laughter and the voices and the soft sounds of the fiddle. Ote picked up a tobacco stick and held it firmly gripped in his hand but the dog did not come any farther along the path and presently a door opened and a boy's voice rang out: "Shet up, Billy . . . shet up now, you durned fool. . . ." The door shut on the dog still barking violently and then the clamor died down as suddenly as it had risen. Ote could hear the rustle of dead leaves as the dog crawled back to his bed under the porch.

He waited for a moment and then walked on along the path. Coming to a fallen log on the edge of the woods he sat down and taking out his sack of tobacco rolled a cigarette. It was dark here on the edge of the woods but the little hollow where the cabin stood was full of light. Ote could see the corner of the mantel shelf in one room and the lamp sitting on it. There was a pink china vase beside the lamp and directly below that a man's head was visible over the high back of a rocking chair. A bald-headed man with a little fringe of gray hair hanging down over his shirt collar. He held a fiddle thrust into the hollow between his neck and shoulder and his left hand kept tightening the strings while his right hand would bow for a moment, then fall to picking. Presently the tune started up, steady and rhythmical.

Ote leaned forward on his log, listening. "Hit's 'The Downfall of Paris,' " he said, "that's what he's a-playin."

A shadow fell athwart the window. Somebody, a woman by the figure, was standing behind the fiddler's chair, reaching out to lay a hand on his shoulder. He shook his head but did not stop playing. His voice drifted to Ote's ears above the fiddling: "You lemme 'lone. I'm gittin tuned up now for 'Darlin Honey.' "

A young boy's hoarse voice rang out: "Idelle she always wants 'Darlin Honey.' She thinks Pap cain't play no other tune."

The girl's voice came to Ote clearly through the still night: "It's a good dance tune. What I say, goin to fiddle might as well fiddle something you can dance to."

The fiddler had ended "The Downfall of Paris" and was breaking into another tune. Ote listened with his head cocked to one side. "Hit's 'The Saints Go Marchin In,' " he said, " 'When the Saints Go Marchin In. . . .' "

The boy in the house was laughing. "You kin dance to that, Idelle. You and Buck kin dance to that."

There was no answer from the girl. The door had opened suddenly and two people came out on the porch. A man and a girl—or was it another boy? Ote half rose and then sat still. He was afraid the two on the porch might hear him if he moved now. The cigarette butt glowed in his hand. He dropped it on the leaves and crushed the spark out with his foot. "They'll think I'm spyin on 'em," he told himself. "They'll think I'm just settin here to spy on whatever goes on in that house," and then in self-defense: "I got as good a right to set on this log as anybody else, ain't I? This log it don't belong to anybody in that house nor these woods either. They belong to Mister Ben Allard and I'm croppin on his place same as they are. . . ."

The two on the porch were invisible but the sound of their voices came to him, a gentle murmur broken now and then by the girl's excited laughter, and once the sound of a little scuffle ending in sudden silence. "That boy he's a-courtin her," Ote thought, "he's a-courtin her hard but she ain't made up her mind yet whether she'll have him or not." He had a sudden desire to see the face of the girl on the porch. Her shadow there by the chair had been light and wavering, a thin girl, maybe, with yellow hair and light on her feet. Her imagined face rose up before him. He could see the hair shadowing her brow and the sweep of the eyebrows across her forehead and from under the brows the eyes looking out steadily as if she knew that he was watching her here in the dark.

"Spyin," he said distastefully, "Spyin. That's what you're doing." He got stealthily to his feet and stepping backwards over the log moved slowly off through the woods. Behind him the fiddle music rose and fell airily.

"Darlin Honey," he said to himself as he moved off through the trees, "Darlin Honey . . . a good tune to dance to. . . ."

CHAPTER FIVE

THE SHEELER boy stepped back out of the plant bed and leaning down wrung out the bottom of his flapping pants. "I declar," he said, "we might as well a gone down to the creek."

"You better be glad of the chance to git wet," Ote told him. He looked around at the wall of undergrowth that fringed the bed on three sides. The buckberry bushes shimmered with moisture as if they had been touched by frost and water hung from the tip of every dogwood and sassafras leaf. The whole wood was soaking wet. But it had been raining hard since some time early in the night. A ground soaker. He had been waked by the sound of it and had lain awake at intervals during the night, rejoicing in the steady pattering sound. A month now since they had had any rain. It had lasted until nearly morning and had fallen off then to a light drizzle. It seemed to him that he had hardly turned over in bed before his father was hollering at him from the next room. They had breakfasted by lamplight and had been out in the field long before sun up. Mister Ben was already there, rearing to go. He had sent Ote and this boy out to the plant bed with the wagon while he and Joe went around and got the rest of the folks up. That had been two or three hours ago. When he and this boy, Random, came in here for the first load of plants it was still dark. They had had to leave the wagon at the edge of the woods and they had been able to find the plant bed only by the glimmer of the white canvas thrown back along its sides.

Random straightened up and passed his dirty hand over his forehead. "Hit's hot in these woods," he said. "Hotter'n 'tis in the field and that's a fact."

Ote looked at the bunch of plants in the boy's hand. They had been drawn carelessly. Little clods of earth still hung on some of them, twisting and straining the delicate roots and the stems of one or two of the plants had been mutilated in the drawing.

"You don't pull 'em clean enough," he said. "See here." He knelt down on the edge of the bed and sliding his hands gently under the leaves drew two or three plants with a swift, sure motion.

The boy looked on uninterestedly. "Hit don't make no difference," he said. "You take a season like this ever plant you set's goin to live." His eyes left Ote's face and ranged over the green wall of undergrowth. "I be dawg," he said suddenly, "if that ain't a ole owl a settin up thar in that tree."

He threw his plants down and plunged off into the bushes. A moment later he was visible, standing at the foot of an elm tree, his little, thin ferret's face turned up, his eyes fixed on something that lurked in the upper boughs. Without turning his head he called back to Ote: "You come gi'me a h'ist up the trunk and I can git him."

Ote shook his head. "I ain't got no time to be foolin with owls. You come on. Them hands waitin now for these plants."

He picked up one of the tubs and heaved it on to the wagon. When he turned around the boy's face had disappeared from the undergrowth. There were noises as of a dog plunging through a thicket and the boy emerged from a clump of saplings.

Ote had finished loading the tubs and was jerking the pole to which his lines were tied. "You gee up, thar, John!" he said. The lead mule plunged to the right and the wagon came slowly off the stump it had hung on. The boy sat on the side swinging his feet and giving free advice.

"You better keep on geein him now or you goin to get hung again. . . . Watch out thar. . . . Cain't you see that stump?" He broke off, to look up at Ote who was eyeing him sternly over his shoulder. "Why'n't you come to our house Sat'day evening?" he demanded. "Most everybody around here comes."

Ote manœuvred the wagon slowly off a stump, then reached around and ran his hand roughly over the boy's head. "I'll come some time when you ain't home. I ain't got no time to be foolin with scopankers."

A low-hanging branch caught both of them and threw them back upon the tubs. When they stood up they were both drenched. The boy laughed gleefully. "That's what you git fer bein so smart." He jumped off the wagon and ran through the underbrush. Ote watched the sumac rustling where he made his way. A likely boy, he thought, even if he was something of a limb. He wondered why his father was so prejudiced against all the Sheelers and decided that it was because they were restless. Joe Mortimer thought that it was a disgrace for a man to be always changing his home. He ought to stay at a place three, four years even if he didn't like it, just to show that he didn't have to leave.

The wagon lumbered on. They were not out of the woods yet but he caught glimpses of the field here and there through the sumac and sassafras bushes. A broad expanse of red brown earth in the foreground and beyond that the lespedeza clover was already showing pale green. A good stand. They had put in thirty acres after all. His father had grumbled but Mister Ben had stood by him and they had sowed it all down. A mixture of lespedeza clover and timothy. That was the way to do it, Chance Llewellyn said. You could cut a good crop of timothy before the lespedeza was ripe. Hay was going to be high this year, everybody said. Tobacco ought to bring a good price too. The crop was bound to be short, the time everybody was having to get his crop in. The ground was dry when they first broke it, those clods as hard as steel. One light rain had come, enough to allow them to finish preparing the ground and then after that no rain at all for three weeks. Most people got tired of waiting and had gone on setting their plants, watering them by hand as they set, but Joe, and Ben Allard, too, had held out that there was bound to be at least one good "season" before the spring was over and here it was, by golly. The ground would be wet for days, long enough to get all the tobacco on the place set. They would finish setting this field today—there were only thirty acres with the half of it in lespedeza and timothy—and tomorrow they would set the Sheelers' tobacco and after that the Davenports' and the niggers'. The Sheelers didn't have all their land ready yet but it was too wet to plough today so they were helping set along with everybody else on the place.

He drove the wagon up over a little rise and across the road. The huge field lay before him, steaming delicately in the morning sun, rows and rows of tobacco hills laid off as regularly as if on a checker board. Here and there in the light mist figures could be seen moving about or standing in groups. The Sheelers, the Shutts, all of Uncle Jim's children. Every hand on the place out to set plants. Ote felt a sense of power rising in him as he watched the figures detach themselves from the mist, move towards the wagon. It was as if they were all there awaiting his pleasure, as if in a way it was he and not Mister Ben for whom they were all working.

Old man Sheeler was calling to his oldest boy. "Here, you, Wallace, take them plants down the row and git them women started to dropping."

The boy was lifting another tub off the wagon. Two of the women caught hold of its handles and a group of four moved off towards the far end of the field: a gaunt old woman, a younger woman who held a baby astride her hip and a girl in a pink, striped dress. A slim girl, older than the boy Random but still not what you'd call grown. That would be the one they called Idelle. A sleepy head evidently. They had all hollered at her when she came to the field early in the morning. "You up? Well, it's shore time to start work then." A half-grown girl like that ought not to be working in the field really. His sisters never had, except once or twice in a rush season. But Old Man Sheeler was hard put to keep a place anyhow, he supposed. He and all his boys had the name of being shiftless. When men were like that the women of the family always had to help out.

Mister Ben was approaching the wagon with his rapid yet sauntering gait. He lifted off a tub of plants himself. His face, whipped red by the wind, was lifted to Ote's. "These are better plants than Mister Chance's, Ote. Woodier."

Ote nodded. "They touched up a lot them three days we left the canvas off."

He threw the lines down and jumped off the wagon, aware that his father was already calling to him fretfully: "Hey,

69

Ote, you git a move on you now. Which way you goin?"

Ote indicated the direction, took up his load of plants and moved off towards the opposite quarter of the field. The lean, oldest Sheeler boy was striding beside him. At the end of the row they stopped and set the tub of plants on the ground. The boy stopped and taking up a handful of plants started swiftly off down the row. "I'll drop a while," he said, "and we can change around when I come back."

Ote squatted down on his haunches and began setting. The earth was wet through, every hill a loblolly. He worked swiftly with the ease of long practice, his left hand reaching out automatically for the plant that the Sheeler boy had thrown down while his right punched the hole in the hill. Back and forth, back and forth, his arms flinging out in almost the exact circumference each time, his two hands coming together simultaneously to push the dirt in around the roots of the plants. It was almost as monotonous as tending some piece of machinery. And it was awkward for a heavy man to squat down this long. The backs of his legs and his knees were already feeling the strain. He shifted his position, dropping forward on one knee, but he could not reach the plants as well that way. The Sheeler boy was dropping them carelessly, some of them flung so far that Ote had to get off his knees to reach them. He was already at the end of the row and starting back down another. In the next row a gaunt old woman was stooping along, old Mrs. Sheeler. One thing you could say for them they had every hand out this morning, setting. The married daughter's baby was even bobbing about there at the other end of the field. Old Mrs. Sheeler was setting herself and letting the younger woman drop. But the baby's mother was fat, it was easier for old Mrs. Sheeler to bend down, thin as she was. He wondered if they noticed his own mother's absence. It had been years since she had done anything in the field. She was so unwieldy that she was no help, really. Pap always said he'd rather have her room than her company.

He got to his feet and standing with his legs wide apart threw his arms over his head and stretched himself until he had brought every muscle into play. The Sheeler girls had stopped work and had taken up a bucket and were moving off towards the spring. He watched them walking across the field. The older woman shuffled along heavily in a man's run-down brogans. But Idelle was barefooted. Idelle was standing aside while her sister got over the fence. She was over, too, now, quick as a flash. It occurred to him that she was quicker on her feet than any girl he'd ever seen. He had been watching her all the time, yet his eye had hardly followed her movements.

He was aware of voices beside him. Old Pap Sheeler was coming down the row. A bent old man with a long, dirty yellow beard, wearing an army overcoat that must have belonged to Wallace Sheeler and an old-fashioned fur cap. He was having an argument with one of the Sheeler boys about the accuracy of his dropping. Suddenly he tilted his bald head and looked at the sky. "Hit don't make no difference whether you drap 'em or don't drap 'em. Every one of these plants might as well be left in the bed."

Ote smiled good-humoredly at the old man. "You think we ain't goin to git another season?"

The old man withdrew his gaze from the sky, fixed his bleared eyes on Ote's face. "I was settin by the fire the fifth day of the new year when the sign come into my mind. I called that boy, Random, to me. 'Boy,' I says, 'look in the almanac and tell me what day of the month it is.' 'Hit's the fifth day of January, Granpap,' he tells me. 'The fifth day of January,' I says, 'and hit ain't rained today nor yesterday nor day before.' " His cracked voice rose shrilly. "I tuck notice after that. And it didn't rain till the fifteenth. During none of them twelve days didn't e'er drop of water fall."

Ben Allard had come up behind them humming his tuneless, abstracted song:

> "Jim, crack corn, I don't keer,
> Jim, crack corn, I don't keer,
> Jim, crack corn, I don't keer,
> *Old Marster's gone away. . . ."*

"It's the first twelve days of the new year, that's the sign, is it?" he asked.

The old man nodded. "They's a day for every month of the year." His cracked voice rose shrilly. "Warn't a drop of rain e'er one of them twelve days and yet here y'all go setting out tobacco same as if you hadn't had a sign."

Ote laughed. "What about this here ground soaker we got now?"

Pap shook his head. "Hit don't mean nothing. A morning's favor, that's all."

Ote withdrew his gaze from the old man's face, looked past his shoulder. Idelle and Myrtle had climbed the fence and were coming back down the rows. Myrtle had stopped and was setting plants again. But Idelle walked on down the rows the bucket swinging in her hands.

"Well," Ote said, "I reckon I'll git me a drink of water."

He went towards her down the rows. She had stopped and was setting the bucket down. As she bent forward the black shadow of a sailing crow fell across her face, slanted down over her body and rested for a moment on her instep. Ote

72

looked down at the arched bare foot that had resting, on either side of it, outstretched wings. "You gettin ready to fly?" he asked.

She laughed. "I ain't a ole crow."

He laughed too. She had raised her hand and was pushing back her hair from her forehead. He could see the line where the tan ended and the white began. He thought suddenly with excitement that if she were not so tanned she would have the whitest skin he had ever seen on a woman. Delicate too. That was why it tanned so easily. And it was the brown skin that made her eyes look light. He had thought they were blue but they were really gray. Gray and fringed with long golden brown lashes. She could handle 'em too. She was making a play at him right now. He laughed again. "I thought you might be," he said and bent and dipped up some water. While he drank slowly his eyes sought hers boldly over the dipper's tilted brim. A faint flush had risen in her cheeks but she stood immovable, her eyes not leaving his. "I like a woman that can look you in the eye," he thought, and realized suddenly that here before him in the flesh was the girl he had pictured the other night, the same shadowed brow, the same steady gaze.

She was speaking nervously with a little bubble of laughter. "We goin to have some music at our house tonight. You want to come?"

He leaned towards her, still looking deep into her eyes. "I'd be proud to come," he said.

CHAPTER SIX

THEY HAD pushed all the chairs
back against the wall and had cleared the floor for dancing.
But nobody was dancing yet. They were waiting on Old Man
Sheeler. To tune up. It took him a long time. It took him as
much as an hour sometimes. Idelle had said that a moment
ago, drifting by, laughing, with Buck Chester. "Pap, you
goin to take all night to tune up? Keep everybody waiting?"

Old Man Sheeler sat with his eyes half closed, the fiddle
shoved up under his chin. The fingers of his gnarled right
hand touched the strings every now and then but the music
came only in snatches. A few bars of "Money Musk" and
before he had got started on that it would turn into "The
Arkansas Traveller." As if he himself didn't know what he
wanted to play. Next to him Claude Trivers, Ed's black-
haired brother, leaned forward into the circle of the lamplight, his black hair falling in one great tousselled lock over his
forehead, his deep-set, green eyes twinkling. Ote looked at
him incuriously. He was thinking that Claude was a regular Trivers. Same kind of hair as Ed and same eyes, only a
different look out of them. Like Ed he would rather talk
than eat. He was arguing with Wallace Sheeler now, saying
niggers didn't have souls. Ote shifted his gaze to the other
room, where the women still moved about. Old Mrs. Sheeler
and the married daughter worked steadily, the one washing,

the other drying the dishes that were stacked at the far end
of the oilcloth-covered table. Idelle had been helping them
for a while but she had disappeared, out the side door, probably with that Buck Chester.

Wallace Sheeler stoped whittling, stretched and yawned.
"Uncle Jim Allard?" he said. "Good a ole nigger as ever
breathed. Don't teil me he ain't got as much a chance of going
to heaven as a whoremaster like Ote here."

Ote brought his chair down to the floor with a bang while
he leaned over to cuff Wallace around the neck. "I'll break
yo' head for you," he said.

Claude waited till their scuffling had subsided, then he
struck the mantel shelf with his pipe. "Naw," he said, "they
ain't a chance for a nigger to go to heaven. Ain't a chance.
You know why? A nigger ain't like us. He's been bought
and sold. Like a hawg. . . ."

Ote tilted his chair back against the wall. By turning his
head a little to the left he could see into the other room out
of the corner of his eye.

Idelle had come back and was standing in the doorway
again. She had on a red dress with a black patent-leather belt
and high-heeled slippers. Buck Chester was with her. Ote had
not seen Buck in five or six years but he would have known
him for a Chester anywhere. He eyed the boy now, noting
the pasty face, the slightly protuberant blue eyes that some
of the girls found so handsome and the black hair that was
always plastered smoothly down over his skull. Buck was all
dressed up tonight, in a white belted suit. One end of a laven-
der-colered handkerchief peeped from his breast pocket, his
tie was lavender-colored and his gray socks had lavender
stripes running through them. Ote wondered how he had
got the money for such an outfit and decided that he must

have turned bootlegger; no Chester had ever been known to do an honest day's work.

Ote's eyes went back to the girl. Buck kept catching at the dish towel she held over her arm, and she would lean forward to pull it away from him. Her yellow hair fell forward in a wave and hid her cheek each time she leaned forward. When she straightened up again it was like a cap fitting close over the back of her head. She must brush it a lot; it shone in the lamplight like gold. . . . When he had entered the room a half hour ago she had not spoken to him, had not even looked his way, just gone on about her business as if she had not invited him to come. But a few minutes ago he had felt somebody looking at him and had looked up in time to catch her eye. He had given her a bold stare. It had been in his mind: she thinks she's going to play with me like she's playing with that Chester boy. He had not spoken or made any motion towards her and after a second she had looked away.

Wallace Sheeler got up and dusted the shavings from his whittling off his knees. "You know what I hearn a feller tell once? I hearn him tell how the niggers come over to this country. Some folks went over thar in a boat and they had fiddlers on board and they started up a lot of fiddling and all the niggers come on board to dance and soon as they got to dancing them folks just rowed off with 'em. And when they got to this country they put 'em up and sold 'em. Just like you say, Claude. Just like they was hawgs. . . ."

Claude nodded. "And all the niggers in this country is the children and grandchildren of them original niggers. Uncle Jim, Aunt Pansy, all the niggers on this place. . . ."

Wallace grinned. "Thar's some of Uncle Jim's folks didn't come over in no nigger boat. They was some of them here before the niggers." He got up and walked across the floor to where two or three of the girls sat in a group.

Old Man Sheeler's pale blue eyes lightened. His hand stopped bowing a minute. "That so, Ote?" he asked. "Is Uncle Jim Allard got white blood in him? Your folks been here on this place a long time. You ought to know."

Ote shook his head. "I dunno," he said politely. "Looks to me like he had a lot of white blood in him, but I dunno."

He got up and followed Wallace. Idelle and Buck were standing in the doorway. Pearl Lightwood was with them. Ote paused before Pearl and bowed. "Would you choose to take a turn outside?" he asked. "Would you choose to take a turn while the music's starting?"

She turned about, a dumpling of a girl with stupid brown eyes and too much coarse black hair. She put her hand on his arm promptly. They went out on the porch. Outside in the cool night air he leaned against the railing, listening to the girl's chatter, answering her in monosyllables. "No ma'am, I ain't been back here long. I reckon that's why you ain't seen me at any of the dances. . . . Yes, I liked it in Detroit all right. But I figured it was about time for me to come home." He kept his tones even and polite but he was furious with himself. He ought at least to have taken one look at the girl before he brought her out here. A plain girl like this that probably nobody else ever looked at. That little vixen in there must be laughing up her sleeve at him this minute.

The music had started, clear and sustained this time. The old man was tuned up at last. Ote caught at the girl's arm, brought her briskly forward. "I reckon we better be goin in," he said.

Inside the house they were forming quickly for the reel. Wallace Sheeler had the black-haired, red-cheeked girl he'd

77

been with a few minutes before. Idelle was still with Buck Chester. Claude Sheeler had gone into the other room and had brought his wife out from where she was putting the babies to sleep.

"I reckon we ain't too old to dance, Mary," he said. "I reckon we can still show 'em." He stood there a moment, balancing awkwardly in his rough work shoes that had lumps of red clay sticking to them, before he began calling the figures in a rich, sonorous voice:

"Bow and balance all. . . . Bow and balance to me."

Idelle in her red dress was advancing mincingly from the end of the line. She was bowing to her brother Wallace. Then she was back at her end of the line. It was *dos à dos* now. Laughing, her arms folded over her breast, she revolved around her partner and now he and she were coming down the line on opposite sides. She was extending her hands to him, Ote. He took them and she swung him, no farther, no less, than the others. Buck Chester was patting and calling louder than anybody else. The dance progressed by couples. Ote and his partner had taken their turns twice before Old Man Sheeler stopped fiddling abruptly.

The young people surged towards him pleading, but he shook his head. "That ain't no dance tune. I don't feel that fer no dance music. That's all now. That's all fer the time being."

They were breaking up into couples, some moving towards the front door, others sitting down in the chairs that were ranged along the wall. Wallace Sheeler standing in the doorway was beckoning. Ote followed him down the steps.

They walked across the yard and out of the clump of oak trees that surrounded the house. On the edge of the woods Wallace paused. Standing still he looked back towards the house, then bent and pushed a rock aside from the stump of an old tree. He lifted something out of the hollow stump. "Here you are," he said.

Ote uncorked the bottle and tilted it to his lips. New corn but pretty good. He took a long drink, then handed the bottle back to Wallace. "Whar'd you git it?"

"Buck Chester brought it," Wallace said. "He's got a still running in one of them caves on the Adams place." He slipped swiftly to the ground. "Sit down," he said. "If you sit down here they ain't so likely to see us from the house."

Ote sat down beside him in the shadow of the stump. The bottle lay between them on the dead leaves. Ote picked it up and took another swig. Then he realized that he was drinking Buck Chester's liquor and that for years he had disliked Buck Chester. He couldn't remember when he had started disliking Buck. Was it the day he drove his new Ford car up to church with something so arrogant and swaggering in his manner that the boys leaning against the wall had broken out into loud laughs? No. It went farther back than that. Long ago. He couldn't have been more than fifteen and Buck not much younger. At meeting in August. The preacher had been pretty hot that night. The boys, all of them, had had swigs at the fruit jars hidden around the corner of the church, before they went inside. They came out looking for girls. Buck Chester had steered Ote around the corner to where one of his sisters waited.

There was a tight feeling at the base of Ote's neck. The hair on the nape was rising, stiff as a dog's. He got up. "Come on," he said, "let's git in the house."

Wallace was leaning sidewise to peer around the stump. "Wait a minute," he said. Ote looked over his shoulder. The yard was full of dark, moving forms. Through the hoarse shouts of young men came the steady sound of leaves being trampled under foot. Wallace watched them shaking with mirth. "Lissen at 'em," he said. "They think I ain't got no better sense than to hide it in thar in the yard."

"Ain't you goin to give 'em any?" Ote asked.

Wallace shook his head. "I done hid one bottle in that old hollow oak on the aidge of the woods. They'll find that before the night's over. I ain't goin to have 'em gittin into my liquor. They'd t'ar that house down."

"Well, come on," Ote said impatiently.

They walked off stealthily through the woods and re-entered the house the back way. Most of the young men were still out in the yard hunting the liquor. The girls had all disappeared into the other room. The older women sat ranged in chairs along the wall, keeping up a light hum of talk, turning now and then to look into the other room where before the dresser a knot of girls were primping. At the far end Old Man Sheeler sat in his corner, his fiddle across his knee. In the corner beside the window Claude Trivers was telling stories in the midst of a group of young men, about Morton Seay, who had got religion last fall.

"... And the first thing anybody knowed he jumped right up in meeting. Didn't fool with no mourner's bench. Jumped right up, saved and sanctified. 'Come on, Jesus!' he says and grabbed a holt of the stove pipe. He grabbed a holt of it but he turned it loose mighty quick. 'Go 'way, Jesus!' he says, 'You too hot for me!'"

The loud laughter ran through the room, against the background of the women's chatter. In the little silence that followed Mrs. Sheeler looked down at the floor and spoke plaintively: "I declar, next time we have a dance at this house I hope it ain't going to be right after a tobacco season. This floor hit'll be a regular loblolly before they git through."

Claude leaned forward, the smile still on his ugly, loose mouth. He clapped Old Man Sheeler on the shoulder. "Come on now, Old Man, give us a tune."

The strains of "Darling Honey" rose on the air. Claude Trivers had sprung into the middle of the room and was cutting a pigeon wing. When the music lulled he ran over and fetched old Mrs. Sheeler from her corner. The old woman protested but he swept her out into the middle of the floor. "Hurry up now," he called, "Miss Mary's coming down the lane."

The young men were coming in from the porch, the girls drifting back from the other room. Wallace Sheeler's black-haired girl was standing on the threshold looking about her. Ote went towards her. "Will you do me the favor?" he asked.

She laughed and nodded. A reel was forming but Ote and the girl disregarding the others began to two-step. The reel broke up. The room was full now of revolving couples. Ote's partner danced with abandon, her body swaying in double time to the measure, her hair fluffed out about her face like a Circassian lady's. Ote put his hand up and pushed it away from his cheek. "Here," he said, "keep yo' hair out of my eyes." She laughed and pressed herself closer to him. Their steps grew wilder. Soon they gave up all pretense at formal steps and careened about the floor, wildly jigging. The black-haired girl's laughter died to hoarse shrieks. She argued against him, clutched his arm. "Let's go outdoors," she gasped. "Let's go out and git some air."

He shook his head curtly, detached his arm from her grasp. "You don't want to go out thar. You'll git cold." She was looking up at him in surprise, her mouth half open in remonstrance. He detached his sleeve from her grasp and walked across the room. Idelle and Buck Chester were coming towards him, sauntering down a lane that had opened for their progress. Buck, half turning around to say something to Willis Morton behind him, had not seen Ote. But Idelle stopped short. She stood there looking at him but she did not speak. He laid his hand on her arm and walked her towards the door. "Come on," he said. "Come on outside and git some air."

CHAPTER SEVEN

Outside in the dark they stood facing each other. The girl spoke first. "Well," she said, "there's a whole lot of it."

"Whole lot of what?" Ote asked.

"Whole lot of air," she said and laughed. "Warn't that what you brought me out here for?"

He interrupted her to speak passionately. "I wouldn't keer," he said, "I wouldn't keer to see you goin with a feller that had something to him, but that Buck Chester . . ."

"What's the matter with him?"

"Plenty," he said.

"Well, what? How you come to know so much about everybody's business, Mister Otho Mortimer?"

"I know about him," he said slowly.

"Well, whyn't you tell it?"

"I ain't goin to tell it in front of you. It ain't fitten for a girl to hear."

She had jumped up on the railing and sat there, her legs dangling, her hands flung out on either side to steady herself. "I like to know what business it is of yours," she cried shrilly. "I like to know how come you and your folks set yourself above everybody else. Your pappy's a cropper on this place same as everybody else. I like to know how you think you can come it over me. . . ."

83

Ote stood looking at her. He put his hand up and wiped the sweat from his forehead. "Christ!" he thought. "Here we are quarrelling like an old married couple and we ain't even started goin together yet." It occurred to him that he had hardly said three words to the girl. Four: "Yes ma'am" when she asked if he wanted a drink and "I'd be proud to come" when she asked him to the house. He laughed out loud. Grasping her arm he pulled her down off the railing. "Come on," he said, "let's take a turn in the yard. All them folks'll be out here in a minute."

She sat back on the railing stubbornly. "What if they are?" she asked. "They all folks that come to see me. I ain't goin to run away from them."

He pulled her gently down to her feet. "Come on," he pleaded. "You know I got to talk to you."

She suffered him to lead her down the steps and out into the yard. Under the shadow of an oak tree she halted, mocking him. "We can talk here," she said.

"Lord," he thought, "now I got to start in and court her. Court her proper." It had been a long time since he had had to court a girl. Mamie Hawkins, that was the last one. Mamie, that lived on the Howard place when he was sixteen years old. But Lottie and that Simmons girl he'd had for a while. He hadn't had to fool around long with them. They knew what he wanted, right from the start.

He smiled back at her. "I'm a old man," he said, "gittin along. I cain't talk standin up."

It occurred to him that he was indeed much older than this girl. She couldn't be more than seventeen while he was twenty-four his last birthday. Twenty-four. He wondered if that seemed very old to her. That fat, yellow-bellied Buck

Chester was more her age. He ground his teeth. "Lemme catch him 'round one more time," he thought.

She had turned and was entering a little path into the woods. "Where she brings 'em all," he thought with swift jealousy. But the path ended abruptly on the edge of a blackberry thicket. She stood as if bewildered, looking back towards the lighted house. "Looks like it ain't anything but briers," she said.

He caught her arm and led her to the right, skirting the stump where the liquor was hidden, past the thicket and a good way into the woods. Under a cedar tree he paused and took off his coat and spread it for her, then motioned to her to sit down. She hesitated, then sat down. He dropped down beside her. He held her small hand in his and caressed it gently. She did not withdraw it but her body beside him was erect and unyielding. "You know," he said, "first time I seen you I said to myself, 'There's my girl.'"

She was laughing. "Barefooted, dropping tobacco plants. I must a looked a pretty sight."

He shook his head. "'Twarn't then. I was lonesome one night, lonesome for music or something going on and I walked clear up here. Late at night it was but your pappy was still fiddling. I saw you through the window and then I heard you come out on the porch. With one of your beaux. I heard him a-courtin' you but I said to myself, 'He may think he's going to git her but he ain't. That's my girl.'"

She had twisted her hand out of his grasp and was looking back towards the house. "They's somebody comin," she said. "We better git up from here. They's somebody comin."

Ote threw his head back and listened. From the house came cat-calls and prolonged whistlings and then voices:

85

"Idelle. . . . I—Idelle! Whar's that girl gone to?"

"You better ask Buck. He keeps up with her."

"I wouldn't 'low no girl of mine off in them woods with Ote Mortimer. . . . That low life son of a bitch, he . . ."

And then Buck Chester's voice, braggart but trembling, cutting across the others. "Will ye shet your mouth or will I have to shet it fer ye?"

She sat erect, trembling. "They goin to fight," she said, "reckon they goin to fight?"

Ote laughed. "If he fights anybody it ought to be me."

She was on her knees, getting the coat out from under her. "Here," she said and thrust it at him. "You better cover up that white shirt. They'll see it in the dark, even."

He took the coat, then mechanically put it aside. She was still on her knees. Her face was a white triangle before him in the dark. He put out his hands, set them surely on her waist, warm and incurving under the cool leather. "Come over here," he whispered, "come over here to me."

CHAPTER EIGHT

M̲ʀ. A̲ʟʟᴀʀᴅ put on his yacht-
ing cap. "I better be getting back to the field," he said.

Bill Fauntleroy said, "Yes, sir," respectfully, and added:
"I reckon you're pretty busy, setting tobacco."

The corners of Mr. Allard's mouth twitched. "We set our
tobacco a good while back," he observed gently. "We're poisoning now. I got a good deal of flea bug and Blackfire too."

Bill shook his head sympathetically. "I heard there was a
good deal in the country. What do you do for it?"

"Comes with the drouth," Mr. Allard said. "There ain't
anything much you can do for it once it gets in." He felt his
head to see if the cap were really there and started at his long
trot across the yard. "You young folks better pray for rain,"
he called back.

Bill Fauntleroy stood there in the hall. He was a tall young
man of twenty-three, lean and big-boned. His long face had
a humorous expression which would become fixed as he grew
older. His eyes, gray and lively under the beetling brows,
characteristic of his family, were fixed on Letty's face. "It's
hot," he said.

"It's fairly cool in the parlor," she offered.

He shook his head. "Let's go outside."

They went down the steps and across the lawn. At the
lower end there was a grove of trees. A hammock was swung

there between two maples. The place was cool, shaded by the maples and by a hedge of althea which had grown up under them. Bill Fauntleroy walked sedately beside Letty until they were around the corner of the hedge, when he took her in his arms and kissed her. "Lord," he said, I thought I never would get here."

Letty disengaged herself from his embrace, smiling. "Was it very bad?" she asked.

They sat down in the hammock His weight made it sag heavily in the middle. As she slid down against him she was aware of the pressure of her thigh upon his, aware, too, of the scent of fresh shaving soap and talcum, mingled with a faint odor of perspiration. He had stopped at home long enough to bathe and change but he was perspiring again in this unnaturally hot weather.

He was drawing her closer to him, bending to kiss her again. "You had me nearly crazy there for a while," he murmured.

She drew a little away from him, widening her eyes. "I? Why, Bill!"

"You didn't write for a week," he said; "nearly two. Ten days, anyhow."

"Was it that long?" she said. "I didn't realize.... But Bill, I didn't promise to write every day."

His eyes were on his ring, gleaming on her finger. "No," he said slowly, "you just said I could write every day. Still, I thought you'd answer my letters."

"But, Bill, you write a good many letters."

He turned his head so that he could look into her eyes. "Too many?"

She said, "Bill!" in a tone that she tried to make tenderly

indignant but his level, unhumorous ɑaze held her. "Letty, I'm crazy about you."

"I know it."

"That's the devil of it," he said.

"But I couldn't be crazy about a man who wasn't crazy about me."

He laughed out. "Then I ought to be the most attractive man in the world," he said, and, taking her face between his palms, looked into her eyes and slowly approaching his face to hers, kissed her so hard that she felt her lips bruised. "My God," he said, "how'm I going to keep my mind on torts?"

"What are torts?"

"I don't know," he said impatiently. "Don't talk about 'em. . . . Letty, these last few weeks have been hell. You know, I thought I wasn't going to get by. . . . I got Sam Sloane to help me. We boned every night till two or three. For a week . . ."

"Poor Bill!" she said, and laid her hand lightly on his. Glancing at his face in profile she noticed how his bushy eyebrows jutted out. When he was old he would look exactly like lean old Judge Fauntleroy, his father. She reflected that there was no danger of his not passing his examinations. All the Fauntleroys made good lawyers. "I like lawyers better than doctors," she thought. "They aren't always out delivering babies at night."

"My brain feels like jelly," he said.

"Poor Bill!" she said again and, because she wanted to hide her face, bent and laid her cheek gently against his lean hand. He waited until the caress was ended, then drew her to him so that she settled in under his shoulder. He clasped her waist with one hand while with the other he stroked her cheek.

"Like jelly," he repeated. "Lord, it's fine to be here."

Letty sat quiet, prisoned by his arm. Her eyes roved over the lawn. The grass at this end looked as if it hadn't been cut for weeks. Tomorrow she would ask her father to send a man in with a mower. He would say, "Certainly," but it would be weeks before the man and the mower would appear. The hands were always busy, setting tobacco or something, whenever you wanted anything done around the house. . . . The grass in this corner of the yard was as tall as hay, some sort of wild grass with a silvery sheen on it. She watched the heavy beards sway under the breeze and saw silvery, bearded grasses like these parted by a black foot, a flag-stiff tail. *If I was any good I'd go up there. . . . Why? . . . She's on a point. You ought to shoot over them when they're on a point. . . .*

Bill was talking about one of his professors. "We had a row the first day I was in his class and he's been out to get me, for two years now."

"What did you row about?"

"He asked me if I knew who Blackstone was and I asked him if he knew who Jesus Christ was.

She laughed because he expected her to. "He didn't know your father was a lawyer."

"My father was a better lawyer than he'll ever be," Bill said belligerently.

"Aren't all law professors just broken-down lawyers?"

"No. Some of them are damn good. This fellow's good. But he's an S O B."

"Bill, do you reckon you're going to like being a lawyer?"

"Oh, I don't know," he said. His lips were at her throat, coming up over her cheek, passing her mouth to press her brow, coming back to her mouth. She parted her lips for his kiss, thinking, "That's the first time today he's kissed me

like that. I wonder why." Then, aware that her body had
grown rigid in his embrace, she forced herself to relax, put up
a hand to touch his cheek. "Bill!" she murmured.

"I wouldn't want to be a lawyer or anything else without
you," he said.

She moved a little way from him and as she did so realized
that her skirt was damp where their two bodies had pressed
together. "Let's sit on the grass," she said and rose. He got up
too and flung himself down beside her. She thought for a
second that he was going to put his head in her lap and was
glad that he didn't. She sat with her short linen skirt spread
out, looking about her out of self-contained, watchful eyes.

There was a gap in the althea hedge. She could see the old
cook, Aunt Pansy, waddling from kitchen to out-kitchen and
back again, could hear the old woman's muttered soliloquy.
She was talking to her old mistress, Miss Fanny, Letty's
grandmother. Miss Fanny had been dead five years but Pansy
kept her alive in these muttered conversations.

"You right about that, Miss Fanny. Way I was going to
do anyhow," or "Look here, Miss Fanny, I warn't born yestiddy. I know as much about that as you do." And once Letty
had heard her say as she strained the milk, "Naw, I ain't.
I ain't goin to put it through twice. Don't keer what you
say...."

Letty looked away. "Everybody on this place talks to himself," she thought. "Pretty soon I'll be doing it too."

Her eyes returned to the old woman. Aunt Pansy did not
admire her, Letty; had not admired her for several years—
ever since she grew up, in fact. Aunt Pansy took a cynical
view of Letty's visits away from home. These visits, accord-
ing to her, had only one purpose, the pursuit of eligible
men. "Ought to stay home and take keer of your pa. Ain't

got no business flying around the country after the men."

Letty was irritated. "Aunt Pansy," she said once, "I don't have to go away from home to get beaux. I have plenty staying right here."

"I ain't saying you don't have plenty," the old woman had retored. "You the kind of gal always goin to have plenty of beaux, but you the kind cain't git enough of 'em. No matter how many you have you all time got to be foraging for more. Ought to stay here and take keer of yo' pa. He gittin old and nobody round him but niggers."

Letty at that point had walked haughtily out of the kitchen but Aunt Pansy had the last word. "Ought to git married and settle down. . . . Better watch out now. You the kind'll go through the woods and pick up a crooked stick. . . ."

Another saying of Aunt Pansy's came into the girl's mind: "The biter bit." That was what she said when Edmund ran off with Clarence's wife. If Aunt Pansy knew that she, Letty, was in love with a married man who didn't care anything about her, that's what she would say: "The biter bit."

Bill Fauntleroy rolled over in the grass. His face for the moment was serene. He gazed idly after the waddling form. "Old Pansy's faithful, isn't she?" he said. "Mother changes cooks every month."

"She's about as faithful as an old rattlesnake," Letty said, "and as mean."

"Whew!" Bill said. "I never knew you felt that way about her."

"I never could stand her," Letty said absently, "from the time I was born. . . ."

Her own thoughts echoed in her mind. . . . "A married

man who didn't care anything about her was a crooked stick, all right . . . but he wouldn't be picked up. . . ."

She had thought for a minute that he would—for just about five minutes. The day she left Countsville Frank had gone to the office as usual, but he was to come back at eleven to take her to the train. Her luggage was all downstairs in the hall. She was in the living room when the bell rang. They heard old Joe go to the door and then she heard Jim Carter's voice in the hall: "Are the ladies in?"

She was talking to Elise. She finished what she was saying. But Elise wasn't listening. She said, "Who is it? Who is it in the hall?"

Letty said, "I don't know," and then, thinking fast: "It sounds like Jim Carter."

Elise gave her one quick look and was going towards the door. But Carter was already inside the room. His eyes were fixed not on her but on Elise. He said: "I've come to take Letty to the train. . . . I just saw Frank. . . ."

She thought: "He did that well, but it would have been better if he'd looked at me first," and then: "Oh, I don't want to be thinking about that now. . . ."

Elise was worrying about time. "Then you ought to start, Jim. . . . You ought to start now. . . ."

Old Joe was carrying out the bags. The last one was in. Jim was standing holding the door for her. She turned to kiss Elise. ". . . Such a good time. . . . Daddy. . . . Yes, I'll write the day I get here. . . . If I left anything you keep it till I come back. . . ."

"You have plenty of time," he kept saying.

She was in the car beside him. Old Joe shut the door on the hem of her skirt, opened it and shut it again. Elise was standing there, the smile on her face. Then the car started. Letty waved. Elise waved back, waited a few seconds, then turned around and started for the house.

He drove fast down Broad Street. It had turned leafy overnight. The petals of the dogwoods in Mrs. Miller's yard were whiter than any paper. They came into Franklin. He was slowing up. "The train doesn't go till ten past. We have plenty of time."

She said, "Yes. . . ." They passed the Reid place where the gingko tree heaved its enormous trunk out of the sidewalk so that people passing by had always to step around it. She watched a woman wearing black patent-leather pumps hesitating whether to step out into the street or up on to the Reid's lawn, and thought in terror: "Twenty minutes and part of that spent in checking my bags. . . . Will he make me speak first?"

The woman decided in favor of the street. He said: "I thought I'd come by this morning. I wanted to talk to you again."

"Talk to me . . . talk to me. . . . Well, talk. . . . Yes," she said, and felt her breath die on the words, "Yes . . ."

"I got to thinking about things after we talked the other day and I got to worrying about you. I don't want you taking this too hard."

A child came out of the Campbell house and turned on a sprinkler. It sent a shower of drops into the air. The child dashed through the shower, shrieking. She was going to speak when its shrieks died away, but she opened her lips and no sound came.

He was slowing up still more. "Well, what about it?"

What about it? . . . About what? Oh, yes, he didn't love her. A moment ago, a long time ago, she had thought that

94

he did. But he didn't. He might have said so sooner. Back there on Franklin Street or before they passed the gingko tree.... "No," she heard herself saying, "no, I don't think I'm taking it hard."

He said, "I was a little worried," and then he was laughing, queer, awkward laughter. "I'm no sheik, but I've had crazy kids in love with me before."

Her body that had been all limp a moment before was taut now. She moved a little back and as she did so was conscious of her slim, flat haunches, of her little belly. . . . She turned her head and looked him full in the eyes.

He looked away. "The Roberts girl," he said, "she took a notion she was in love with me. Two or three years ago."

She continued to look at him. "Do you make notches on your belt?" she asked and heard how hard and crisp her own voice was.

They were at the station. She opened the door for herself before he could get around to her side. A Negro had come running to take the bags. She walked slowly ahead into the vast, cool building, fast at first then slowing up politely as she heard his footsteps behind her. He was touching her arm, indicating a seat, ". . . a minute . . . get the ticket . . . check your bags."

She nodded and sat down obediently. A seedy-looking little man, smoking a cigarette, fixed her with a suddenly bright stare. She gave him a level, arrogant look, rose and strolled over to the magazine counter and stood with her back turned, confronting the array of faces. Clark Gable, Myrna Loy, Simone Simon . . . "Can I help you?" the clerk was asking. She bought a package of cigarettes, then stood there, holding the cigarettes in her hand. Feeling the bum's eyes on her again, she drew the toe of her slipper across the slick floor so that she might feel the taut line from flank to ankle. "There's not anything the matter with me," she thought, "I have a good figure. Jane Morrison's is better. No, it isn't, either. . . . I have as good a figure as anybody I know. . . ."

He was coming towards her, the checks for her bags in his outstretched hand. She took them and slipped them into her purse. He was holding out something else. A magazine with a red, no, an orange cover. She stared down at black ink: Contributor's Column . . . My Winter in the North Woods. . . . She took the magazine from him, then turned back to the counter. Her eyes slipped past Myrna Loy, past Clark Gable to a pink-fleshed, petticoated child of eight. "Yes, the Dotty Dimple cut-outs," she told the clerk and when the paper-covered book was in her hand she handed it to him. "For your little girl," she said, smiling.

He said "Thank you," but he did not throw the book on the floor. He stood, breathing hard, holding it. When the caller announced her train he walked beside her through the door. He walked with her down the windy tunnel between the trains and helped her up the steps into her pullman and found her chair for her. He said, "Good-by," then and left her. She did not look out of the window for several seconds. When she did she saw him walking rapidly towards the escalator, the garish cover of the paper-doll book visible under his arm . . .

Bill Fauntleroy was sitting up, chewing on one of the long, bearded grasses. He was repeating something he had said before, about February. ". . . Yes, it was about February, I should think," he said.

"March," she thought, "March. That club dance had been

on a cold night in March. Aloud she said: "What *are* you talking about, Bill?"

"The change in you, he said, "I noticed it in your letters—even before you stopped writing."

"I didn't stop writing."

"No," he said patiently, "not entirely," and fixed her with a shrewd gaze. She did not trust herself to meet his eyes. She edged herself nearer to him, laid her hand on his arm. "Bill!" she whispered. He bent and kissed her quickly. She allowed him to draw her closer and laid her palm against his cheek, a gesture that she had found he liked.

"I know I get crazy ideas," he said.

"Let's don't talk about it," she murmured.

They sat quiet. Letty stared out over the waving grasses. She was wondering if he really was all right now or whether she would have to soothe him again before the evening was over. He would stay to supper. It would be eleven or twelve o'clock before he even thought of leaving. She might say she was tired. A headache would be better. She would refuse to eat any supper on the ground that she had a headache.

There was the sound of wheels at the gate. Bill rose to look over the hedge. "Who in hell is that?" he asked. She rose, too, and saw two men descending from an automobile. One of them was of ordinary size. The other was enormous. She watched the enormous man waddle towards the house, followed by his smaller companion. She sighed. "It's Cousin Rock," she said, "Cousin Rock Winn from Alabama. He'll stay a month."

CHAPTER NINE

Oꜰᴇ ʟᴇᴀɴᴇᴅ against a tree, smoking, and watched Ed hitch his horse to one of the stunted saplings that fringed the bare ground around the meeting house. He turned back to the buggy. May was clambering down off the high seat, one child in her arms, another clinging to her skirts. The four of them were making their way up the path.

The boys gathered on the hard-beaten ground in front of the church moved to one side, scuffling and laughing. The little, worm-eaten Sessons boy guffawed and smothered an oath. Bob Davenport cuffed him over the head carelessly.

"If you ain't an ornery little cuss. Cain't you see the preacher comin?"

They surged across the path and came to rest, sprawling against the side of the church, ten or twelve young men and a sprinkling of half-grown boys. The girls and the older people had already taken their seats inside. Bob Davenport moved nearer Ote. "How's it feel to have a preacher in the family?" he inquired.

Ote spat onto the ground, not taking his eyes from the moving figures. "D'know," he said. "He ain't never preached yet."

They had passed the big hackberry and were within a few feet of the church now. May and the children were lagging behind, but Ed walked with measured steps, his head held high, his features solemnly composed. The boys had begun shuffling again at his approach. The older boys and those in the foreground bent their heads and gave him the respectful salutation they would have given any other preacher, but a few faint catcalls came from the rear, and one of the smaller boys called out Ed's nickname: "Baldy Trivers. Hey, Old Baldy Trivers!"

Ed stopped sort. His blue eyes roved over the group with their odd, intent gaze. He raised his right hand, palm held stiffly upright. "Come in, boys," he said. "Come in. There's somethin inside fer ye."

He had passed on, into the church, an awkward and yet commanding figure, in his rusty black Sunday clothes, May and the children following on his heels. The group of boys hung back until they were well on their way down the aisle; then they all slouched into the church and fell heavily into the back seats. Ote had taken his place with the rest when he saw that his mother had turned around and was beckoning to him. He got up, walked down the aisle, and took his place beside her and May, midway of the church.

Nora Mortimer had lifted the baby onto her lap and was settling the little boy, Beulah, beside her. She leaned over now to whisper to Ote. "Looks all right, don't he?"

Ote's indifferent gaze rested on Ed. They had been going on all week about whether Ed's Sunday suit was good enough for him to preach in. His mother had been on the point twice of going up to the house and asking if Mister Ben didn't have a black suit Ed could have. Ed had restrained her. "Hit don't make no difference what I wear. Hit's the message. Hit come to me in overalls. I reckon hit ain't going to leave me 'cause I ain't got a new suit."

99

He was walking up the aisle now, past the knot of giggling Davenport children, past old Mr. Billy Rodney's out-thrust, goateed chin. Brother Wickersham, who was to introduce him, had risen from his seat on the platform and was coming forward to meet him. The two men stood in full view of the audience holding each other's hands in a close, lingering grip, peering into each other's eyes. Ed's gaze was serious as always, compelling, but there was a sudden bright flicker of malice in the deep-set eyes of the older man. Ote remembered that Brother Wickersham had experienced sanctification years ago, here in this same church.

"He's jealous of Ed," he thought, "jealous as hell."

He shifted his cud of tobacco in his cheek and settled himself more comfortably on the hard seat. His glance went swiftly over the church, came to rest on the back of a girl's neck a little to the right, three seats ahead. Idelle and her two girl friends had passed the group of boys lounging in front of the church without a look to left or right, a moment ago. She had not even looked up when he and the rest of the boys entered the church, but she knew that he was there. She was turning this way now, leaning over to whisper something to Corrie Wall. The brim of her blue straw hat came down so far that he could not see her eyes, only the curve of her cheek and her chin. She knew he was there, but she had not located him yet. She was turning still farther around now, giving a quick, searching glance to all the back seats. Her eyes had found his. She was looking straight at him. Her face, framed in the blue hat, was tilted back over her shoulder, her lips were wreathed in the conventional smile of the churchgoer, but her eyes had plunged straight into his. He sat stiffly erect, his locked hands swinging between his spread legs. He was aware that his mother and May on either side of him were looking first at the girl and then with quick side glances at him. A little sweat broke out on his forehead. His teeth, clenching suddenly, bit his plug of tobacco in two, but he held the girl's eyes with his until, her lips still fixed in the faint half-smile, she looked away.

Ed had come forward to the edge of the platform and was giving out the lines of a hymn:

> "Maree had an onlee son,
> The Jews and the Romans had him hung. . . ."

The women had started it off, a thin, quavering strain. His mother's voice soared high above the other sopranos. Her big body, quivering, shook the wooden bench. He turned sidewise to steal a glance at her. Her mouth was opened wide as if to loose all the music that was in her. Her eyes, wide open too, seemed to be fixed on some point beyond the whitewashed wall. She was nudging him now, wanting him to sing too. He opened his mouth, dutifully joined in the second verse:

> "They took him off to Calvaree
> And thar they nailed him to a tree. . . ."

He fell abruptly silent as the wailing swelled into the chorus:

> "Keep your hand on the plough,
> Hold on . . . hold on . . . hold on. . . .
> Keep your hand on the plough . . .
> Hold on. . . ."

Idelle had turned around and was facing the preacher. But one arm lay along the back of the bench. A thin, bare arm, only faintly tanned as yet, delicately splotched with freckles.

His eyes followed its curve, from the sharp elbow to the bone that sprang out on the wrist. Idelle's wrists were so slender that they looked as if they would break under any weight, yet he knew that she carried heavy buckets of water every day from the cistern at the big house and chopped in the rows, too, all day long sometimes. A little thin girl like that ought not to work in the field. But Old Man Sheeler was always behind with his crop. The women folks had to help out. . . .

She had shifted the position of her arm slightly along the back of the bench. The cheek that was turned towards him was stained suddenly with color. He watched the flush rise slowly until even the nape of her neck was red. She would not turn around, but she knew he was looking at her. She felt his eyes on her arm as if they had been his hand! It was almost as if he had reached out and touched her and she had drawn a little away . . . as she had always done . . . until last night.

A flush swept over his own face. He folded his arms tight across his chest, straightened up in his seat, and stared hard at the preacher. Ed had come to the edge of the platform and was speaking in a hoarse, earnest voice:

"I'm glad to see you here today. I've got a message fer ye. Old folks, little chillun, men and women in their prime. Thar ain't one of ye here today that I ain't been wantin to see. . . ."

He stopped speaking abruptly, paced the length of the platform, then whirled about suddenly to face his audience:

"I was down in Mister Ransom's new ground when I got the message. Sat'day morning it was. Nigh on to twelve o'clock. I was mighty nigh ready to take out. I was a-standin thar by one of them old stumps . . ." He stepped down off the platform, advanced until he was within a foot of the faces in the first row. "I was a-standin thar by one of them old stumps," he repeated, "not thinkin about nothin no more'n whether to take out now or plow another furrow before dinner." His eyes went to the face of a man on the extreme right of the third row. "Monroe Travers," he said sharply, "you know that old mule I bought off Mister Robinson last spring?"

The man spat out of the open window beside him. "I advised ye not to git him. Past his prime and warn't no 'count to start with."

Ed nodded impatiently. "That thar old mule, Frank, was a-standin thar at the aidge of the field sound asleep when suddenly he picks up them years of his like he heard somebody call him. I didn't think nothin of it, but a minute later that mule he starts off across the field hard as he can tear . . ." His voice sank to a whisper. "He didn't travel across it like no mule. He went across it like a horse. He went *aginst* the furrows and he went fast as any horse could travel. . . ."

A sigh ran through the audience, thin and sibilant like the murmur of the wind through ripe wheat. Ed put his hand up and dashed beads of sweat from his forehead. "I don't know how long it was," he muttered. "When I come to myself, me and that mule was down in the hollow by the spring. I don't know how we got over the fence or how we got down the side of that hill, but thar we was by that spring. . . ."

The sighing ran through the crowd again, deeper this time and more sustained. As it grew stronger, old Mrs. Agrew heaved her enormous bulk halfway up in her seat, fell back as if overcome by her own weight, then heaved herself up again. Broken, indeterminate sounds came from her lips.

Ote looked out of the open window, into a mass of dogwood blossoms. He noted mechanically that the woods were pressing closely on this side of the church, a whole thicket of dogwood and sassafras springing up right at the window. But the stiff, paper-white blooms, the black branches were like something remembered, not seen. He saw more plainly the hollow where Ballard's spring bubbled up between two leaning black rocks. They had come along there last night right after supper. A clear pale light still lingered in the open field over which they had come, but dark was already gathering in the hollow. They had stepped down the path slowly, clumsily in the gathering dark, their arms wrapped about each other. Idelle had made him take her up the ravine on the far side of the hollow. When he wanted to stop at the spring she had said it was too light. People coming along the path might see them. They had gone finally to the top of the hill where a big hemlock tree swept its branches low on the ground. . . .

Ed had stepped down off the platform and was standing at the head of the aisle. His voice, rising and falling, filled the room:

"It warn't like no feelin I ever had before. It were a kind feelin, a gentle feelin, and yet it were joyful too. I jumped right up thar in the hollow. 'Sing,' I said. 'Sing. Make a joyful noise unto the Lord!' " He stopped and looked about him as if bewildered. "Warn't nobody there but me and that mule and an ole crow. But I want you all to hear me now. I want you all to know what happened to me thar in that hollow by Ballard's spring."

He raised his hand and gestured sharply to the right. The eyes of the listeners followed his pointing finger to the field that was framed in the open window. A level field, bright with new green, hedged at the far end with dogwood blossom and the yellow tassels of new sassafras. "That ar field of Mister Ben's," he said, "hit's a pretty sight. Thar's some of you'll say thar ain't no prettier sight than a field like that covered with new rye. Thar's some of you workin from sunup till sundown to git a field like that of your own. Some is saying Ed Trivers'd do better to save his breath to try to git ahead hisself. . . ." He shook his head while his eyes held theirs. "Hit ain't nothin," he said. "This world and all its pleasures. . . . Hit ain't nothin." He ran his hand through his shock of auburn hair. His voice broke hoarsely, sank to a murmur:

"You old folks ain't the only sinners. Thar's some of you here before me still young enough to be studyin meanness. I know ye and I know the kind of meanness you're studyin . I'm a-gittin along but I ain't forgot how it was." He paused, levelled a finger dramatically at the listening faces. "Thar's a woman settin right here before me. She might not tell ye if ye asked her, but she ain't forgot the night me and her was settin down thar on the creek bank. Settin thar clost to each other and both of us studyin the same thing. She turnin to me and me turnin to her. I ain't sayin we done any meanness that night. Hit don't make no difference. Hit was in our minds to sin. We mought not a called it that, but that's what it was. . . ." He paused again, raised himself on his toes and flung his hands wide:

"Oh, brethren and sistren, sin can taste mighty sweet. Hit can be so sweet on the lips you'll say to yourself hit cain't be sin, but sin it is. . . . Sweet while you're tastin of it but after you've savored of it, it'll turn to ashes . . . dust and ashes. . . ."

The little rustling sounds made by people turning around had died away. Ote sat looking straight in front of him. He did not need to turn around and scan the faces. He knew the woman that was down on the creek bank with Ed that night.

Rob Traylor's wife. She sat there now beside her husband, her worn, sallow face upturned to the preacher.

Ote stared at the woman while Ed's words echoed in his mind: "Settin thar clost to each other . . . she turnin to me and me turnin to her. . . ."

He could see the creek, a silver line on the black, and the dark forms of the man and woman on the bank, but in his mind they remained immobile. He could not picture them turning towards each other. But the hemlock tree was a black cloud on the side of the hill, its branches feathery to the touch, wet already with dew. He and Idelle had had to crawl to get in under them. They had sat there close together, their legs touching in the little space made by two great, down-sweeping boughs. The hollow that had seemed so black a few minutes before took light from the open fields. He could see the white trunk of the sycamore that grew beside the spring and make out the outline of the two rocks that leaned over the water. Her face beside him had been just a splotch in the dark, but he had had the warm pressure of her knee against his thigh. He had sat there rigid, silent, while the fire rose and spread over his body. It was she who moved first. She had reached over and laid her hand on his knee. He had found himself pleading with her, stammering: "Idelle, I can't wait. Idelle . . ."

He had not needed to plead. She had come straight into his arms. She was trembling all over but her mouth had sought his eagerly. The hemlock branches had been all about them like dark plumes. . . .

Ed's hands, that had been raised high over his head, were sinking. He held them tight, clenched against his breast. "Hit's like them days in spring. Hit'll be cloudy when you git up and you know it's goin to rain before night. Thar'll be flashes of sun off and on enduren the day, but they don't mean nothin. You know it's goin to rain and rain all night. . . ." His clenched hands sprang apart, extended themselves pleadingly. "Sinner . . . Sinner. . . . Hit'll be a long night."

Ote shifted himself in his seat, fixed his eyes on the toes of his boots. Idelle had been afraid to go home last night. "I'm afraid. . . . I'm afraid they can all look at me and tell what I've done. . . ." She had cried a little and had talked about her sister, Nelsie, the one the old man had driven away from home. But she had been happy again by the time they got out of the hollow. He had helped her up onto the stile. She was standing on the top step when she turned to him again. They had slipped down together into the wet grass. A lightning bug flitting over the meadow had seemed a lantern swinging in a moving hand. Idelle had laughed recklessly. "Let 'em look. I know what to tell 'em."

He had known swift jealousy. "I reckon you do. I reckon you been at it long enough to know all kind of tales to tell 'em."

She did not draw away and did not speak but she trembled and her body grew rigid in his arms. He drew her closer, asked forgiveness by the pressure of his arms. She had put her head down against his breast. . . .

Ed had stopped gesturing and stood now, his hands hanging limp at his sides. His head was thrown back. His blue eyes shone. He spoke earnestly, his lips seeming to linger over the words. "Hit ain't nothin. This world and all its pleasures. A flash of sun on a rainy day. . . . A mornin's favor. That's all. . . ."

His voice died away. Silence flowed into the church, settled over the bending bodies, the upturned faces. An old man on one of the front seats sighed deeply. Somewhere in the back of the church a child wailed. On the murmur of its mother's hushings a woman's voice rose, full and rich:

"Oh, ye young, ye gay, ye proud,
Ye must die and wear the shroud. . . ."

Mrs. Traylor rose to her feet and lurched stiffly out into the aisle. Her husband, slumped down in his seat, did not move. The little boy who had been sitting beside her slipped from his place, stood a moment staring solemnly about him, then followed her uncertainly down the aisle.

Ed came to meet them. He took the woman's hand in his, laid his other hand on her shoulder. Around them the chorus swelled:

"Time will rob you of your bloom,
Death will take you to the tomb. . . ."

Ed had led her to the mourner's bench and was coming back to greet the other sinners who came crowding now from all corners of the house. The music was drowned in the shrill cries of children and the excited whispers of onlookers. Ote became aware suddenly that in the seat in front of him old Mrs. Agrew's voice had been going on all the time:

"Oh, Lord . . . Lord . . . Jesus. . . . Sweet Jesus. . . ." She was on her feet and had whirled about to face the congregation. "He said, 'Come,' she shouted, 'Come out from amongst 'em or you're lost.' He spoke to me by night and I'm buildin. I'm buildin high. I love Jesus. . . ."

She slumped sidewise suddenly and fell between the seats. There was a light froth on her lips and her eyes were closed, but her lips did not cease their mumblings. Her hands upraised, the fingers stiff and bent like talons, seemed to clutch something out of the air. The woman sitting next to Ote groaned suddenly.

"She's laid holt," she shrieked. "She's laid holt and she's a-bringin it down. Oh, God, I'm a sinner and I always been a sinner!"

Nora leaned forward, her right hand cupped behind her ear. Her face was bent upon Mrs. Agrew for a moment; then she turned back to May. "Hit's tongues," she said, "the unknown tongue. She's speakin."

Ed raised his hands and smote them sharply together. His voice, high and thin, pierced the label of voices around him. "I heard ye, God," he cried. "I heard ye in the wilderness. Come down . . . Sweet Jesus. . . ."

Nora was getting heavily to her feet. They were all singing:

"Then you'll cry, I want to be
Happy through eternitee. . . ."

Ote stood up beside his mother. Ed had stopped in his progress down the aisle and stood now not three feet away from them. He rocked a little on his heels. His lifted hands, swaying now to the left, now to the right, wove patterns in the smoky air. His lips, moving, half formed words: "A long night. . . . Sinner. . . . Sinner. Hit'll be a long night. . . ."

Ote looked away. Idelle was standing up between the two Cottar girls. She was singing. He could see her shoulder blades move under the thin blue dress. She had turned her head. Their eyes met while her lips still moved in the song. *Tonight,* she had said. The same place. But he must not come to the house. She would come across the pasture to meet him. The fiery-sweet sensation swept over him again, almost to the point of bliss. He raised his head, stared straight ahead of him. The church was not there nor the people, nor Ed's rapt face, only the hemlock branches that sweeping low to the ground were parted by the impatient hand.

CHAPTER TEN

Ben Allard, at the head of the table, bent sidewise, proffering a piece of ham to the setter dog who lay at his feet. "You have a little piece of ham, Miss?" he enquired. The dog gave a whine which Allard paraphrased in a high falsetto voice: "If you cain't do no better, Mister Ben."

Letty, at the foot of the table, bit her lip. During these weeks at home this habit of her father's had annoyed her more than anything that went on in the silent house. He would come in from the field at eleven o'clock and take a seat on the porch, the dog at his feet. An animated conversation would ensue, Allard making his remarks and then answering in quite another voice for the setter. There were jokes, it seemed, shared by Allard and the dog alone. There was one long duologue about a time when she got hung in a fence and he was always teasing her about being a tree dog and not a bird dog. The first time she heard the voices Letty had come downstairs, thinking there was company, and had been surprised to find her father rocking placidly, the half-blind old setter lying at his feet. The conversations during the last week had been so many and so prolonged that Letty felt that the dog really was answering her father and had come to dislike Old Sue as one dislikes a person who breaks in on one's train of thoughts with unnecessary chatter.

Allard, having ministered to the dog, turned his attention

to his guests. He carved ham, so expertly that each pink slice curled a little as it fell from under his knife. He disregarded his daughter and addressed himself to Cousin Rockingham Winn, who had come that afternoon for an indefinite visit. "Rock," Ben said, balancing several wafer-thin slices on the point of his long carving knife, "Rock, have ham?"

Cousin Rock shook his head, so vigorously that his pendulous jowls quivered. A morose expression came on his face. "Can't eat ham at night," he said.

Ben, too, shook his head. "That's bad." He put the ham on a plate and sent it around to Letty by the house girl. "I reckon I ought to be thankful to the good Lord," he said. "My stomach's never given me a moment's trouble in all my life. In all my life," he repeated. "Yes, I remember now. I gorged on peaches once when I was about ten years old and had a right bad night."

"You're the lean kind," Cousin Rock said. "I'm a Baswell. No hope for me not to have dyspepsia. I'm a Baswell."

Ben laughed. "All of 'em dig their graves with their teeth," he admitted. "Never saw a Baswell yet didn't think a lot of food. . . . Rock, you remember that nigger, Joe, you had once? Made the best gumbo I ever put in my mouth."

"He got cut," Cousin Asa said, "cut into ribbons one Saturday night. Little yellow nigger named Sam did it when he was drunk. He cried when he come to. Joe was laying out there on my lawn. They knew how much I thought of him, so they brought him to the house and then went and hid in the bushes. But that little yellow Sam stood right up and said he did it—something I never saw a nigger do before. Said 'Marster, I done cut Joe all to pieces but I never went to do it.' 'You may well cry,' I told him. 'Done killed the best cook in Alabama and then stand up and tell me you never went to do it. Ought to think twice before you get out that razor.' "

Letty looked at the enormous old man with curiosity and aversion. All her life she had heard of Cousin Rock Winn, of his prodigious appetites and his peculiar, solitary life. The old man's appearance exceeded her expectations. "He looks like a rhinoceros," she thought, eyeing the mottled skin that hung in pouches below his small blue eyes, "a dissipated old rhinoceros. I don't care if he is kin to me!"

Bill Fauntleroy, delighted by the eccentric, was laughing though he kept his tone respectful. "I don't reckon a nigger does much thinking when he has a razor in his hand."

"They don't do much thinking any time," Cousin Rock observed. "Seems to me I got the worst crew last few years I ever had. Got some of those mean niggers from over at Pisgah. Albert went out in the stable the other morning and one of them come at him with an axe."

"That so?" Allard said heartily. He turned to Albert, regarding him as if for the first time. Albert, a blue-eyed, solemn-faced man of forty, stared back with no change of expression. Allard shifted his gaze to his cousin. "How long you had Albert, Rock?"

"Ten or twelve years," Cousin Rock returned. "No, more like fifteen."

"Fifteen, come Christmas," Albert observed in a hoarse rumble.

Letty regarded him, too, with disfavor. Anywhere else in the world, she thought, Albert would not appear at the first table but here one had to have him sitting at the table, saying, "I don't choose any," to almost every dish that was handed him. She wondered why poor white people were so finicky about what they ate. You'd think they'd be glad to get anything. But Albert probably fared very well at home. Cousin Rock kept two cooks, one for meat and pastries and one for fish and game, and he had a four- or five-course dinner served up every night, even if there was nobody there but himself and Albert. In summer he kept a chair out under a shade tree and every hour or so a little Negro brought a bucket of cold water and poured it over him to cool him off. She had heard other things, too, of Cousin Rock. There was something strange, perhaps even a little sinister, about his *ménage*. No white woman had set foot on the place in forty years, it was said. But ten or twelve beds were kept made up for visitors. Sometimes visitors would go there and stay a week or so and leave without seeing their host. At such times he was supposed to be shut up in one of the upper rooms, gambling or drinking or Heaven knows what. He had a set of young niggers to gamble with him when there was no company on hand.

"Well, he ought to like it here," she thought; "nigger cooking if I ever saw it." She refused fried chicken and helped herself to cucumbers from the glass bowl that was set in front of her. She put a dab of mayonnaise on the cucumber, thinking as she did so of the remark Aunt Pansy had made to the house girl: "Set that ar axle grease in front of Miss Letty. Don't put it down thar where the gentlemen can get at it." She was tired of Aunt Pansy, tired of her old-fashioned cooking and her bossy ways. She wondered if she could persuade her father to get rid of Pansy then decided that she had better not try. After all, Pansy did take good care of Mister Ben and she, Letty, couldn't be here all the time.

She glanced up at her father. He was not eating much, either, tonight. He was too excited. All through the meal he had been plying his guests with food, and now that every plate was heaped and nobody could be induced to have any more of anything, he sat back in his chair, smiling.

She watched him lean sidewise the better to hear what Cousin Rock was saying. His face ordinarily wore an amiable expression except when he was peremptory with Negroes or white tenants but tonight there was a glow upon it she had never seen before. He was listening intently to what Cousin Rock was saying but his eyes meanwhile darted from face to face about the table as if while he were listening to one person he did not want to miss what anybody else was saying. She realized suddenly that this was a great occasion for him. "It's the first time he's had company in the house for months," she thought. "It's like Aunt Pansy says: he never sees anybody but poor white folks and niggers unless Chance Llewellyn or somebody rides over to ask his advice about something. He's lonely. That's why he talks to the dog. . . . I never thought of his being lonely before."

The house girl brought around the dessert, apple snow which Aunt Pansy had seen fit to serve in finger bowls, and a rather heavy cake. Letty refused hers and waited impatiently until Cousin Rock had had a second helping, when they all went out on the porch.

Ben Allard lit his pipe and sank into his chair with a sigh. "It's mighty nice having you all here," he observed, and then as if he had read his daughter's thoughts of a few moments before, "I declare, sometimes I go for months without seeing anybody but poor white folks and niggers."

Cousin Rock gave a sympathetic cluck. "Same with me. I stay down there on Acacia until sometimes I feel like I'll take root. Albert, he says to me day before yestiddy, 'Mister Rock,' says he, 'you stay here much longer and you'll take root.'"

He laughed chokily. "Said he believed I'd take root. 'Albert,' I said, 'I believe you're right. I sat down and I thought over all my kin folks and I said, 'Albert, there ain't anybody much I want to see but Ben Allard. I'd like to see Old Ben Allard,' so we got in the car and come right on. . . . ."

"It was time," Allard said heartily. "How long since you been on this place, Rock?

"I came to your mother's funeral," Cousin Rock said. "She was buried in February, warn't she?"

Allard nodded. "And you came home and spent the night with me, but you hadn't been here for a long time before that."

"Ten or fifteen years," Cousin Rock said. "Last time I was here—before the funeral—there was a peach orchard started out there at the corner of the yard. One of the best orchards in this country but ain't a sign of it left."

"Two, three old stumps," Allard said. "I've got that field in corn this year."

"How much is it going to make?" Cousin Rock enquired with interest.

Bill Fauntleroy had waited until Letty sat down, then dragged a chair close to hers. Under the cover of the half dark he was gently pressing her hand. The pressure grew stronger. She interpreted it as "Let's go out to the hammock." She gave him an answering pressure of the hand which meant, "I have to sit here with them a little longer."

"After all," she thought, "I was out there with him almost the whole afternoon."

Bill subsided. He was capable of sitting for long periods, silent and respectful while older people talked. He liked listening to old men like her father and Cousin Rock he had told her once, liked just the flow of their voices, no matter what they were saying. It reminds me of Father," he said. Letty knew that he had been genuinely devoted to the old judge and conceded as she had mentally conceded a hundred times before that he had an affectionate nature. "I like him as well as anybody I know. Why is it I hate to have him touch me?" For she knew now that she did hate to have him touch so much as her hand. "How will it be when we're married?" she wondered. "How will I stand it?"

She thought in desperation of a man she had known in Baltimore two years before. She had dismissed him rather sharply then. Two years was a long time, but she believed she could whistle him back if she wanted to. But did she want to? She summoned up his plumpish face with its mild blue eyes, his drawling voice, remembered mannerisms that she particularly detested. No, she thought. I'd rather have Bill.

She wondered how it would be if she never married, just stayed on in this old, moldy house with her father, making occasional visits to Baltimore and Louisville. But the visits would grow fewer with the years. She had been very popular the last time she was in Baltimore but would she be as popular if she visited the Slaydens next year and the year after that? People didn't want an unattached girl around forever, no matter how pretty or pleasant she was. No, she thought, I'd have to quit going around and get interested in something. That was the phrase her grandmother always used. Cousin Matty at Peacholorum was interested in chickens and took prizes at fairs with Buff Orpingtons or was it Plymouth Rocks. Cousin Elizabeth at Sycamore was not interested in anything, just mildly insane. "I might be like that," she thought and remembered a man once who had told her she was oversexed. "Yes, I'd be the kind that goes coo-coo. . . . I'll have to take Bill."

"But I won't marry him till he's through law school," she told herself rebelliously. "I'll have this one more year. No matter what he says."

One more year. . . . Who knows, she asked herself, what could happen in one year. The most important things in your life happen in a day, a minute, a second, even, so that afterwards you wish you could have been two persons, one to participate, and one to observe what is going on, for the sake of memory. But nothing—nothing at least that could delight her or interest her—could happen. Everything, as far as she was concerned, was over. She might as well go on and marry Bill this fall as he wanted her to.

Ben Allard was getting to his feet. "There's somebody stopped at the gate," he said.

The others looked and saw the lights of an automobile go out suddenly and then heard the slamming of its door. Two figures were striding across the lawn. As they watched, the figures passed the dark shadows of the sugar trees and came out into the shaft of light from the hallway. Letty, who had risen too, and was standing beside her father, saw her brother, Frank, step up onto the porch. Behind him came Jim Carter.

CHAPTER ELEVEN

THE PLANTATION bell rang as usual at four o'clock. It waked Jim Carter. He sat up in bed, thinking that some one had called him. Then he saw the pale light at the window and he realized that it would not be breakfast time for hours yet. He fell back upon his pillow and closed his eyes, but sleep did not come. After a little he turned over on his side and looked out of the window. You could see the stable lot from here. In one corner two or three men moved slowly about, throwing gear on mules. In another corner three young Negroes squatted beside cows, their heads dug into the animals' flanks, their hands moving rhythmically to bring milk down into the buckets. Suddenly Mr. Allard appeared moving along the path that led from the house. He came almost on the run, as if he could hardly wait to get where he was going. He had his funny old cap stuck on the back of his head and he wore a white suit that must have been Frank's originally from the way it hung on his gaunt limbs. As Jim watched he stepped lithely over a broken panel in the fence and was into the group of figures. They all began to move faster. The mules, as if realizing that the master had come, settled themselves under the gear and stepped off without waiting for the slap of the trace over their backs. A few young Negroes picked up hoes from where they had been set against the stable wall, and followed the mules off to the field.

Mr. Allard, now that they were in motion, seemed no longer to be in a hurry. He leaned against the fence. One hand went down into his pocket, brought out his pipe. He filled it in a leisurely way and began to smoke.

Jim closed his eyes and turned over on his back but under his closed lids he could still see the gaunt, agile figure striding down the path. Jim had not seen Frank's father for ten years. Yes, it would be all of ten years since the old man had visited in Countsville. He, Jim, had been married that same spring and Frank and Elise couldn't have been married more than a year. But the old man didn't look much different now from the way he had looked then. There were a few more lines in his weathered face, and his mouth was a little sunk in where he'd had some teeth pulled, but his figure was the same, and his walk as he came down that path a few minutes ago was the walk of a young man. Well, he, Jim Carter, wasn't as light on his feet as he'd been ten years ago, and as for Frank, Elise was after him all the time to take some extra turns at those pulley things to keep his waistline down.

He thought of Frank Allard as he had been when he first knew him, that spring he came home from St. Louis. Frank had been living in Countsville three years and had his insurance agency well established. He had looked young to be at the head of such a concern. He didn't look so young now. His hair was beginning to thin on top. Well, the last three or four years had been enough to age any man. Frank was four years younger than he himself was, thirty-one to his thirty-five.

Thirty-five! He hadn't realized his age or thought about his age, really, in all his life until the other day when he climbed into the dentist's chair. Nothing wrong with his teeth that he knew of. Still he wanted Ogden to take a good look at them. He had good teeth and he wanted to keep them looking good, so he went every six months whether there was anything to be done or not. Ogden was one of those philosophizing birds, liked to stop and smoke a cigarette and talk between rounds. He filled one cavity and tapped about a bit on the others. There was one tooth he said would have to have something done about it but nothing urgent. There were still one or two others that didn't look so good but they would hold up a while yet. Something in his tone made Jim uneasy. He twisted around in the chair. "Say, are all my teeth going to drop out on me?"

Ogden laughed. "Your teeth are in unusually good shape, for a man your age."

"You talk like I was Methuselah," Jim said.

Ogden laughed again. "No, but you're nearly forty years old." With his blunt, clean-smelling fingers he pried Jim's mouth open and tapped one of his teeth. "You're nearly forty and your gum line is receding. There's no disease of the gums. They're just shrinking, that's all."

He let Jim shut his mouth, pulled out his cigarette case, proffered a cigarette, then took one himself. He gazed out of the window where, far below, the city shimmered blue in the smoky light. "Nature," he said. "You see up to the time you're forty she's on your side. Everything is for building up. You can get a lick on the jaw bone, a cut, anything, she'll take care of it, as long as she's interested. But after you pass forty or forty-five, after you get on the wrong side of the slope, it's different. Everything's giving way then. It's slow, so slow you can hardly notice what's happened from year to year, but it's going on all the time. It takes almost as long as the first building-up process and when it's finished you're old—or dead." He smiled, ground his cigarette ash out and dexterously flipped the white napkin from about Jim's neck. "I reckon we'll both last a few more years," he said.

"I don't know," Jim told him. "When a guy gets through talking to you he feels like John D. Rockefeller, Senior."

The dentist laughed and pushed him out into the anteroom where half a dozen people were waiting. Jim, as he went towards the elevator, felt sorry for poor old Dave Ogden, who had to stand humped over for five or six hours every day prying into people's mouths. He was not a reflective man, but often during the next few weeks the dentist's words came back to him. It annoyed him to think that inside his splendidly built, well-conditioned body the mysterious disintegrating processes might already have begun. He could not get out of his mind the picture the man had painted: himself coming up over the crest of a hill and then without stopping even to look around him, starting, being propelled, relentlessly downward. "Why, damn it," he thought, "I've hardly started living yet!" And it was a fact that until that moment in the dentist's chair he had always thought of himself as a young man starting out in the world.

Jim Carter was the youngest son of an Alabama circuit judge. Marshall Carter enlisted in the Confederate army when he was fourteen and fought under Breckinridge. At nineteen he came home with four fingers shot off one hand, and began to read law in old Judge Shaw's office. At thirty-five he was a judge of the circuit court and he died at his desk of heart failure when was fifty-eight. In his middle years, after he retired from the bench, he made a good deal of money by the practice of law. He bought land with the money—to the day of his death he was as much farmer as lawyer, and even after his practice grew he continued to live on the old Carter place on the outskirts of Countsville, riding in to his office every day on horseback.

The Carter house, an ugly red brick mansion, sat far back from the road in a grove of maples. In the judge's day the house and its many outbuildings were well kept, but Jim could hardly remember back that far—his father had died when he was five. The judge's widow, Josephine, had as much as she could do to feed and clothe and, as she said, "half educate" seven children. Robert, the oldest son, had studied law at the University of Virginia, Edward had got an appointment to Annapolis, Bob had got through medical school, partly working his way and partly through the aid of a rich cousin. The girls each had a year or two at Ward's or Sweetbriar, but when Jim came along the money and the education too, the widow said with a deprecatory laugh, had just about run out. "It was easier with the other children," she had once explained to rich Cousin Alfred who had come down from St. Louis for a conference. "They all seemed to have a bent towards something, but Jim doesn't have any bent."

Edward, on leave from the Naval Academy, laughed at her. "Mama, I heard Uncle Joe Burden say the other day that Jim was as gifted a boy as he'd ever seen."

Mrs. Carter looked at Cousin Alfred. "He means with dogs," she explained. "The boys are over at Uncle Joe's half the time."

Cousin Alfred's faded eyes kindled—he had been raised on a plantation near Grand Junction. "Do you mean, Josie, that Joe *Burden* lives neighbor to you?"

"For three years," she said. "He had some kind of fuss with the Whitleys and moved over here."

Cousin Alfred heaved himself out of his chair. "No use discussing the future of these boys," he said. "They will all turn out professional handlers. Joe Burden could train a stick." He was calling to Ned: "Boy, fetch me my hat." The widow heard him slap Ned on the back as they went down the hall. "Boy, do you realize Joe Burden is the greatest trainer ever lived in this country? He knows more'n you'll ever know if you live to be a hundred."

Jim, lying in the bed, was thinking of those old days now. Something about this house he was in reminded him of the Carter place, the high ceilings, worn furniture, bare floors; or perhaps it was just the way the fields sloped away from the house. Tobacco in most of the fields, of course, but the field outside the window, in hay this year, tilted up and outward just like the big south field at Carter's. A wonderful piece of breakaway ground, that field. It was through that field the Carter boys had come to know Uncle Joe so well.

He had had a spectacular quarrel with the rich Yankees who employed him as trainer and had gone to law with them. He had been defeated, of course, and had lost his house at Grand Junction as a consequence of the suit, and because he had a married daughter living in Countsville he had moved to a little farm on the outskirts of the city.

There were only thirty acres, hardly room, Uncle Joe said, for a rangy dog to turn around in, but he had had the run of all the Carter fields. Jim was twelve that year. Out of the four Carter boys Uncle Joe had picked him to help with the dogs. Marshall Carter had been a good shot but his youngest son, Uncle Joe said, was a natural. In addition to bringing down the birds he knew how to get all there was out of a dog. He helped Uncle Joe train Tribulation—he was fourteen that year—and handled him when he won the North Carolina Sweepstakes and handled him again in the Inverness trials in Mississippi.

A boy's family knows very little of what he is doing. Mrs. Carter knew that her son was considered a fine shot. She knew too that he spent a good deal of time at the kennels but she had no idea that at seventeen he was a professional trainer with responsibilities that weighed heavily upon him. That was Trib's third season. Jim and Uncle Joe, too, expected him to win the National championship.

When the telegram came from Cousin Alfred saying that a friend of his had an opening in his office and Jim was to come to St. Louis at once, she went in—it was early in the morning—and waked Jim up with the news. He sat up in bed, a heavily built, darkly sunburned boy of seventeen. He stared at the wall, his under lip a little thrust out, then looked up at the woman standing beside the bed.

"The National field trials are next Monday," he said.

Mrs. Carter was a tall, high-headed woman who wore her abundant gray hair pushed back from her face and carelessly knotted at the nape of her neck. She had large gray eyes which had a peculiarly intent gaze, but her voice was drawling and weary. It held nearly always an ironic note as if the things she commented on were beyond her understanding and therefore no concern of hers. She looked down at Jim now in surprise. "Don't you *want* to go to St. Louis?"

"No," he said.

She sat down suddenly on the foot of the bed. She put her hand up over her face. Under the half-shielding hand her fine mouth twisted uglily. Jim looked at her, then leaned forward and put his hand on her knee. "You want me to go to St. Louis, Mama?"

She let the hand fall. Her eyes looked directly into his.

There was accusation in them and hatred. "Haven't you any mercy?" she asked. "Don't you think there's any limit to what I can stand?"

Jim was known as the slowest-witted member of the family. He shut his mouth now and swallowed in the effort to follow her. "You mean I've got to get to work and make a living?" he asked.

"You've got to start," she cried harshly. "A great, hulking boy of seventeen!"

He got out of bed. He stood there, barefooted in his gray striped pajamas. He stared at her, his brow furrowed. "I haven't asked you for any money for three years," he said slowly.

Her hand came up sharply to her brow. "And do you suppose I haven't worried about that? You gamble for it, I reckon. God knows what you do!"

He was stooping to slide his old leather slippers out from under the bed. "I get it out of the dogs," he said. "Uncle Joe has been giving me a fourth of everything for the last year."

She cried out again at that. "Great God!" she cried. *"Dogs!* Don't you want to *help?* Do you realize that Helen is thirteen this month and Cissy has to have a new evening coat for that dance? Transparent velvet. It's six dollars a yard."

"I don't know anything about transparent velvet," he said, "but if you all want me to go to St. Louis I'm willing."

She got up from the bed. She passed her hand over her brow where a lock of gray hair was straggling. She held her hand for a moment before her mouth. When she took it down her face was quite composed. She said: "How do you want your eggs? . . . Alfred's telegram said 'immediately.' You reckon you can catch the noon train?"

He said, "Fried. . . . Yeah, I can make that all right."

She moved towards the door, then paused. "Bring what soiled shirts you have down with you. Dilse can wash them and they'll dry quick in this wind. I'll have to send some of your things to you by parcel post."

He said, "All right." Then, before the door closed, he moved forward. "Mama," he said, "you understand about this dog, don't you? Uncle Joe says he can't help but win the National. You know the stud fees alone'll run into money."

She looked at him. Her eyes were dull, her voice was as calm and weary as usual. "You do just exactly what you want to do, Jim," she said. "Of course, this is an opportunity that may not come again, but I wouldn't want to influence your decision in any way."

She was gone. Jim stood looking at the closed door a second, then he began to dress. Ten minutes later he was downstairs. He ate his breakfast, then went across the fields to Uncle Joe's. As he went he noted automatically that the weather had changed. It had been burning hot all through September, too hot even to take the dog out most of the time. But there was a wind stirring this morning and the air was cooler, an ideal day to exercise, what Uncle Joe called "good working weather."

He unfastened the gate, entered the little yard. Trib, who was sunning himself in a corner, saw him and came loping over. Jim put his hand down, then raised it quickly as if the dog's head had been hot. He went around the house and through the side door into the little room that Uncle Joe called his office. Uncle Joe was wiping a gun with an oiled rag. He looked out of the window as Jim came in.

"Nice wind stirring," he said. "Less take him over in that south field of y'all's today."

Jim stood in the doorway. He said, "Uncle Joe, I've got to go to St. Louis."

Uncle Joe's hawk face swung away from the window. "What would you be going to St. Louis for?"

"Cousin Alfred telegraphed," Jim said. "He's got a job for me."

Uncle Joe leaned over and stood his gun in the corner. "Alf Marshall's got a job for you!" he said. "Doing what?"

Jim made a slight, controlled gesture. "Writing advertising or something. It's in his office."

"Don't he know you wouldn't be any good at that?" Uncle Joe asked.

Jim did not answer. After a second the old man slid from the desk, stood erect. His gimlet eyes bored into the boy's face. "Look here," he cried, "they been talking to you about me. They been saying Joe Burden's done for, on account of that law suit. I know. I know what they all say."

Jim remembered his mother's face as she had raised it when she was sitting there on the foot of his bed. It seemed to him that Uncle Joe's face had the same expression that hers had had. He had thought, coming across the fields, that he would have to stay with Uncle Joe a while, an hour maybe. It would take time to make him see that he, Jim, had no choice, that he had to go. Now he knew that he must get out of the room as soon as he could. He said:

"Cousin Alf doesn't even know that you had a law suit with the Whitleys. He . . .," his voice broke . . . "he thinks you're the greatest handler ever lived."

Uncle Joe had picked up his gun again from where he had stood it in the corner. He stood looking down at the barrel that glinted in the morning sun. When he spoke his tone was even. "Alf Marshall always was a fool." He turned the gun stock, laid his finger on a spot that might have been duller than the rest. "Don't you worry about us, boy. We'll git along."

"We'll have to dissolve the partnership," Jim said. "Trib is going to win. I know that, but I don't want any of the money."

The old man slid the gun into the crook of his arm. "Let's talk about that later. What train you going to make?"

Jim told him that he had to make the noon train. They shook hands. The old man gripped Jim's hand hard, but he said only, "Good-by. I'll let you know how Trib makes out. But you'll read it in the papers." Then Jim was walking back across the field, and four hours later was on his way to St. Louis.

He stayed in St. Louis eight years. When he was twenty-five Alfred Marshall decided to open a branch of his agency in Countsville and Jim was sent there as its head.

He arrived home on a blowy morning in May. There had been a heavy rain the night before. The taxi driver who brought him from the station was afraid he would get his car stuck in the muddy avenue that led up from the highway, so Jim got out at the gate and walked, carrying his suitcase. He could still recall his feeling of surprise when he came upon the house at the end of the long avenue of maples. It was larger and so much shabbier than he remembered it. He thought that it must have gone down a great deal in the years that he had been away, but after he had been at home a few days, moving among remembered objects, he realized that it was he and not the place that had changed.

His mother was a little thinner, her hair a little grayer; otherwise she had changed little. On the first morning he was at home she said: "Well, Jim, I reckon you'll be going over to see Uncle Joe Burden?"

His sister, Helen, looked up from her grapefruit. "He'll have to go a long way," she remarked.

Uncle Joe, it developed, had moved two years ago from the Sloane place. "He quarrelled with Mr. Sloane," Helen remarked, "like he does with everybody."

Jim looked at her attentively, but said nothing. He had not seen the old man since he left Countsville. There had been a brief exchange of letters. Uncle Joe, in writing, had confined himself strictly to business and he had not written until after the National field trials were over. Trib had won, all right. It gave Jim a funny feeling when he saw the pictures of the field trials in a St. Louis paper: Trib breaking away, Trib on a point at the edge of a plum thicket that Jim knew well, and last of all Trib, with his handler, the Warner boy. Uncle Joe had got Ed Warner to handle Trib when Jim let him down.

But that was eight years ago, the same spring he left Countsville. There was a lot of Trib's get scattered over the country, but Trib, himself, was dead—run over by an automobile—and Uncle Joe moved away, getting ready, doubtless to quarrel with somebody else. Jim knew all about the old man's quarrels, starting with the famous and ruinous altercation with the Whitleys. Jim understood how in a way Uncle Joe had to sue those people. He was good, Uncle Joe was, the best there was in his line. Some people thought he was the greatest handler ever lived. It was galling to Uncle Joe's dignity to have to take orders from a man like Whitley—or worse, from Mrs. Whitley—those rich Yankees had a way of turning sport over to their women. Uncle Joe's quarrels with people like that were all part of his touchiness and his dignity. When you came down to it he ought not to have to take orders from any of them. . . . But Jim was not thinking of Uncle Joe as he sat at breakfast that morning. That all seemed very long ago and part of a life that did not now interest him. He was looking at his youngest sister with some curiosity.

She sat, leaning slightly against the table. One hand supported her chin, the other reached out from time to time to convey a morsel of grapefruit to her mouth. She had refused toast and scrambled eggs with a little shudder. Jim saw that there was a faint beading of moisture on her upper lip and that the corners of her pretty mouth were drawn as if even sitting at the table took an effort of will. "She must have been on one hell of a binge last night," he thought, and, seeing that her glass was empty, unobtrusively poured it full of iced water and set it in front of her.

She thanked him with an upward flicker of her long lashes. He watched her as she continued a conversation with her mother. Helen was not an absolute knock-out, but she was undeniably a pretty girl. She had her mother's coloring, the gray eyes and the blonde hair—Mrs. Carter's hair had been ash blonde before it turned gray—but Mrs. Carter's skin was tanned and leathery from working in the garden, while Helen's was so white that the veins showed blue at her temples and wrists. The odd thing, though Jim did not realize it, was that the voice of mother and daughter had the same dry note of disillusion though Helen was twenty-two to her mother's sixty-five.

They were carrying on a conversation now in which neither of them seemed interested. Helen said that she would stop at Black's and get the picoting and Mrs. Carter said that in that case she would try to get at the dress tomorrow morning. She had to go over to Mrs. Moore's this morning on church business. Helen nodded and rose. "I'm staying at Sara's for lunch, Mama. We're playing tennis."

"Are you staying there for dinner too?" Mrs. Carter enquired.

Helen essayed liveliness. "Heavens, no. I haven't been asked. I'll be back by two-thirty, three anyhow. You'll leave those curtains for me, won't you?"

"Yes," Mrs. Carter said drily, "I'll leave them."

When Helen had gone she sat staring at the tablecloth a moment, then raised her head and looked about the shabby, sun-lit room. Her eyes had a fierce, resolute expression, but her voice was calm. "I'm glad you're here, Jim. Helen never brings any of her company home. I don't even know where she is these days." She laughed, a faint, unpleasant laugh, "I mean nights."

"Does she run with a wild crowd?" Jim asked.

She shrugged. "I don't know whether they're wild or not. There is a young lady who is dictatrix—social dictatrix of Countsville. They run wherever she leads them. . . . Do you remember the Camps?"

He shook his head.

"Kampschafer," she said. "That was their name, but they've changed it."

"Are they Jews?" Jim asked.

"No, but they are people who can change their names as easily as they can change their clothes. They are very rich. They make—products. I remember your father tried hard to prevent these very people from coming into this town."

Jim, as he pushed his chair back, suppressed a grin. He had placed the Kampschafers—or Camps as they were called these days. He had never seen their factory—it was over in

Milltown somewhere—but you could not drive through the country without being made aware of their "products." On the road he had come out on this morning there was a huge billboard advertisement, a young girl smiling vivaciously and leaping high into the air. "Be as gay as the rest," the caption said, and below that, "Use Fascinex. In three sizes." Jim remembered also to have seen a fat, healthy baby crying from his billboard: "I—Want—a—Camp Diaper."

He grinned again as he went up the stairs to his room. His mother, with her old-fashioned ideas, connected the Camps so intimately with their products that she couldn't meet them without embarrassment. But they themselves probably didn't give a whoop. After all, he thought, somebody has to make the laxatives and contraceptives and baby pants, just as somebody on the farm has to butcher the hogs.

As he got ready to go to the office he was frowning. His mother's eyes this morning had had an expression in them he had seen only once before in his life, that day he went off to St. Louis. He rarely reflected upon that experience. He had pushed the whole business out of his mind, but he realized now that he had gone to St. Louis just because of the way his mother had looked at him. The expression in her eyes this morning had not been quite the same, but it was enough alike to set dim memories stirring. Now as he swung down the stairs he told himself that if they—and Helen was somehow included in the accusation—if they started "that" again he wouldn't stay here. He would leave, that was all. He wouldn't stay here a minute.

He came in at five o'clock, tired out. It was hot, even in the airy upstairs rooms at the Carters'. He took off his shirt and undershirt and lay down on the bed. In a few minutes he would get up and take a shower and dress. He would call up somebody—he didn't know just who—and make some kind of date for the evening. He was tired, but after he was rested he knew that he wouldn't want to stay at home.

There was a light tap on the door. He sat up in bed, reached out and getting his shirt, draped it shawlwise over his shoulders. "Come in," he called.

Helen stood in the doorway. She looked better than she had this morning, freshly made up, in a cool-looking linen dress. "Do you want to go over to the Camps' tonight?" she asked.

He had dropped back upon his pillow and did not answer for a second. He was wondering what had become of his own old crowd. After all, he didn't want to trail around with kids Helen's age. Still, he had nothing on for tonight and his mother would be pleased to see him going out with Helen. "What are you going to do?" he asked.

She shook her head. "I don't know. Just sit around." The door was swinging to in her indifferent hand, then her voice came from the other side. "They have very good liquor."

He nodded. "All right," he said, "I'll come along."

CHAPTER TWELVE

T HE CAMPS, ten years ago, had bought the old Taylor place. The square red-brick house stood there at the end of the avenue just as it always had, but it looked different. The tall white pillars still ran across the front, but a glassed-in porch had been added at the side and a pergola hung with vines ran off from that down the slope.

Helen was stopping the car on the gravelled circular drive.

"We'd better go in the house," she said. "Mrs. Camp's fussy about that."

Jim wondered if Mrs. Camp were in the habit of receiving her guests on the lawn, but he followed his sister into the house without comment.

She was evidently a frequent visitor here, for the middle-aged, serious butler smiled a welcome before he conducted them through the hall and one of the large parlors to the glassed-in sun porch on the south. An elderly man and woman sat here. He was sunk in an armchair, reading. She sat in a low chair near by. There was a bowl of white freesias on the table beside her, and behind her cactus leaves were green against the clear glass of the window. She was a small woman whose hair shone like silver in the light. She wore a gray dress and her little, beautifully shod feet rested on a hassock. Her needlework lay in her lap. As Jim and Helen crossed the wide expanse of floor she raised it to draw a colored thread slowly through a piece of coarse net.

She heard them coming, looked up and smiled. "Father, here's Helen."

The little man was on his feet and coming towards them. He had bright blue eyes. His hair rose in a white wave above a high forehead, the only part of his face that was not as brown as a gypsy's. He smiled absently and said, "Good evening, my dear. And is this the brother?"

Jim said, "How do you do, sir?" and shook hands.

Mrs. Camp was calling: "Has Jim come? I'm so glad."

They went over to where she sat. Helen dropped down on the hassock and Mrs. Camp made Jim sit down too so that she might "get a good look at him."

Helen, whose manner had changed for one of great animation, leaned over and raised the needlework in Mrs. Camp's lap. "You're doing the chair-back after all," she said. "It's going to be lovely, Mrs. Camp." And she held the netting up against the light.

Mrs. Camp regarded it, her head a little to one side. "The pattern is nice, isn't it? It's taken from a sixteenth-century *prie-dieu,* one that Mary Queen of Scots is supposed to have used." She looked over at Mr. Camp. He had surreptitiously begun reading again, but he seemed to feel his wife's glance, for he put his newspaper down and turned his bright blue eyes affectionately upon her. She shook her head at him as if in answer to something he had said, though he had not spoken. "No," she said, "you musn't offer these young people a high ball. If they have anything they'd rather have it out there with the others."

Mr. Camp looked at Jim. "Quite sure?"

Jim, who would have liked a high ball, said he was quite

sure he wouldn't have one. Helen rose to her feet. "We'll run along," she said. "You two have a better time alone, anyhow."

Mr. Camp was reading again, but Mrs. Camp turned her pretty, faded cheek slightly so that Helen might drop a kiss upon it. "Tell Sara I'll be out after awhile, will you, dear?"

Helen said that she would. Jim bowed and walked beside her through the glass doors out onto the lawn. The weather had changed overnight. It was as warm as June though there were no leaves out as yet and only spring flowers showed in the borders.

They came to the end of the slope and started down a long flight of stone steps set in the hillside. Jim involuntarily halted at the head of these steps, surprised by the prospect before him. He stood on one side of a deep ravine. On the other side was a long, low lodge built of brick with a wide terrace in front of it. Immediately below the terrace was a pool. It was rather narrow but, long and curving around the side of the little valley, gave the impression of a miniature lake. Jim's eye followed it till it was lost around the bluff. He knew this ravine well. He had often hunted rabbits in it when it was just a neglected part of the Taylor grounds. He would never have recognized it in its new aspect. He gave a low whistle. "Taylor's gulch?" he said. "Pretty slick."

Helen was already descending the steps. "It's the nicest pool anywhere around here," she said. "Sara planned it all herself."

"Well," Jim said, "she's done a good job. Still, I reckon I could have done it myself if I'd had the money. Must have set her old man back a notch or two. I suppose they have reservoirs up above here. But grading this slope must have been a job. What's that house over there?"

"It's the guest house," Helen said, "bathing house, really. But we use it for parties in the winter."

"Well, you tell Sara it looks all right to me," he said.

She did not answer as they walked around one end of the pool. It was set with ferns and rock plants and a reddish climbing vine was flowering in the crevices of some of the rocks. He admired the natural beauty of the setting, then found himself again calculating the cost of the operations. "They must have money to burn," he thought.

Helen, ahead of him, was ascending a low flight of steps. They came up over the little rise onto the brightly lighted terrace. Deck chairs and tables whose chromium frames shone in the light were set about here. At the far end of the terrace a group of young people were gathered about a larger table where a Negro servant had just set down a tray of drinks.

A young man standing on the edge of the group turned around and saw Jim and Helen. He was coming towards them. Helen introduced him: Joe Camp. He had a narrow, tanned face and weak blue eyes. A plump man in a deck chair was waving his hand without rising. Jim's eyes went from Joe Camp's face to that of the man in the chair. He knew him—Seely Latham. Seely was opening cotillions when Jim's oldest sister, Anna, came out. He must be forty if he was a day. Jim wondered what he was doing in a crowd as young as this.

The young people on the fringe of the group were standing aside. Jim went up and spoke to Latham. In his confusion he called him "Sir"—then acknowledged the other introductions: "Bitsy" Trabue, a pretty little blonde girl he had known since the days when she played dolls with Helen, a blue-eyed boy he remembered as a member of a scout troop he had talked to once about dogs. And there were two or three whose family names, even, he had never heard before.

They all sat down. The servant had remained standing near the door, waiting to see if anything else were needed. Seely Latham picked up his glass, took a few sips, then motioned the servant forward. "John," he said, "John, this is right. I don't mind telling you, this is exactly right. Now you going to remember exactly how you made it?"

The Negro bowed, too low, and allowed himself a sudden, roguish smile. "Yes *sar,*" he said. Jim realized that he was a Jamaica Negro. "Now what in hell is he doing up here?" he thought.

Seely let himself farther down into his chair. He sighed contentedly, then leaned towards Jim. "You see that Negro?" he said.

Jim inspected the Negro.

"His father," Seely said, "no, damn it, it was his grandfather, used to be head bartender at the St. Charles. This boy makes a perfect Planter's Punch. He understands about the grenadine."

"It's the grenadine does the trick, is it?" Jim asked.

"It's the grenadine," Seely said, "but it isn't the grenadine itself. It's the moment of fusion. No, you can't call it fusion when the grenadine meets the rum. There must be no mixture of the liquids. The grenadine, when you start drinking your punch, must be still superimposed upon the rum, must be just spreading out into it. . . ."

"I see," Jim said. "Well, a good Planter's Punch means a lot."

"It means everything," Seely said.

"I always liked it better for an afternoon drink," Jim said.

"The thing is to prolong the afternoon into the evening,"

Seely returned. "A good Planter's Punch will do that, for me, for you, for any man."

"I always liked 'em better than mint juleps," Jim said.

"You are quite right," Seely said. "The mint julep is like the bison of the plains. Its day is over. In the first place you can't get the whiskey. In the second place people don't know how to make one these days and after they've made it they don't have time to sit down and drink it." He leaned towards Jim again. "Do you know what happened to me not two weeks ago, in this very town?"

"Somebody give you a mint julep?" Jim enquired.

Seely nodded impressively. "A lady here in this town gave me a mint julep which she had made from ice cubes which she had taken from her electric refrigerator."

Jim shook his head. "She ought to have crushed the ice," he said tolerantly.

Seely sank back in his chair. "This house," he said, "is the only place in town where one is safe. I relax when I come here. I know that I am safe. And I am keeping an eye on that boy. As good as he is, a little judicious direction helps him now and then. . . ."

Bitsy Trabue had dropped down on the arm of his chair while he was talking. "It's hot," she said.

Seely nodded. "It makes the punch taste better, Bitsy."

"It's *awfully* hot," the girl said.

She got up and walked to the edge of the pool, sat down and took off her shoes and stockings. A young man rose and followed her. In a minute he too was barefooted. They dabbled their feet in the water.

Joe Camp had come up and was standing beside Jim. He said: "When did you get here?"

"Last night," Jim said.

"Are you going to take over the *Star Ad* office?"

"That's right," Jim said.

He did not like Joe Camp and suddenly he thought of the boy's father. The old man, sitting under the lamp, reading, looked as mild as milk, but in his brief business experience Jim had found that these gentle-looking old boys could be pretty snappy. This boy here didn't look dumb but he was too high hat. "He isn't on to himself yet," Jim thought. "Well, I reckon he's the Prince of Wales around here, all right."

Bitsy Trabue and her beau were coming up from the pool, still barefooted. "Anybody want to go swimming?" Bitsy asked. Nobody answered. The youth who was with her yelled, "Where are the bathing suits?"

Joe Camp and Helen were walking to the other end of the terrace. Without turning his head Joe called, "In that long chest on the balcony."

Bitsy and the boy went on into the house. There was the sound of a fall. Jim, seeing that nobody paid any attention, got up and went inside. Bitsy was sitting at the top of a short flight of steps staring down at her escort, who had fallen halfway up. Jim after a glance at them stood and looked around him. The balcony which Bitsy and the boy were trying to reach ran on all four sides of the enormous room. He could see doors, some of them shut, some of them ajar. There was another flight of steps on the east side of the room; there were rooms up there too. Downstairs there was an immense expanse of polished floor and over in the corner what looked for all the world like a bar. Jim had never before seen a bar in a private house and he stared at it to make sure. It was a bar, all right. His eyes picked out familiar labels on the bottles that gleamed on the long row of shelves, and the nigger was just then polishing some bottles with professional briskness. Jim walked over. He grinned a little as he put his foot on the rail. "I'll take Scotch and soda," he said.

The Negro said, "Yes *sar,*" and quickly set out bottle, siphon and glass.

Jim poured out the whiskey and put the soda in it, took a long drink then started for the stairs. He leaned over and with one muscular hand brought the sprawling boy to his feet. "Come on," he said, "get upstairs."

Bitsy rose and went slowly up the stairs ahead of them. On the balcony she paused and pointed to a long chest. Jim lifted the lid. A tangled mass of clothing was revealed. Bitsy leaned over and picked up several garments. "Here's some trunks, Eddie," she said.

Eddie took the trunks and began unbuckling his belt. Jim laughed. "No, you don't," he said, and shoved the boy into one of the dressing rooms and closing the door turned to Bitsy. "Want me to help you put your rompers on?" he offered.

"No, thanks," she told him and disappeared into one of the dressing rooms."

He stood on the balcony and drank the rest of the whiskey and soda. He drank it slowly and thoughtfully, gazing down at the room below. He had been about to down it quickly as he did most prohibition drinks but palate and memory arrested him. It was not Scotch at all but Bourbon, old-fashioned Bourbon. He had not tasted whiskey like this for a long time, not since he was a child and used to go with his father out to Cousin Edward Marshall's. A servant would bring a decanter and glasses out under the trees. Cousin Edward as he mixed his toddy—he put sugar into whiskey as so many old-fashioned Southerners did, a thing Jim couldn't abide—Cousin Edward before he mixed his own drink would pour out into another glass as much as a table-spoonful of amber liquid. "Smell that, boy. Taste it," he'd say and when Judge Carter protested: "Well, I want him to know what good whiskey tastes like, Marsh."

Bitsy and her beau emerged from the dressing rooms and passed him. Jim finished his drink and went downstairs. He paused at the bar long enough to get another one, then went out on the porch. Bitsy and the boy were already in the pool. Several people had gone over and were standing on the edge watching them but Seely Latham still lay stretched out in his long chair. Jim took a chair next to him. When he had taken his first drink he had told himself that he would have to get organized quickly in order to stand these kids, but now he had almost forgotten that he was on a party. The Bourbon was an old friend. He just wanted to sit alone with it quietly.

Seely glanced towards the pool. "Crazy kids," he observed tolerantly. "But that cold water won't do 'em any harm. Eddie was a little too high."

Jim shook his glass gently so that it caught the light from the window and reflected that he might take the next shot neat. "The old man's got some good stuff," he observed.

"It's Joe's doings," Seely said. "Joe has a palate. Yes," he continued with enthusiasm, "I think you can say there isn't its equal in the state. I take some credit for that. I helped form the boy. Still," he added judiciously, "it's not a thing to be imparted. One has it or one hasn't."

"Trouble these days is getting something to put on it," Jim replied. "Does the old man just turn this liquor loose for these kids to guzzle?"

Seely laughed. "Joe carries the keys to the cellar. Mr. Camp is indulgent with his children," he added after a pause, "but he's such a splendid fellow. I don't know any man I have a higher regard for than Mr. Camp. That's one of the nice things about this house," he continued with animation, "Mr. and Mrs. Camp are truly civilized people. They like to see gayety around them."

"Well, I bet they see plenty if they put out liquor like this."

Seely did not answer and Jim himself did not speak for several minutes. He was watching his sister and Joe Camp. They were standing at the other end of the long terrace. Helen's back was to Jim but Joe stood, facing Helen but a little to one side so that he could look down the length of the terrace. They were talking in low tones but Jim fancied that Joe was not as interested in the conversation as Helen was. He kept glancing towards the others and then some remark of Helen's would fix his attention again. Helen finally turned around. They both strolled over to where Jim and Seely were sitting. Helen's face was flushed, her air animated. Jim looked at her with curiosity and a little resentment. She was making too obvious a play for Joe Camp, he thought. Joe, aside from his money, was nothing to get excited about.

Joe and Helen sat down. Seely was talking when Helen interrupted him: "There comes Sara." Jim saw a young man and a girl coming around the end of the terrace. He rceognized the man as Rice Bolling, the youngest and most do-nothing of old Judge Bolling's four handsome, scapegrace sons. The girl, Sara Camp, did not look at all like Joe. She was small and dark, slight, too, though her broad shoulders gave her the effect of being more heavily built than she was. Her best features were her eyes, very large gray eyes set under rather heavy brows. Above the brows was a bang of black hair which made her look like a little girl. She came up to them with her escort and without speaking dropped into the chair next to Jim. Rice Bolling, after speaking to Jim, went over and stood leaning against a pillar. He was always like that in a crowd, silent and carrying himself with a slightly superior air. The girl, on the contrary, seemed in high spirits. She looked about the group as if she were seeing them all for the first time, then her gaze fixed on Jim. "When'd you come?" she asked.

"About half an hour ago."

She nodded, then leaned towards him. "Have you ever been here before?" she asked in a confidential tone. She had approached her face rather close to his. Jim looked into her eyes and saw that she was drunk. "No," he said quietly; "but I'd like to come again. May I?"

She considered this for a moment, then sank back in her chair. "You may," she said with exaggerated dignity.

Seely reached over and patted her arm. "Here come your mother and father," he said in a low voice.

The girl sat where she was. Seely and Joe rose and went to meet Mr. and Mrs. Camp, who were coming down the long flight of steps. Mrs. Camp came slowly, supported by her husband's arm. When she reached the end of the flight she walked a little way around the pool. Seely walked beside her, head bent attentively, while Joe walked behind with his father. Once Mrs. Camp motioned to a flower that grew among the rocks. Seely stooped and picked it for her. She took it with a nod and stood holding it in her hand. Her low voice fl.oated across the water: "So pretty—but I hate to bruise the stalk."

Seely laughed at her gently. Then they had turned and,

walking around the other side of the pool, began to ascend the last flight of steps. Sara suddenly got up and started towards them. Jim repressed a smile as he watched her put each foot down with a drunkard's care. Then he realized that, moving in circles as she was doing, she would fetch up some feet away from them. He glanced at Helen. She gave him back a deliberately non-committal look. He rose and went quickly across the terrace. He came up to Sara and laughing and slipping one hand under her elbow steered her to where Mrs. Camp was standing. Mrs. Camp did not seem to notice that anything was wrong. She talked to the three of them for a few minutes then said she believed she would sit down a while before going back to the house. Seely escorted her across the terrace. Jim was left standing with Sara.

Helen, followed by Joe, was coming towards them. She bade Sara an affectionate good night, then turned to Jim. "You can take the car, Bud," she said, using his old nickname. "Joe and I are going to run out to the club for a few minutes and he'll bring me home."

Jim said, "All right." He stood there looking after the departing couple, then turned to the girl beside him. She was staring after them too. She was frowning. There was a hostile look in the gray eyes that she raised to his. She was drunk but she knew what was going on and she didn't like Helen any better than he liked Joe.

CHAPTER THIRTEEN

THE next night Jim went out with three of the boys. They drove out to Sam's place on the river and had some drinks. A poker game started up but he and Ed and Tom Gray didn't feel like playing, so they came on back to town. It was eleven o'clock by that time. They drove around the square, looking into the poolrooms to see if they could find Jim Bass, the bootlegger, but they couldn't. Tom ran out of cigarettes, so they stopped at Franklin's drugstore. Old Doc Franklin had gone home to bed. There weren't any customers and a Negro boy had already started mopping up the floor in the back but the soda-jerker was still standing behind the fountain, a cute-looking girl in a man's white coat. She had on white trousers too but she was built so she looked good in them. Ed and Tom went over to play the machine for their cigarettes. Jim dropped down on a stool at the fountain. The girl was wiping the nickel bar with a cloth. Jim had not intended to have anything and then he saw that she had put the cloth down and was looking at him. At the same time he realized that he had the beginnings of a headache. "I'll take a bromo seltzer, please, ma'am," he said.

The girl drew some water into a glass, then took a spoonful of Bromo Seltzer from a big bottle behind her and dropped it in. She let it fizz up, then as she bent forward to set it before him she said with a husky laugh, Hello, Jim!"

146

He said, "Hello there!" quickly and looked up. He had to take a good look at her before he knew who she was. Evelyn Worsham. She used to sit in the seat in front of him at assembly that year he went to the public high school. Her old man was a barber in Pete Johnson's shop. He said, "How long you been working here, Evelyn?" using her first name to show that he knew who she was.

"Ever since I graduated from high school," she told him, adding with a laugh, "and that's a long time ago."

He had drunk off the seltzer and he slapped his nickel down on the counter and stood up. "It sure is," he said. As he spoke he looked at the girl more closely, noticing how pretty she was. She had a broad, squarish face, pink even where it wasn't rouged. Her eyes were brown. Her hair, which grew very low on her forehead, was tossed straight back in what his sister Helen called "a wind-blown bob." It was brown, too, and curly. It looked as if it would be as soft as a baby's to the touch and it had a beautiful sheen to it.

"What become of all those people, all that crowd?" he said vaguely.

The girl had just taken a look through the open front door, as if wondering whether any other customers would come in that night. She was taking off her mannish jacket and now she reached up to a hook behind the counter and took down a light coat and put it on. "Well, Bud Dawson is our pharmacist," she said. "Here he comes now."

Jim stepped up and greeted the young man who was approaching. Bud lingered to exchange a few words about school days then strode to the front door. He halted there, looking back. Tom and Ed had gone over to gamble on the golf machine but when they saw he wanted to lock up they picked up their cigarettes and came on. The girl came too.

147

Bud locked the door behind the five of them, said good night and went on down the street.

"How about going over to Kelly's now?" Tom asked. "Jim Bass is sure to drop in there before bedtime."

The girl with a murmured good night had started off down the street. Jim turned to Tom. "You all go on over," he said; "I'll be along directly."

He hurried after the girl and caught her just as she was about to cross the street. "Does that Bud Dawson let you go home by yourself every night?" he demanded.

She laughed. "I'm just going over to the taxi stand. Old Mike Ginley drives me home."

When he had started over towards the girl, he had been genuinely indignant with Bud Dawson for letting her go home by herself, but now another thought struck him. He had taken her arm in a familiar, casual clasp. He tightened his clasp on the round arm and reaching down, lifted her chin with one finger so that his eyes looked boldly into hers. "My car is just around the corner," he said. "What say we go get in it?"

Her upward glance flickered over his face. "I'd just as soon walk," she said composedly. "It isn't far. I just make Mike take me because I don't want to walk by myself late at night."

"Where is it?" he asked.

"Hyacinth street," she answered. He recognized the name as belonging to one of the small, obscure streets down near the river.

"All right, then," he said, "we'll walk and let old Mike get his sleep out."

They crossed the square and started out. The streets were deserted at this time of night. On their way across town they met only one person, the policeman, Bradley, who at first touched his cap, then as he came abreast of them swung his night stick fraternally and called out, " 'Night, Babe."

" 'Babe,' " Jim said; "is that what they call you now?"

"Almost everybody does," she said.

"That wasn't what they called you in high school," he said. "There were three, four of you girls used to run around together. A tall girl named Miller and another one that had red hair. I remember now. You were on the basketball team. What was it they called you?"

" 'Florence,' " she said. "I was on the team that time we beat Florence so bad."

"I saw you," he said. "Their guard was a big girl, had arms like a gorilla, but you just kept shooting 'em past her. How many baskets did you make that night?"

"Oh, I forget," she said.

They began the descent of the steep, rocky street which led to the river. He relinquished her arm and slipped his arm about her waist and as they walked kept drawing her to him. He was going through motions which he would have said meant business. At the same time he was speculating about this girl. He remembered now hearing Tom and some of the other fellows talking about a girl they called "Babe." He had only half listened to what was being said but he had got the idea that the girl was one of the town chippies or if she was not a professional that she certainly took money from men on occasions. He was wondering now whether this Babe Worsham was the same girl and whether she *was* a chippie or just a girl that liked to have her fun.

They came out onto the main highway. The river was before them, a placid expanse dotted with the reflection of those lights that still burned in the town. Between them and the river was the main road and, straggling uphill away from the road were half a dozen little streets. Jim remembered that they all had flower names—the lady of some forgotten city father had had a fancy so to name them when the town was young.

He remembered, too, that in the old days many of the best residences had fronted the river. That was all changed now. The mansions, those of them that hadn't been demolished, had rotted down. Cottages, inhabited mostly, he supposed, by mill workers and river rats, had sprung up all around. They were small and for the most part shabby but there were flowers in many of the yards and some of the cottages were shaded by fine old trees. He had not been along here for years but when he was a boy he used to come here often with Uncle Joe Burden to see old Bill Tripp, a wary and knowledgeable river rat with whom Uncle Joe sometimes had dealings.

Jim had always liked this part of "The Bend." When he was a kid he used to wonder why everybody didn't have houses here instead of stuck off in the duller parts of the town. He slowed their pace to look about him. "It's nice and quiet down here, isn't it?" he said. "Which way do you live?"

She pointed to a side road which could hardly be called a street, for there were only three houses on it. Two of them were dark. He was able to see the third clearly, for it had a light burning in an upper window. A story-and-a-half cottage. It sat in the shadow of a giant silver poplar. There were no flowers immediately about the house but the lower half of the small yard was crowded with a jungle growth of bulbs and shrubs.

The girl had paused and was looking into the lighted

windows of a house on the other side of the road. "That's George Robey's place. You ever go there for a drink?"

Jim imagined the crowded back room in which one would sit to drink cheap whiskey. "Not if I can help it," he said. "I don't like George's stuff. Say, I've got a bottle on me. If you'll ask me in I'll give you a drink."

"All right," she said and passed before him through the little gate. Jim stumbled over a thick clump of spring bulbs. "Say," he said, "somebody around here sure does like flowers."

She laughed. "It's Dad. Since he quit work he don't think about anything else."

There was a path leading around the side of the house. As they came along it under the drooping branches Jim saw that an outer flight of stairs led up to the room that was lighted.

"Pretty nice for you," he said, "having your own entrance."

She laughed again. "I have to, coming in all hours of the night."

They mounted the rickety wooden stairs. When Jim stood on the top step his head brushed the poplar boughs. He was stooping to enter the door which the girl had just unlocked but she hurried in ahead of him and came swiftly back with a tray which had on it two glasses and a pitcher of water. She set the tray down on the top step and then dropped down beside it. Jim sat down too and poured whiskey into the glasses from the bottle he had in his pocket. She put water into hers but he drank his neat. It was not bad stuff. He was glad to have a drink. The whiskey he had had earlier in the evening was beginning to die out on him. He looked over and saw that the girl was just starting her drink. He poured himself another and drank it off, then moved so that his leg was close against hers and he could put his arm around her. He looked down the road where the lights of George Robey's place were still visible. "I'm glad we didn't go in there," he said. "Much nicer out here. Just like summer, isn't it?"

"Yes," she said dreamily, "it's just like summer."

She was leaning, still in the circle of his arm, a little backward so that her head was supported against the wall. The light fell on her square little chin and arched throat. He could see the pulse in her throat play each time she swallowed. The thought came to him again: was she a chippie or wasn't she? Well, he would soon find out.

She had finished her drink. He took the glass out of her hand and set it on the tray. He tightened his arm about her waist, then leaned over and kissed her on the mouth. "What about us going inside?" he whispered.

She straightened up. As she turned her head the light from the window made her eyes flash tawnily. He thought for a second that she was going to throw him out. Then he realized that it was desire that lighted her eyes like that. She was on her feet. "All right," she said and led the way into the house.

CHAPTER FOURTEEN

He made himself stay away from Babe Worsham the next night but he was with her the night after, and during the ensuing weeks he formed the habit of going around to the house on the river two or three nights a week. Once she kept him waiting on the stairs for several minutes and when she came out spoke up harshly in answer to his murmured greeting, saying that this was not the Kelly House but the residence of Mr. Worsham. He imagined that she had a man in there with her and turned with a grin and a loud, "Thank you, ma'am," and ran down the steps. He did not see her again for several days until they met by chance on the street and made an appointment. And after that he went to her only by appointment.

He did not question any of his friends about the girl but he continued to speculate about her a little. She was no virgin. In fact she had told him that she had been promiscuous for years. Still he knew girls in his sister's crowd who must have had as many men as Babe. She was a mighty loving girl; she made him as welcome as the flowers in May. But she wasn't a chippie. He asked her once if she made enough at that soda jerking job to live on and told her he'd be glad to help out, any time. She seemed embarrassed and said she got by, all right, and said something about her father having a pension when he retired. Still there was something funny about that house. Old Mitch, working his garden, when Jim came down the steps once just as day was breaking, just looked up to grunt "Hello," and Mrs. Worsham the few times he had encountered her seemed to take his presence there for granted. The really funny thing was that except for that one night he had never seen a sign of any other man about the place. A girl as attractive as Babe ought to be having beaux in her own class. Still there were her working hours. She couldn't go out with men as other girls do when she worked at night as she often did.

He didn't want to pry into the girl's affairs. He really hadn't any curiosity about them. In his experience with women, as soon as you got to know them at all you knew too much about them. Babe was a silent girl as girls go, but even she talked, on occasion. One evening—it was Sunday, her day off from the drugstore and he had come over early —they were sitting on the steps under the poplar tree and she got to talking about two mill girls who had just gone past.

She told him to look at their clothes. He said they looked all right to him. After all, those girls couldn't make more than six or seven dollars a week. He didn't suppose they could buy Paris models on that.

"They *like* cheap things like that yellow dress," she said, suddenly, fiercely.

He did not answer. She talked on, as if to herself. "I never thought I'd get anywhere. It's just that I couldn't stand to be like them."

"Well, you aren't like them," he said. "You're different from any girl I know."

She laughed a short laugh. "You don't know what it's

like. Now, take my clothes. You wouldn't know, being a man, but I wear good clothes. I don't buy cheap things, like those girls. I save up enough till I've got enough to buy something good."

He had been gently stroking her arm. His hand paused in its motion, arrested by a sudden memory. He had heard his sister, Helen, say "I saw that soda fountain girl on the street the other day. You know she has real style," and she had gone on to comment on the girl's costume.

His fingers slipped down over her wrist, closed on her hand. "You look mighty pretty in those clothes," he said.

She said, "Oh, go on," and gave him a push, then her mood changed abruptly. She shook her hair back from her face with a shrug. "You know how I started?" she said. "I went with a boy named Joe Robey. . . . He got killed when a vat exploded over at the plant."

The hand he held was tense in his, the fingers suddenly began straining as if they wanted to get away. He dropped her hand with a gentle pat. "That was tough on you," he said.

Her lips parted. She swallowed as if she had tasted something bitter. "You know I've heard people talking about not feeling the shock till it's all over and all that but I never knew what it meant. I went around just the same, I reckon, but you know it was two or three years before I felt like myself." She looked up at him intently, *"Like myself. . . . You understand?"*

He nodded. "It was a tough break," he said.

She was still looking at him as if he might understand what she was saying better than she herself could. "You know, I remember the first time I felt like myself? I was walking down Market and I saw a gray dress in McClure's window. It had a black astrakhan collar and cuffs and patch pockets. I stopped to look at it and it was just like somebody said 'There, Babe, there's something you want.' You know what I did?"

He looked away, uneasily conscious that he had rather not hear what was coming. "I reckon you bought it if you had the cash," he said.

She disregarded his facetious tone, continuing in the same strained voice. "There was a rich man coming to see me then. A rich man. I made him buy me that dress. I thought he'd never miss it and I thought as long as I wanted something that bad I might as well have it."

"Didn't you want the man?" he asked.

"No," she said. Her eyes, still fixed on his, were somber, her tone flat. Her lower lip wried suddenly in distaste. "No," she said, "I didn't want *him*."

He felt that this had gone far enough. "Well, there's something I want mighty bad right now," he said, "and that's a drink. Come on." He stretched out his hand and pulled her to her feet and they went inside the house.

One Saturday afternoon a few weeks later he was playing tennis with Sara Camp on the courts back of the pool. He had beaten her two sets and they had sat down to rest. It was an off day, somehow, for company, nobody there but Sara and himself. It was in June. The leaves had been out for weeks but you still had that feeling of new green all around you. They flung themselves down, panting, on the thick grass of the western slope. Sara had on shorts. Her legs were already as brown as they'd be in midsummer. She took her yellow silk bandanna off and mopped the sweat from her face and neck, then flung it down on the ground beside her. He was lying on his back with his eyes closed, getting that good, burning summer feeling into him, when he realized that Sara had sat up. He sat up too. Sara was plucking off pieces of grass, holding them a second, then throwing them away. He watched the brown hand move in and out of the green grass and thought that she had the prettiest hands and feet of any woman he knew.

He stretched himself, yawning. In a minute they would be going across the lawn to the guest house and that yellow Negro would fix him a long Tom Collins. Sara's hand in the grass was suddenly still. She said, without looking up, "You know I like you."

He smiled. "I like you too."

She looked up. She had gray, very clear eyes, with pupils that grew dead black when she was excited. "I know you do," she said, "I knew the very minute you started liking me."

"When was it?"

"The first night you ever came here."

"Well," he said, "that's right." He laughed. "You were dead drunk and you were trying so hard to be a little lady so as not to worry your mother. You know what you reminded me of? A hen. A little Banty hen."

"I like that," she said.

"Did you ever see a hen drunk?" he asked. "We had a little Banty hen named Sophia. Ned and I gave her a tablespoonful of whiskey once. You ought to have seen her. She stepped around that yard, and she'd lean over and look at every place before she put her foot down, just like you did that night."

He was laughing but she remained sober. "I remember you came up and put your hand under my elbow," she said. "That was nice of you."

"I didn't want to see you spill in the middle of the floor," he said. "Didn't your mother really know you were drunk that night?"

"I don't think so. Mother's funny about her children. Now, she thinks Joe has wings and as for me—well, I suppose she doesn't think about me any more than she has to."

"I think she's crazy about both of you," he remarked.

"Oh, she's awfully fond of me but I imagine I'm sort of a disappointment. I ought to make what they call a brilliant marriage and I don't seem to get around to it."

"Well, there's time."

She nodded. Her hand went back to plucking the grasses and then she looked up again. "You know sometimes I think I may not marry at all."

He laughed. "They all say that."

She laughed too. "I know. But I mean it. I wouldn't cry if I didn't. I can think up plenty of things to do."

"Well," he said matter-of-factly, "it *is* kind of hard on you. All these people around here, like Seely Latham, drinking up your liquor. It's hard to tell the sheep from the goats. And you know—" he, too, had an impulse towards confidence —"I find there's blame few sheep in this world."

"Seely's all right," she said. "He's a real friend of ours. He's devoted to Mother."

Jim looked at her. "I reckon he is," he said. When he had first come home he had regarded Seely as a toady, hanging on to the Camps for what he could get out of them. He saw now that the thing wasn't as simple as that. For one thing, Seely was a eunuch. That, and not his limited income, was the reason he had never married. He didn't want to have anything to do with women, really, but he liked all the flutteration. Men like that always hung around older women.

You could see how Mrs. Camp aroused Seely's admiration.
She was a lovely lady, all right. He thought sudddenly of
how different she was from his own mother. When the man
hadn't come to fix the rose bushes the other day Mrs. Carter
had got down in the trench and spaded the green manure
in herself. She had told them about it later with a faint air
of distaste and yet there was a sparkle in her eye. You could
see she rather enjoyed pulling off something as disagreeable
as that. But you couldn't imagine Mrs. Camp doing it. She
loved flowers; in fact, apart from her children they seemed
to be her whole life. But you couldn't imagine her even
digging up a clump of jonquils.

Sara was leaning towards him. "I'm going to tell you
something *horrible* about myself."

"Whoa!" he said. "You're sure I'm safe?"

Her expression remained serious. "You know Rice Bolling.
Have you noticed that he doesn't come here any more?"

"Well, now that you mention it, I had."

"We were engaged last spring—for about a month. I
thought I was in love with him and then I got to thinking.
. . . Oh, it's horrible, but I'd look at him sometimes and I'd
begin to wonder. . . ."

"I know," he said, "Papa's money."

She shook her head to and fro, mournfully. She made a
mouth. It was almost the same expression that he'd seen
recently on somebody else's mouth. "There's probably something wrong with me," she said. "I ought to be able to tell
whether a man's in love with me or not."

He felt genuinely sorry for the girl. He was about to lay
his hand over hers—it was his weakness that he could never
see a woman in distress without wanting to comfort her—

but he held his hand back. "There's nothing wrong with you," he said. "And if it's any comfort to you you can take it from me: you've got a hell of a lot of sex appeal."

She said, *"Jim!"* Her tone was affectionate, conventional, but the pupils of her remarkable eyes had gone dead black. He felt his own face reddening. And then somebody was coming across the grass calling to them.

They got up and went over to the guest house. Sara went up to the house to change. The yellow Negro mixed Jim a long Tom Collins. He stretched himself out in a deck chair. He was moved by his talk with Sara, perplexed, too, and a little excited. As he sank deeper into his chair, the cold glass clasped in his hand, he admonished himself: "Look here, Carter, you'd better watch your step. All these women telling you their hearts' secrets. First thing you know you'll be like Seely Latham!"

CHAPTER FIFTEEN

T HE AFFAIR with Babe Worsham lasted, all told, less than a year. In the meantime he was seeing a lot of the Camps. The old man offered him a job in the smaller plant, with a chance to learn the business, and he took it. He always remembered the interview he had with Mr. Camp the day he accepted the offer. Joe, who in those days made quite a stir about being an up-and-coming business man, was just leaving the office as Jim came in. The old man did not ask him to stay. He invited Jim to sit down and pushed a box of cigars across the table towards him. He himself lighted a cigar and turned his swivel chair so that he could look over the tops of the willows out to the yellow river. Jim was silent, smoking his cigar. As the old man turned around finally, Jim observed the changes that a year had wrought in him. His blue eyes were not as keen as they had been a year ago. The veins at his temple showed through the brown, parchmentlike skin.

He said: "I was thinking about your father. You know, Jim, he was a very intelligent man."

Jim had been a child of ten when the Camp factories moved to Countsville, but he remembered that there had been a lot of talk about it. The local chamber of commerce had agreed to raise a certain sum of money to induce the factories to move there; they had also remitted their taxes for ten years and the city had floated a bond issue to build the very road that ran along the river. Judge Carter had been the bitterest opponent of the whole scheme and of the road in particular. Jim remembered some of his arguments. The people in the town who had a little money would buy the bonds, he said, and thus make a little profit. But the bonds would be redeemed ultimately out of tax money; so it was the poor people of the county who were building that road along the river for the Yankee manufacturer. He had felt so strongly about it that he had got on the train and had gone to Camden, New Jersey, to see if he could not dissuade the manufacturer from moving south.

Mr. Camp was thinking of that interview now. He said: "I never saw your father but once, to talk to." He smiled. "We were enemies in a way for, though he always spoke to me very politely when we met on the street, he tried to keep me from moving to this town. Came up to see me in New Jersey. Did you know that?"

Jim nodded. "I remember something about it," he said.

Mr. Camp was smiling again. "You know, Jim, it's a wonderful thing when a man knows his region intimately. I was just thinking about your father as I was sitting here and I reckon I've thought of him a hundred times since he died. You know that man sat there in that hotel room and told me exactly what we'd be up against if we moved our factories south."

"What did he tell you you'd be up against?"

"The people, mostly. He said the Southern hill-billy was not suited temperamentally to the work. And he was right." He sighed. "I've been down here among 'em fifteen years now and I've honestly tried to better living conditions

162

among those mill workers but I can't see that I've made any progress with them. I even offered at one time to turn over that tract of land out there beyond the Bend and to advance money to build cottages to each man who would conform to certain conditions. For one thing I wanted them to raise more vegetables. It's their diet that's the trouble with most of them."

Jim laughed. "They wouldn't take you up on the proposition. They'd rather live out there in the Bend where they can raise hell with one another." He became expansive. "And you know poor white people are choosy about their food. There was an old bird from out in the hills used to come to see Father twice a year. He never would touch English peas because he didn't have them at home."

Camp nodded. "Your father knew all that and tried to tell me. He told me that our production would be cut in half if we came here. He said he'd known them all his life and you couldn't get them to work a single lick faster than they wanted to for any amount of money. He said that if I paid them big wages they would make up for it by working only two or three days a week."

"They're hard to handle, all right," Jim said.

"Your father was right about most things," Camp observed. "But we have accomplished something in the fifteen years we've been here. For one thing we've got young people now who've been bred up in the factory. They've got ambition." His manner changed, became brisker. "Now, what I wanted to see you about was this: we've got a good man out at the little plant, Jim Rogers. Fine, upstanding man who knows the business from A to Z but he's getting old. I'm getting old, myself. Joe will have his hands full with the big plant. I want a young fellow—I prefer to get one from Countsville—who'll go out there and learn all that Jim Rogers can teach him. If you get on to the job I'll see that you get advancement rapidly. What do you say?"

"I say I'd like to try it," Jim said promptly.

The details of the job and the salary—more money than Jim had ever made before—were settled very quickly. He had started in a week later, driving the two miles out to the Little Bend factory to report to the foreman. Jim Rogers made him keep going around the plant with him for months to get the hang of things, then he settled down to supervision of the cutting room. They were making baby pants then. Fascinex was still a side line. The cutting-room boss was a good man. Jim got on to things quickly. In those days he'd rather liked it. Seeing anything—even babies' pants—getting made was better than selling advertising space.

It was that May that Helen announced her engagement to Joe Camp. Her announcement to the family was made characteristically, on the evening of Bitsy Trabue's dance. They were having a late dinner and Helen would just have time to dress before the dance. Polly had brought in the dessert. Helen waited till the door had swung to behind her, then turned to her mother. "Mother, Joe and I have decided to be married this summer."

Mrs. Carter had a spoonful of pudding halfway to her lips. She seemed to flinch for a second, then she put the spoon down carefully on her plate and fixed her large gray eyes on her daughter's face. "Will you have a June wedding?" she asked.

"I don't see how I could get ready before August," Helen said.

"An August wedding is a trial to everybody concerned,"

Mrs. Carter said. "Still, the really hot weather usually comes in September. I suppose you'll want to start planning right away. Can you stay at home tomorrow?"

Helen said that she thought she and her mother might begin to look around to see if there were any things she could buy in Countsville. She hesitated, then said, coloring, "Sara wants to give me my dress."

Mrs. Carter was silent a moment, then she observed: "You will still have to dress the bridesmaids."

Helen said that she and Sara had been talking it over and had decided that the bridesmaids would appear in silk muslin, with lots of ruffles. "My dress will be a contrast, very severe. I think I'll wear a Mary Stuart cap."

"I do not see the connection with the Queen of Scots," Mrs. Carter said.

Helen laughed. She was rising to leave the room. Suddenly her lip trembled. "Mother, *please* don't be difficult. It's going to be hard enough as it is."

When she had left the room Mrs. Carter began to eat her dessert. Her face was composed and her voice ordinarily calm as she made some flat remark, but Jim saw that each time she lifted her spoon her hand trembled a little. He observed awkwardly that the wedding would be a considerable expense. He would be glad to help out a little from his salary.

Mrs. Carter put her spoon down with a gesture of finality. "A wedding is always a strain," she said. "This wedding will be harder than the others but that was to be expected."

"Well, I'd like to help out," Jim said again.

Mrs. Carter looked at her son. There was a tender note in her usually hard voice. "No," she said, "you may give Helen a wedding present. I think a hundred dollars would be generous but I am not going to allow you to make any sacrifices for Helen. You have already made enough sacrifices for the girls."

"Why," Jim said, surprised, "I haven't done anything for 'em. Sent 'em a Christmas present now and then but that's all."

Mrs. Carter continued to regard her son. "You gave up your education for them," she said. "You may not realize what that meant but I do. I wish I could make it up to you in some way but I never can. . . ."

There was a note in her voice that made Jim nervous. He was glad she was rising. He rose too, quickly. "It'll be an expense," he said, "but I reckon we can pull through. I bet Cousin Alfred will send a good cheque."

Mrs. Carter was now as calm as he. "I'm counting on that," she said, "and there's that paid-up policy. I'm going to see about cashing it tomorrow."

He told her that it was a bad idea to cash the policy. She listened, smiling absently. He knew that she was paying no attention to what he said. And a few days later Bob Burton told him that she had called at the office to see about the policy.

The house, from that time forward, was given over to wedding preparations. Mrs. Carter entered into everything and worked like a dog. Jim knew from her dry, hard manner that she profoundly disapproved of Helen's marrying Joe Camp but he never heard her say anything derogatory about the Camps except once and that was by way of a joke.

She was sewing in the sitting room—she made many of the underclothes for the trousseau herself—when he came in from work one afternoon. She looked up. "Sara and her mother were here this afternoon," she observed and then she

166

added, smiling, "I'm glad it's Helen marrying Joe instead of you marrying Sara."

He looked at her, startled. "Why?" he asked.

Mrs. Carter snipped a thread with her tiny embroidery scissors. "Why," she said, "Sara has known us all these years and doesn't know how to pronounce 'Carter.' I'd hate to have a daughter-in-law who couldn't pronounce her own name."

He laughed. He knew that it infuriated his mother to be called "Karter." She said "Kyarter" just as she said "gyarden" and "gyrl." There was something mysterious about the pronunciation of these words among old-fashioned people. They were an indication, he believed, of whether or not you came, as the Negroes said, "out of the top drawer." But times had changed and with them the way people talked. He couldn't see that it made a hell of a lot of difference. He had long ago got used to being called "Karter." In fact he sometimes pronounced the name that way himself.

It became apparent as the weeks went on that the wedding was going to cost more than anybody had expected. Jim thought that his mother might as well have saved her insurance policy. It was just a drop in the bucket. The Camps, when you came down to it, paid for most of Helen's wedding. Mrs. Camp had asked if she might supply the flowers from her greenhouses. It looked as if that would cut down expenses a lot but it didn't work out that way. As Mrs. Camp pointed out once to Helen: "If you have so many expensive flowers for background you will have to live up to them." The liquor would have been the biggest expense, of course, but the Camps furnished that too. It would have been all right if it had just come out of the Camp cellars, but Joe must have champagne flow like water at the wedding reception.

Jim had discovered in the first few weeks he was at home that the boys around town didn't like Joe much. "The twelve o'clock boy in the nine o'clock town," Sam Reid called him. It gave Jim a funny feeling to have his sister marrying a man nobody liked. You could see why they had it in for Joe, all right. Everything he said and did irritated them. He *was* patronizing. You couldn't deny that. That was partly because of his education. He had gone to Harvard, which was bad enough in itself, and then they had sent him over to Oxford. He had picked up some mighty irritating ways there. He used the broad "a" on everything that came along and if he saw you didn't understand him he laid it on thicker than ever. He said, "Oh, blahst," if he missed a shot at tennis and he called a racquet a "bat." It burned Sam and the others up. Sam said he couldn't understand it. Joe was in Oxford only two years and learned to talk British but he had lived in Countsville since he was ten years old and couldn't talk Alabama yet.

Jim never did know whether his sister, Helen, was in love with Joe Camp. Joe, if you didn't take into consideration the Camp money, was not the fellow to sweep a girl off her feet. He wasn't put together right, somehow. He was too long, too thin. His eyes were an off shade of blue and he had sometimes an impediment in his speech. "His tongue," Mrs. Carter said succinctly, "is too large for his mouth."

Helen must have overheard that remark but she made no reply. She had very little to say during the weeks that preceded her wedding. She was as tired as the devil all the time, of course, partying half the night and rushing down to Birmingham to shop two or three times a week. There was something else though. It was as if she knew that nobody approved of what she was doing but she was determined to put it through just the same and knew that the only way she could do that was by keeping a stiff upper lip. Jim felt sorry for her during those weeks. She was up against it. It wasn't her wedding. It was Joe's. And if anything had gone wrong about it Joe would have been pretty sour.

Once it looked like something would go wrong. Cartier's wrote, saying that they couldn't have the favors for the bridesmaids and the groomsmen ready by the date they had set. Joe went straight up in the air.

They were all over at the Camps having drinks to brace them up for the party Elise Allard was giving for the bride and groom. "Oh, for heaven's sakes," Sara said, "what difference does it make?"

Joe looked at her. "When you get married, Sara," he said, "I shall expect you to jump into a car with some yokel and make for the nearest justice of the peace. I happen to prefer to do things properly or not at all."

Sara waved her hand at him. "Don't mind me, Big Boy," she said.

She and Jim—they went about together a good deal that spring—left the house ahead of Helen and Joe. Sara was still laughing when she got into Jim's little roadster. "How about making for the nearest justice of the peace?" she asked.

"It would suit me fine," he said. She laughed some more and then she sighed. "My God," she said, "I don't know how Helen's going to put up with him."

"I think you're a little hard on Joe," he said as he turned the corner into Greenwood. "You know he and I get along all right down at the factory. He's a good fellow to work with."

"You know how to manage him," she said. "He and I never did get along. Even when we were little. I remember when ladies would come calling, Mother'd always have us in to go the rounds. I was never much credit to her—I was skinny and my hair was stringy. But Joe had curls. I remember once there were a lot of ladies there. One of them was talking and she didn't see Joe. He stood there, all right, till she got around to noticing him. 'Oh, the tunning little thing. Tum here and div Mrs. Manning a kiss.'" And she laughed again.

"Well, I'll bet you were as cute as he was," Jim said. "You're always running yourself down." And he took a hand from the wheel to shake her arm gently.

She did not answer. The car came to a halt on the Allards' drive. They got out and went in. There were ten couples, just the wedding party and two or three guests from out of town. Some people played bridge but Sara and Jim were pretty well organized by that time, so they danced. He liked to dance with Sara better than any girl he'd ever known. She looked pretty that night, in a white dress with some sort of silver business in her hair. She had been drinking steadily all that evening but her face never got that mottled look most women's faces get—just two spots of color came out on her cheeks under her rouge and the pupils of her eyes got as black at night.

Some time well after midnight they went out on a veranda to cool off. Drink sometimes made Jim argumentative—in a rather tiresome way, Helen had told him. He had been arguing with Sara, telling her that she was the prettiest girl there. She had been arguing back and then suddenly she got quiet. "To hear you talk anybody'd think you were crazy about me," she said.

"You know perfectly well I'm crazy about you."

"Since when?" she asked pertly.

"Since the first time I saw you," he said. "Since—" and at the time he was proud of himself for remembering— "since that time I saw you walking across the terrace like a hen, a little Banty hen," and he tried to kiss her. He had kissed her often enough before but this time she resisted. "Oh, for God's sake," she said, "go in and get me a drink, will you?"

He steadied himself with a hand against the balustrade. "I'm not going to do it. I'm not going to move from here till we get this thing settled."

She was leaning up against the railing, looking off over the dark garden. She turned around and looked at him. "What thing?" she asked.

"About when we're going to get married. We ought to stand up with Helen and Joe. Make it a double wedding."

"I wouldn't get married with Joe," she said. "I wouldn't have all that fol-de-rol."

He became angry with a drunken man's quick anger. He spoke coldly. "Does that mean you won't marry me at all?"

She moved a little away, picked a leaf from the vine beside her. "I wasn't aware that you had asked me to marry you."

"Oh, you weren't? How many times have I got to ask you?"

She must have been soberer than he. She dropped the leaf, came over towards him. "You don't have to ask me but once, Jim," she said quietly, "that is, if you mean it."

"Mean it?" he said. "My God, what does the girl want?" And then he was kissing her.

Sam Reid came out on the veranda just at that minute. He said: "What do you two think you're doing?"

"We're going for a drive," Jim said. "Going to hunt up a justice of the peace. Want to come along?"

Sam said he would be delighted.

Sara looked from the one to the other and then down at her white dress and bare arms. "I can't go without a coat," she said.

"Get you a hundred coats," Sam said. "Want anything else?"

"You'd better get one of the other girls," Sara said.

"Get three or four."

"No. Get Lucy Childress but don't get anybody else."

Sam stayed away for ten or fifteen minutes, long enough to get himself and Lucy a drink. She came out a little scared but very excited. The four of them got into Jim's car and drove over the line. Sam had a bottle on him. They passed it around on the way. It was four o'clock when they got there. Old Squire Hicks was just getting up. He came to the door, fastening the top button of his trousers, but he welcomed them as if it were mid-morning—he was used to this sort of thing. The whole business could not have taken more than ten minutes but it was light by the time they came out of the house. They got into the car. Everybody had another drink around and then they drove like hell for Countsville. It was seven o'clock when they got there. Sam, who was driving, was the first one to consider the difficulties of the situation. He halted just as they came into town. "Which way?" he asked. Jim, sunk down in the rumble, his arm about Sara, raised up. "Just keep on driving," he said.

"Which way?" Sam insisted. "Bride's house or groom's house? May make a lot of difference which you strike first."

Sara raised up then. "You'd better take me straight home," she said.

172

Jim did not dissent. He had drunk so much that his head was getting clear. He had an instant's vision of his mother's face if he should appear at the door with his bride of the night. It wouldn't be fair to expose Sara to that meeting. At the same time he didn't like the idea of appearing on the Camp doorstep with Sara at that hour of the morning.

She settled it by jumping out when they got to the Camps'. "I have a key," she said. "You'd better not come in now, Jim. But call me up as soon as you've had breakfast."

He drove Sam and Lucy home and then drove out to the Carter place. The door was locked and he had lost his key but he shinned up by the wistaria vine outside his window and was in bed by half past seven o'clock.

CHAPTER SIXTEEN

He had no intention of going to sleep but he must have slept an hour, for there was old Viny at the door with her regular, "Git up, Mister Jim. Batter bread's in."

He said, "All right," and jumped up quickly. He had slept so hard that for a second he did not know where he was and though he knew that something had happened he did not know what it was. Then he remembered. He was married. He remembered everything that had happened, even Sam's hesitating over that last turn in the road, but he could not recapture the mood of the evening. He thought of Sara. He must get over there as soon as he could. . . . But there was something he had to do before he saw Sara. . . .

He bathed and shaved, dressed hurriedly and went downstairs. His mother had finished her breakfast but she was still sitting at the table, the morning paper open before her. The news was evidently not in the paper. The face she turned to him was composed, her "Good morning, Jim," was bland.

He came up to the table and stood with his hands on the back of his chair. He said: "Mama, I've got a bad surprise for you."

Her gray gaze flickered, then became steady. "What is it, Jim?"

"Sara Camp and I got married last night."

It seemed a long time before she answered. She sat looking down at her plate. Once she raised her eyes and looked about the room as if it had become strange to her. "Was there any reason for such suddenness?" she asked harshly.

For a moment he did not know what she meant, then he said with equal harshness. "Good God, no! We just took a notion."

"You couldn't wait to tell me what you were going to do?"

"It was in the middle of the night," he said lamely. "I didn't want to wake you up."

She laughed. "I was awake. I was lying there thinking about this. I've known it was going to happen, for a long time."

"Well, I didn't," he said doggedly. "I tell you we just decided last night."

The little mulatto house girl came in with scrambled eggs and a plate of hot batter bread. The sight of the food sickened him. He turned away, muttering, "I've got to get to the office."

His mother said: "Please sit down, Jim. Please eat your breakfast."

He sat down, ate a slice of batter bread and some scrambled eggs and drank a cup of coffee. While he was eating his mother left the room. When he went out into the hall to get his hat he found her standing there. She said: "I suppose you're going over to see Sara now. I hope to see her later in the day. Tell her . . ." her voice faltered. . . . "Tell her I . . ."

"Sure," he said hurriedly, "I'll bring her over to see you," and he ran down the front steps and around the corner of the house.

He got into his car and drove downtown. He parked it in front of Simpson's drugstore, went in and got a Coca-Cola.

He asked the boy who brought him the drink to bring him a sheet of paper also. He wrote a note:

"I want to see you right away. Make some excuse and get off for the day. . . ." He hesitated and during the interval spoke to three people passing by. "Walk down Market Street," he wrote, "as far as the square. I'll be waiting there and will pick you up." He folded the unsigned note, got up and left the store. At the end of the block he found an idle Negro boy, gave him the note and asked him to take it to Miss Worsham at Franklin's soda fountain.

He got into his car; then, driving out Market Street, made a circle around the town until he came out on the river road. She was there, walking slowly along the side of the road. She had on a green summer dress. She must have known who it was coming. She did not turn her head until he had drawn up beside her. She said, "Hello," and got in.

He had intended to drive out towards the plant, as they would not be likely to meet many people on that road at this time of day but as they drove down the river road she suddenly put her hand on his arm. "Let's go up to the house," she said.

He nodded and turned into the little side road. Mrs. Worsham was not visible but old Mitch was working in his flowers. He looked up as they came through the gate but did not speak. Babe said, "Hello, Dad," and went past him swiftly. Jim said, "Mornin, Mr. Worsham," and followed her.

Babe's room upstairs—Jim had never seen it before except at night or by very early morning light—was in prim order. Babe's bed was made up smoothly with three or four little boudoir pillows in a lacy nest on top of the counterpane. A toy dog with beady eyes and butter-colored hair stood this morning on the mantel shelf instead of reposing among the pillows as he usually did.

Jim went over and stood in front of the mantel. He put his hand on the dog's silky hair, wondering idly for the hundredth time just what sort of breed he was supposed to be.

Babe had taken her hat off and flung it on the bed. She said: "I heard you got married last night."

He was taken aback but he said courteously, "I wanted to be the one to tell you myself, Babe.... Who did tell you?"

Her eyes had been fixed on his. She looked away suddenly. "Pat told me," she said after a moment, naming the Negro boy who ran errands for the store, "and then Bob Guthrie came in at nine o'clock like he always does and he said he'd heard it and Joe Reynolds and Jim Macrae came in and they'd heard it and old Miss Byelow and the Methodist preacher...." Her voice, calm when she started speaking, had risen. She gulped and put her hand to her throat.

He took a step towards her. "Now don't let's get excited about this," he said.

She took her hand down from her throat, moved a little away from him, towards the window. When she spoke, her voice was flat and cold: "*I'm* not excited."

There was a little sofa in front of the window. He went over and sat down on it. He patted the vacant place beside him and after a moment she sat down too. He leaned forward, his hands on his knees. "See here, Babe," he said, "the reason I didn't tell you before.... It was sudden.... We didn't either of us know...."

"It must have been sudden," she said in the same flat tone.

He frowned, looking down at his hands that lay helplessly on his knees. He had been oppressed when he woke this

177

morning but it was because he felt the weight of a task that had to be done. He had thought when he staretd out here that all he had to do was to make a clean breast of the whole business. Babe was a good sport. If he told her how it was she would understand. But he found now that he did not like even to mention Sara's name before this girl, much less to tell her that he and Sara had both been drunk when they were married. He became aware that the silence had gone on too long. He looked up. He said: "Babe, I know I've treated you rotten. . . ."

"I don't think you've treated me rotten," she said. She had turned around so that she faced him but she looked past him, out into the branches of the poplar tree. They sat in silence, he heavily pondering what else he could say. Then, aware that she had turned from the window, he looked up and saw her as he was always afterwards to remember her. She was looking at him but she did not really seem to see him. She had just turned her head in the direction where she knew he was. Her eyes, brown eyes that were never very expressive, seemed today to have no expression at all. The eyeball looked flat, too flat to record any image, and afterwards he remembered that the whole surface of the face seemed withered as if the muscles everywhere had slackened under the skin.

He shuffled his feet. He thought: "I've got to get out of here." Aloud he said, "Well, that's that. I'm mighty glad you don't have any hard feelings."

She did not answer. He stood up. "Well, I reckon I'd better be going."

She stood up too. He said: "Want me to take you back to the store?"

She shook her head. "No, I told 'em I was taking the day off."

"That's a good idea," he said. She moved over to the table, put out her hand to rearrange some flowers that were there in a glass bowl. A shaft of sunlight filtered in through the poplar boughs. He watched the rather plump, square-fingered little hand moving through the dots of sunshine. A moment before he had felt that he must get out of here quickly at any cost but he had recovered from the shock of that instant's vision of her face. He wanted now to prolong the moment.

There was so much that was perplexing in his present situation. He felt that he wanted to get things straight with her at least. He said: "Look here, Babe, I haven't said anything about it but I've thought all along . . ." he paused, finding himself unable to go on.

"Thought what?" she asked patiently.

"Even before this happened I've thought . . . well, I always thought you took things too hard, you and me, I mean. . . ."

She withdrew her hand from the flowers. It dropped to her side. He had looked away from her as he spoke. He had the feeling now that she was trying to look at him but found the effort too great. She said in an exhausted tone: "I know what you mean. I reckon I did."

He had found it hard to open the subject but now he had started it was easy to go on, as easy as sliding over a precipice; for afterwards in rare moments of self-examination he always labelled his next words as the basest action of his life. He said awkwardly: "Are you sure you do?" and when she nodded listlessly he could not leave the subject there. He went on. He said: "Babe, you know sometimes I've thought you might have the wrong idea of me. I feel kind of bad taking up your time and maybe keeping other fellows away. . . ."

"Keeping other fellows away?" she repeated in an odd, harsh voice.

"Yes," he said, "I've been coming around here for a long time but you never let me do anything for you. I mean I'd have liked to buy you things sometimes but you wouldn't let me. . . ." He stopped speaking, aware at last that her silence was ominous.

She was looking at him now, her eyes so wide open that the black lashes stood up as flat as fans. Tears suddenly welled over her eyelids, spilled down her cheeks. When he came towards her she struck at him and she cried out in a hoarse, strangled voice: "Get out of here! Oh, for God's sake, go on and get out!"

CHAPTER SEVENTEEN

FOR SEVERAL days there was confusion. Mrs. Camp was taken aback, all right, but she rallied and behaved beautifully. His own mother did pretty well too. Mr. Camp—he really was a dead-game old sport—at first had nothing to say. Then he intimated to Sara that he had fixed the editors of both newspapers. There would be nothing printed about the runaway marriage. If she and Jim would just stand up with Joe and Helen and go through a second ceremony it would please her mother and be better for all concerned. Sara said, "All right," when it was put up to her that way. That was three days before Joe's and Helen's wedding. A dress was rushed down from New York for Sara, another bridesmaid was found to take her place, and everything went off all right.

Joe and Helen went to Scotland for their honeymoon. Joe had a big catalogue with pictures of noblemen's estates that were for rent over there. They couldn't afford a castle but they secured the dower house on some earl's estate. It had an Adam mantel that Helen admired very much. A staff of servants went with it and there was even a piper who marched around the table and played after the cloth was jerked off. Joe got pretty worked up about the massacre of Glencoe: his landlord was a Campbell. Mrs. Carter—she had always been pretty strong on the massacre herself (on the other side) and referred to the nine of diamonds as "The Curse of Scotland"—Mrs. Carter thought that it was outrageous for a man to rent his piper. "His silver and linen and I suppose even his servants," she said, "but his *piper!*" A branch of her own family had been hereditary pipers to the Lords of the Isles. She couldn't stomach the idea of a piper's being rented out like a piece of furniture, even to her own daughter.

Jim had a funny interview with Joe the day after the runaway marriage. Both of them were pretty embarrassed. In an attempt to break the ice Jim told Joe that the family didn't realize it but that he, Joe, was the man to blame. Joe stared. "What do you mean, Jim?"

"Why," Jim said, you put the idea in her head. You said she'd jump in the car with some yokel and make for the nearest justice of the peace."

Joe turned all colors. He said, "Look here, Jim. . . . For God's sake! You know I think you're a gentleman . . . a Southern gentleman."

"Well, that helps some," Jim said.

He and Sara went to Canada on their honeymoon. Rice Bolling lent them a camp he had up there. At the time Jim didn't know any reason why Rice Bolling shouldn't lend him a camp or anything else he had to lend. Later he wished he hadn't taken it. But it was a nice camp, on the point of a lake, in deep woods. There was nobody around but themselves and two guides. He got in some good fishing. Sara didn't care about casting much but she liked tramping through the woods, getting soaking wet and coming home at night to a roaring fire. They had a good time. But lying here now in the Allard house, remembering these things, he wondered if she hadn't been disappointed in him as a lover right from the start. He wasn't romantic enough to suit her. At the time she had seemed perfectly satisfied, but it might have been that the trouble started right from the first. He was used up, all right, when he got there. That scene with the Worsham girl. He had told himself that he couldn't afford to regard it, that you had to be prepared to be harsh if you had relations with women like that. But he kept harking back to that morning and then one day it came to him, the thing he'd been dimly trying to remember.

It was something that happened years ago, one day when he was out in a boat on the river, fishing. Some hounds were running along the bank and there had been a lot of baying for so long a time that he had stopped noticing it. Then suddenly a rabbit parted the bushes, dove in and began swimming. It swam straight for the boat. As it got near it raised its head a little. Jim saw the thing's eye, glazed from its exertions but with a light in it. When it was near enough he picked it up and laid it in the bottom of the boat. It lay there, panting but perfectly still. The hounds came on, six or seven of them, crowding into the water. A big, rangy fellow was in the lead and close behind him a little lemon-spotted bitch. Jim recognized her as Windy Peters' Judy, as game a little devil as ever struck a trail. They were almost there. He had nothing but his paddle. He knew he'd have a hard time standing them off and he couldn't run the risk of injuring Windy's Judy. He picked the rabbit up and threw it out. They had it torn in pieces before it hit the water. Just something that happened one day when he was out fishing, but the incident had stuck in his memory. It was the look in the rabbit's eye as it neared the boat. That girl had had just such a look in her eye that morning.

He never wanted to see her again. He had had no particular regret at parting from her. But the picture of her stuck in his mind. A man shouldn't be thinking of such things on his honeymoon. The devil of it was that Sara seemed to read his mind in the very moment that he was remembering the incident about the rabbit.

He had been casting in a beautiful pool all morning and had taken some beauties. Sara had cast a while, too, but her arm soon got tired and she had gone off to sit on a rock and smoke. He kept wading out farther into the stream. He was within sound of her voice but she was so good about not talking when he was casting that he had got the feeling that he was alone. His thoughts had been running on as a man's thoughts will when he is alone. When he remembered that incident he must have made some ejaculation or his face must have changed in some way for she said suddenly, "What did you say?"

"I didn't say anything," he answered, stepping back towards the bank.

"What were you thinking about?" she asked in a hard voice.

"Nothing," he answered mechanically, and then he added that it was time to go home. She was angry about something —what, he never knew, unless she had actually read his mind—but she was all right by the time they'd walked back to camp and that night, lying on a big rug in front of the fire, they had as good a time as they'd had on any of the nights they were at the camp.

They went home a few days later—he couldn't afford to be off the job too long with Joe in Scotland and then, too, Mr. Camp was not at all well, Mrs. Camp wrote. Jim and Sara had intended to build a house of their own that fall—in fact, the ground for the site had been broken but Mrs. Camp begged them to stay on in the big house. The doctor had finally diagnosed Mr. Camp's ailment as heart trouble. She was afraid to stay in the house alone with him, she said. Sara had played about enough building her guest house. She said she didn't much care about building a house of their own just then, so they were installed in a suite of rooms in the west wing.

He hated to have his own mother living alone, but she agreed that the Carter house was impracticable for a young married couple and moreover she had never expected him to live with her after he was married. She got a cousin from Maryland to come for a visit which was to extend into years, so that worked out all right.

Rice Bolling came back to town that fall. He was out at the house a lot, of course. Looking back on it, Jim didn't know that he'd have had anything to say about that even if he'd known how things were going to turn out. Everybody knew that Rice had been in love with Sara for years. Well, he, Jim, had always taken it for granted that the girl he married would have had plenty of other men in love with her. Now, looking back, he felt that Seely Latham was as much to blame as anybody. The trouble with Seely was that he didn't have a thing in God's world to do, and no love affairs of his own, so that in the afternoon he was always having tea with some woman and talking to her about her husband or her lover. It was all right for him to hang around older women like Mrs. Camp but he ought not to have kept the younger women stirred up. He had stirred up Sara. He might not have put those nonsensical notions into her head but he certainly encouraged her in them.

Jim and Sara had had words before and once or twice Sara had made veiled remarks to the effect that he was not overwhelmingly in love with her. He hadn't taken her up on anything she said, just told her simply and affectionately not to be a fool.

Then one night—he came upstairs later than she did and found the door of their bedroom locked against him. He thought for a second that she must have done it without thinking and he called out, "Sara, let me in."

She answered at once in a careful, hard voice, "I'm not going to let you in."

He was so angry that the whole room seemed to swim about him. He had an impulse to smash the lock but he conquered that. He went over to the table, picked up a cigarette and lit it. He drew on it several times and then he called, "Do you mean that?"

She spoke in a low voice—she was evidently close to the door. "I told you how I felt the other day but you didn't pay any attention to me."

He had actually to go back in his memory to know what she was talking about and then he remembered that several days before he had touched her shoulder and she had drawn back, coolly, saying, "You needn't do that." He had just stared at her but somebody had come in just then. He hadn't had an opportunity to ask her what in the devil she meant till hours later and then her mood seemed to have changed and he had thought it best to say nothing about it.

He stood there, his hands clenched at his sides. He thought that if he could only get in there to talk to her, and then he knew that it was better for him not to see her face to face. He couldn't trust himself with her just then. But he wasn't going to sleep on a sofa like a tame cat. He wasn't going to spend the night in that house. He looked at his watch. Eleven o'clock. He picked up his hat, went down the stairs and through the silent house where nobody seemed to be awake and out to the garage. When he got his car out he had no idea where he was going but after he had driven for a block or two he headed west, towards the country club. It wasn't midnight yet. Somebody would still be around. He didn't want to be alone. He had to be with people. He didn't much care who they were.

CHAPTER EIGHTEEN

COLONEL ROGERS and old Mr. Slayden who lived at the club were in the big lounge playing chess but he didn't see anybody else around. He sat down, lit a cigarette and told Charley to bring him a whiskey. Then he heard voices down the hall. He took his whiskey and went down there, into a room that was so thick with smoke that at first he thought it was full of people. Then he saw that there were only three—Bess Watkins, Rice Bolling and Sam Reid. They had evidently been there all evening—the ash trays in front of them were overflowing with cigarette stubs. Bess was sunk down in a corner of a big sofa with her feet tucked up under her. Sam was sprawled beside her and Rice had drawn a chair up in front of them. Sam was talking: "Now you take a fellow like me. . . ." It was one of those tedious monologues that he got into when he'd taken a certain amount of whiskey. Rice wasn't saying much, he never did; but Bess kept nodding her head sadly and trying to break in with a story about Henry Watkins. She had divorced him two years ago and had been pretty much on the loose since then. Jim saw that he would have to work fast if he caught up with them. He said, "What are you all drinking?"

Sam looked up indignantly. "What do you have to come barging in here for?"

"I only asked what you were drinking," Jim said.

Bess peered near-sightedly through the smoke. "It's Jim," she said. "Jim, I want gin. I've got a crying jag on and I've got to have gin."

Jim went down the hall and found Charley. He ordered three gin rickeys and a double soda for himself and came on back. Nobody paid any attention to him except Bess, who moved over so that he could sit beside her.

Sam was still telling about his quarrel with Bob Rogers. Rice kept trying to break in and so did Bess, but Sam was a steam roller when he got going. Finally Bess got up and went to the ladies' room. When she came back she was made up all fresh and seemed to have caught her second wind. She called for another gin rickey and then she turned around and concentrated on Jim. Sam suddenly got sore and said he was going home. Rice Bolling got up with him. He must not have been as drunk as the others for afterwards Jim remembered how he stopped in the door and looked at them as he called, "Come on, Bess, and I'll take you home."

"I'm going to take her home," Jim told him. "I'm going to take her home in fifteen minutes."

Sam moved back into the room, knocking a table over and spilling ash trays all over the floor. "I'm not going to take her home," he announced. "Never did have any use for her. Little bow-legged, painted tart."

"You don't need to be insulting," Bess said.

Jim was just beginning to feel the liquor. He hadn't really understood what Sam said but he started up at that point and went at Sam. "Now, listen," he said, "you're going to speak respectfully to Mrs. Watkins as long as you're in my presence. Understand?" He put his hand out and was pushing Sam backwards against the door when Rice Bolling intervened. He got his arm around Sam's shoulders and propelled him down the hall. They could hear the two laughing and quarrelling and then Colonel Rogers' rasping voice. He had a habit of sitting up late in the big lounge just so he could hop on anybody he caught making a noise after midnight.

"He'll be down here in a minute," Bess said.

"That's right," Jim answered. "We'd better go." But he made no move to go, and after a second he sat down beside her. He stretched out his legs and as he did so felt how clear his head was. He looked about the room. It seemed larger and more attractive now that the others had gone. He did not want to leave it. It was as if the peculiar lucidity he felt was circumscribed by these walls. If he went outside them he might lose it. He sank back against the pillows. He looked at Bess. "It took me a while to catch up," he said, "but I feel fine now. How do you feel?"

"I feel fine," she said.

He put his hand up and ran it over her shining hair. "You have pretty hair," he said.

She was crying softly. "I went back to Henry Watkins when he was in New Orleans," she said. "I stayed three months and it was hell all the way. And that last morning he said I was nothing but a clothes horse, that there was nothing to me but a mop of hair. I said, 'Well, I haven't had to blondine it yet.' That little tart he was running around with had one of these long yellow bobs. Color of straw and so rough it looked like it would break in your hand. . . ."

"Henry wasn't good enough for you," he said.

She was crying louder. "I wouldn't care," she sobbed; "I could have stood it if he'd only behaved like a gentleman."

"Henry always had a dirty tongue," he said.

She stood up. "We've got to get out of here."

He got up too and clasped her arm. "My car's on the side drive," he said. She stumbled away from him towards the cloakroom. As he stood there waiting for her he closed his eyes and then wished he hadn't, for the room began to spin around. She was back with her coat. They got into his car and drove to her apartment.

He stayed with her that night. At seven o'clock the next morning he got up, dressed and drove home. The side door was opened as he drove up and old Sam was out washing off the doorsteps. He laughed as he said, "Good morning, Sam." The old Negro looked at him shrewdly and said, "Mornin, Mister Jim." Jim tiptoed through the halls and up to his and Sara's suite. The living-room door was ajar just as he had left it. He went into his bathroom and took a shower and changed his clothes. He ate his breakfast on a tray in his bedroom as they sometimes did, then went out and drove to the office. When he came in at five o'clock Sara was sitting there in the living room. She had evidently just been out, for her hat and gloves lay beside her on the sofa. But she did not seem to be waiting for him. She just sat there staring abstractedly at the floor.

The yellow boy, John, had come in behind Jim. Jim gave him his hat and as he moved off with it he noticed for the hundredth time the boy's gait, a rhythmical glide that had always struck him as more suited to service in a night club than in a private house.

Sara had got up and was walking towards the window. There were four on that side of the house, framed in yellow damask. The carpet was a sort of peach color. It was a color that suited Sara. She turned around. He thought wearily:

"Now we have got to go over it all again." What she said surprised him: "Dr. Morrow says I'm going to have a baby."

His impulse was to go to her but the look on her face checked him. He stopped still, then said a little belligerently: "I suppose you think that's tough luck."

She said: "Under the circumstances, I suppose it is."

"Are you going to do anything about it?" he asked.

"No," she said—"No."

He stood there, uncertain what to do. All morning he had told himself that he would put it up to Sara that they must get a divorce. He was not going to live with any woman who locked him out of her bedroom whenever she took a notion, and then the thought came to him that you didn't divorce a woman who was carrying your child. He said, "Sara, won't you come over here and sit down?"

She moved over obediently and took her place on the sofa, a little removed from where he had sat down. He did not touch her or speak for a moment and then he said, "I wish you hadn't done that last night."

She looked at him, a queer, glancing look and then she was staring at the floor. "This doesn't make any difference," she said.

"Don't talk nonsense, Sara," he said irritably.

She was silent for a long time and then she said, "You've said that to me before."

"I say it to you only when you talk like a child."

She made a little gesture with her hand. Her voice was cold and even. "I want to divorce you but I think it would be better for us to stay together until after the baby is born, for the sake of the family. . . ."

He said furiously: "I don't give a good God damn about the family."

She did not answer. He said with increasing fury, "Sara, for God's sake. What does all this mean? What sort of a bee have you got in your bonnet?"

She was looking at him again, that same queer look. She said, "I haven't got any bee in my bonnet. I just . . ." Her voice broke. He thought that she was going to cry. He thought, too, for a second, that she was going to put her head on his shoulder. He put out his arm. It brushed her shoulder and then fell away as she made a sudden movement—he was never sure whether she had actually shuddered because he was going to touch her or whether it was just that she was trying not to cry. She stood up. She had her hands behind her as if to keep him from touching them. She said, "I can go through this without letting the family know, if you can." And she was gone from the room.

He sat there for a few minutes, then he got up and knocked on her door. There was no answer. He knocked again. He said, "Sara, please let me in."

The door opened. She stood in the middle of the floor. She had a hair brush in her hand and she was brushing her hair and crying. He went over to her. He said, "Sara, you know I love you. Do you want to divorce me?"

She said, "You know I don't."

He put his arms about her. She let him kiss her. Then he picked her up and carried her over to the bed and they lay down together.

CHAPTER NINETEEN

THAT was on Thursday. Everything was all right for a week. Everything would have been all right for good if it hadn't been for Bess Watkins. She called him up at the office the next day and wanted to know if he was free for dinner. He told her he wasn't and added in a formal tone that he hoped he'd see her soon. But she didn't hang up. She hesitated a second and then asked if he could meet her at Cayce's at five o'clock. Cayce's was a sort of tea-room place that was always full of women at that time of day. He went in a few minutes after five. Bitsy Trabue and Nell Watkins were there and Bess was already there, sitting by herself at a table in a corner. He spoke to Bitsy and Nell and made as if to pass Bess, then stopped and said, "Hello, there." She asked him to sit down, in a voice loud enough for Bitsy and the others to hear. He sat down. She had already ordered tea. He told her he was due at home by five-thirty and wouldn't have anything. Her tea came. She drank a little, then she said in a low voice, "I was sorry not to see you at all yesterday." He knew then that he was in for it. He decided to get the whole thing over at one blow. He faced around a little so that his back was to those girls at the next table. He said: "Bess, I was blind the other night. The fact is I don't remember a thing after we left the club. I reckon I took you home, all right, didn't I?"

She said, "Yes, you took me home," and then waited a second and added: "and you came in for a while."

He shook his head. "Is that so? Well, I don't remember a thing after we left the club. If I said or did anything I shouldn't have done I want to apologize. I hope you'll forgive me." He was looking her in the eye as he spoke. His glance, straight and hard as he could make it, contrasted with the meek words.

She returned his glance and then her eyes dropped. "That's the way it takes you, is it?" she asked.

His tone grew cheerful. "Well, I never drew quite that much of a blank before. But as I say if you'll overlook it this once I promise it'll never happen again."

Her face, ordinarily pale under the two spots of rouge, went suddenly scarlet. Her gaze was as hard as his had been a moment before. "Oh, you needn't make any promises," she said.

The girls at the next table were getting up in a flurry. Jim bent to rescue a dropped glove, handed it back to its owner and acknowledged her thanks, then turned to Bess. "I'll tell Sara," he said in a loud voice. "We might fix something up for one night next week."

She bowed, smiling fixedly, managed a wave of her hand in dismissal. The flock of girls had stopped at a counter to buy candy. He got out of the restaurant ahead of them and made for his car which was parked at the corner.

He did not see Bess again for several weeks. Then one night he and Sara and two other couples were at a dance at the Mountain Club. He had seen Bess earlier in the evening and had spoken to her and had received a chilly bow. He and Sara were sitting out a dance when Bess suddenly got up and, walking swiftly ahead of her escort, stopped at their table. She said, "Hello," and then without pausing to engage Sara in further conversation pulled a cigarette case out of her bag and dumped it down before Jim. "You left this that night you were at my apartment," she said, and walked off.

Jim turned the case over, recognizing it as his own. He slipped it into his pocket. Sara watched the silver thing disappear into the black pocket. She said, "That's the one I gave you Christmas, isn't it?"

He said "Yes" and asked her if she wanted to dance. She said that she did. As they moved out on to the floor she asked: "Which night were you at Bess' apartment?" He said—and regretted the words as soon as they were out of his mouth—"If you must know it was the night you locked me out."

She said nothing after that and they danced until nearly midnight. As they started home she said in a strained tone, "I am very grateful to you, Jim, for not lying to me about this."

He said, "Not lying to you about what? Sure, that's my cigarette case and I left it in Bess' apartment. What of it?"

She was silent for a little, then she said vehemently, "I wish to God it had been somebody besides Bess Watkins. She's always hated me and now she's got something on me she won't forget."

"Now what has Bess Watkins got on you?" he blustered.

They were passing under a street lamp. She looked up at him. "Jim," she said, "Bess wouldn't have brought that cigarette case over to you with me sitting there if she hadn't wanted me to know there was something between you."

He broke down then and, like a fool, confessed. She took it very well. At least he thought at the time she did, for they were reconciled that night. . . . Laura was born in January of that year.

From the start she was more Sara's child than his. He had interfered only once in the management of the baby and then he got into trouble.

It was two months after Laura was born. He was going down the street one day when he heard an authoritative voice issue from an automobile that was drawn up to the curb:

"Mister Jim!"

He went over to the automobile. Sitting inside was Aunt Mary Proctor, an old colored woman he had known since childhood. Aunt Mary was a privileged character in Countsville. She was a Negro woman of the old school but she had been shrewd enough years ago to take a course in nursing. The combination of scientific training and old-fashioned respectability was irresistible to the young matrons of Countsville. It was the fashion to have Aunt Mary take entire charge of one's baby for the first two years of its life. She never stayed in a situation longer than two years, there were so many demands for her services.

Jim heard all this later. At the time he knew of Aunt Mary only as a highly reliable old colored woman whom anybody ought to be glad to have as a nurse.

On this morning he exchanged greetings with the old woman and answered her questions about the health of the various members of the family, then stood wondering what she wanted with him. She looked down at the child on her lap, a diminutive, stiffly starched Prentwell. "I'm about through with this here child," she remarked. "Done carried him through whooping cough and measles. Yes, sir. I'm about ready to turn him over to Miss Sally."

"Well, he looks mighty fine," Jim said, sticking out a finger which the child stolidly ignored. "I've always heard you were a good hand with babies, Aunt Mary," and then, meeting the shrewd old eyes he found himself saying the words Aunt Mary wanted him to say:

"Why'n't you come over and nurse our baby?"

That was enough for Aunt Mary. She had sense enough not to pin him down but she came over to see Sara the next morning, observing that she had met Mister Jim on the street and he had tried to hire her. Sara was annoyed. She had told Jim—but it seemed that he had forgotten it—that the Englishwoman Louise Elkins had had for her children was giving up her situation with the Elkins and coming to the Carters at the end of the week.

Jim said that that was all right. He would have preferred having a Negro nurse for the child but he didn't think it made much difference—until the Englishwoman came.

Her name was Strong, Mrs. Harriet Strong. She had eyes the color of the agates he used to shoot when he was a boy. She suffered from the delusion that any one of the Negro servants was likely to come in and cut her throat any night. She had to have a special diet because of her liver and nothing was ever allowed to interfere with her day off. But she was a superior servant, Sara said.

That was the trouble. Jim had found her too superior. It was on Emancipation Day and the Negroes were all off, of course. Sara and Mrs. Camp had gone to Birmingham. Jim was to have had dinner at the club. But he and Sam Reid came by the house to bathe and change after playing golf. It was so cool that they decided to stay there instead of going out to the club. Jim looked about until he found the Englishwoman sitting with the baby in the garden and asked her if she couldn't make a little supper for them out of whatever happened to be in the refrigerator. She stared at him out of those agate eyes, then told him that if she had to go into the kitchen he would have to mind the baby. He told her that he would. He and Sam sat down on the grass and played with the baby for half an hour. At the end of that time Mrs. Strong appeared, announcing that supper—such as it was—was set out in the breakfast room. It was a poor enough supper but they ate it. Jim thought nothing more about the matter until a day or two later when Sara told him that Mrs. Strong was complaining that she had never before been called upon to cook meals.

He stared. "Cook meals? You mean that cold lunch she set out for us the other night? I'd have got it myself if I'd thought it was going to be all that trouble."

"It isn't the trouble," Sara explained. "It hurt her pride. You see, she's really a superior woman."

"She's too damn superior," he said.

"Just what do you mean by that?" she enquired coldly.

"I mean she's tyrannical."

"I doubt if she's any more tyrannical than Aunt Mary Proctor. Sally Prentwell tells me she couldn't call her soul her own when she had Aunt Mary."

"I'd rather be tyrannized over by a good old colored woman than by that ignorant cockney. She couldn't get away with it anywhere else."

"Anywhere else?"

"Yes, you and Louise Elkins think it's smart to have an English nurse, so you put up with anything from her."

"Did you get that idea from your mother?" she asked in a low voice.

"My mother?" he said, bewildered.

"Yes," she repeated and her voice rose. "Your mother.

199

Your mother, who looks down her nose at everybody just because they aren't as poor as she is and weren't born a Kyarter and married a Kyarter."

"Kyarter?" he said.

"Yes, Kyarter!" she cried wildly. "Well, I was born a Camp. No, I wasn't. I was born a Kampschafer. My grandfather was a German immigrant and he came over here and made a lot of money and I'm proud of him. . . ." Her voice broke. There were tears in her eyes.

"Well, I'd be proud, too, if I had a grandfather made a lot of money."

"No, you wouldn't. That old King Kyarter you're all so proud of—I read in a book once that he was mean as the devil and began to oppress labor back in the seventeenth century."

He was even more bewildered. "I don't know what you're talking about," he said, "and if I did know I wouldn't be proud of him. I don't pay any attention to such silliness and you know it."

"Well, your mother does and so does Helen."

"Well, I don't."

With tears in her eyes, she was still looking at him. "You think you don't but you do. Down underneath you despise us and always have. . . ."

"I don't think much of Joe. . . ." he said.

"Me either," she cried and threw herself down on the couch. "Me either! You despise me and always have."

"Oh, for God's sake!" he said and got up and left the house.

That was the summer when Laura had colitis. Sara was frightened out of her wits and took her to Chicago to a baby specialist. He said the baby couldn't stand the Southern heat, so Sara took her to Charlevoix and stayed there all summer. She came home in October. She seemed glad to be at home and glad to see him. . . . But it was that fall that she started going around with Rice Bolling.

He ought to have put his foot down on it at the start, but it was begun so openly—one night when he had to work late and Rice escorted Sara to a dinner party—that he did not have much chance to object. He had his hands full about that time, at the plant. The Camp products had just started on the down grade. . . .

Mr. Camp, as he grew older, began to soften. He began to trust Joe's judgment. When Jim was first taken into the firm Mr. Camp had as good as told him that Joe was no business man and never would make one. But in the last few years Joe had managed to win him over, on at least one important point.

It was Joe—Joe, in collaboration with a high-powered designer they got in from the East—who developed the "Improved Fascinex." It looked like a good thing, all right. Joe wanted to put on a national advertising campaign and manufacture it in large quantities. That called for new machinery and a general expansion of the business and it came at a ticklish time. Mr. Camp was worried when the stock market collapsed in 1929 and he stayed worried, but Joe thought everything was all right when stocks began to climb in the spring of 1930. He finally persuaded Mr. Camp—who had lived through one panic, that of 1896—that things were still on the up-grade and they made a contract with Cantwell and Company of Nashville to float a large issue of bonds in order to get the money to expand. The bonds were sold to the public by Cantwell in the summer of 1930 and the money was credited to the Camp corporation's account in Cantwell's bank until such time as the corporation should check on it to pay for the new construction. They started the new plant in the fall of 1930, with some misgivings. The depression was just getting under way. The cotton market had been declining for months. That was costing them a pretty penny, as they had big inventories of cotton. Mr. Camp was uncertain. But Joe said there was nothing to do but go ahead. Hoover was in the White House and everything was bound to be right with the world. Then, too, the construction had already been let and there was nothing to do but go on or take the losses on a partially completed plant. Furthermore, the contracting company would have had to be paid a sizable fee to cancel the contract. And Joe was still sold on "Fascinex." He had just made a trip up East. A lot of his manufacturing friends up there told him he was mighty lucky to be doing business in Alabama where labor and water power were so cheap. They didn't see how he could fail to clean up on "Fascinex."

There were rumors going around about George Cantwell even at that time but Mr. Camp and everybody who knew him considered the man a financial genius. Then, too, he had the backing of the Countsville National Bank of which his father was president. And about that time his bank merged with a powerful Kentucky bank. After that Mr. Camp felt justified in not withdrawing his support from Cantwell's bank and besides, as Joe pointed out, they couldn't get out; they were in too deep. It was bad luck, though—or bad management—that they had so much money in the Countsville National.

None of this was ever mentioned at home. Jim had yet to hear Mr. Camp mention a business matter in the presence of his wife and daughter. Jim wondered sometimes whether Mrs. Camp thought money grew on trees. She was certainly vague about its origins. And Sara was almost as bad. Jim thought afterwards that it would have been a good thing if the old man's family had known how worried he was those last months, but he had fallen into the Camp habit of being close-mouthed about business and so he said nothing. Sara knew that he and Mr. Camp and Joe worked late at the new plant three or four nights a week all that fall but she did not seem to think there was anything uncommon in that.

Meanwhile she was seeing Rice Bolling two or three nights a week. If Jim himself had been going about as much as usual he'd have heard the gossip. Seely Latham or some skunk like that would have told him. As it was, the thing broke on him like a thunderclap. He had phoned Sara, saying he was going to work late at the office and then Mr. Camp said that he had left some figures that he wanted at home. Jim volunteered to drive in and get them and then he thought that he would run up and see if Sara had gone to bed. Their sitting room door was closed. He pushed it open. There was nobody in there but he knew that somebody had been having drinks because of the glasses on the table. He walked into the hall. A hat and a stick that Rice Bolling always carried were in the rack there. He walked back into the sitting room. He stood there undecided what to do. Then he called "Sara." There was dead silence, then she came out of her bedroom. Her face was flushed but it went dead white when she saw him. She backed up against the wall, trembling.

He said, "I suppose Rice is in there with you."

She looked straight at him then and said, "Yes."

Rice came out of the bedroom. He was trying to fix his tie. His face, too, was flushed. He said, "Hello, Jim."

Jim stood there looking from one to the other. It was plain what they'd been up to, no way in God's world to ignore it,

203

nothing to say, no way to turn. The sweat broke out on his face. He said "You . . ." then stopped. They all stood there, looking at each other, then somebody was moving in the room. It was Rice, walking slowly towards the door. He had picked up his hat and stick. He turned. "Jim," he said, "I reckon you'll want to talk to me about this. I'll be free all morning.

"Where'll you be?"

"Out at the Mountain Club. . . . Say ten o'clock?"

"All right," Jim said. Rice went out and shut the door. Sara walked over and sat down in a chair. Jim still stood there, staring. There was something vaguely reminiscent about the words that had just been uttered. He didn't know what it was for a second and then he knew. In the old days such remarks were preliminaries to a duel. . . . But he was only going over to the club to talk things over.

He turned his eyes to Sara, knowing that he must look foolish and sick. She looked sick too. He suddenly put his hands up to his forehead. He felt his lips draw back in a grin. "I can feel 'em, all right," he said. She stared at him blankly, then a spark of light grew in her pupil. It was terror. She had not understood what he meant. She had thought for a second that he was out of his head.

He thought—it was curious that he should have had the thought at such a moment—"She's still in love with me." Then he thought: *I'm tired of having women in love with me. I'd like to be in love with one myself for a change.*

The door had been shut behind Rice Bolling for a long time. Sara was getting up from the sofa. She put her hands up, held her face in her cupped hands so it was hidden for a moment, then took her hands down and moved on towards her bedroom. Halfway there she paused. "This wouldn't have happened," she said, "if it hadn't been for that Watkins girl."

"Watkins girl?" he said blankly.

"Bess Watkins," she said, "and you needn't tell me that you didn't have an affair with her, for everybody in town knows it."

"I never said I didn't," he replied.

"No," she said bitterly, "you never cared enough to even lie about it."

He put his hand up to his forehead. "She hasn't got anything to do with this," he said.

Her eyes went dead black, the way they always did when she was excited. "Oh, she hasn't, hasn't she?" she cried.

"No," he said. "She hasn't," and then he added after a pause, "It's different."

"I suppose you mean that my going with Rice Bolling is different from your amusing yourself with anybody that happens to please your fancy."

"I wouldn't mind your going about with him," he said. "At least I wouldn't if this hadn't happened. But I'm not going to have you sleeping with him." The sweat broke out on his face again. He repeated: "I'm not going to have you sleeping with him."

She went over to the table and took a cigarette from a box. She tried to strike a match but the head broke off twice. He took out his lighter and held it for her. When she had her cigarette going he said:

"Do you want to divorce me and marry Rice Bolling?"

She looked at him, opened her lips to speak, closed them, then sank down in the corner of the sofa. "I don't know," she wailed, "I don't know what I want to do. But I can't stand this."

There was a soft tap at the door. Jim glanced at Sara. She

sat up straight and made a sign for him to go to the door. He walked over and opened the door.

The house boy, John, stood there. His yellow face was a discreet mask. He spoke softly: "Miss Sara, Mister Jim, Mister Camp's daid. Done dropped daid in his chair."

CHAPTER TWENTY

THEY RAN downstairs. Joe was standing in the hall. He said that after Jim had left, his father suddenly got tired and said that he wanted to go home. Joe had driven him in. Mr. Camp sat down in the library to smoke a cigar. Mrs. Camp was in bed but she got up and came in to sit with them a few minutes. Joe had a drink with his father and was just leaving the house when he heard his mother crying, "Oscar! Oscar!" He rushed back. Mr. Camp was sitting just as Joe had left him with his head fallen a little back and his mouth open. Joe said that as soon as he walked into the room he knew that his father was dead. Mrs. Camp didn't realize it, though. She kept kneeling beside him and chafing his hands and she had the niggers running all over the place bringing hot water bottles and spirits of ammonia. They let her go on that way until the doctor came and told her that Mr. Camp had died of heart failure. She had to believe it then. Poor woman. She was like a crazy person and then the doctor gave her a shot of something and she quieted down. She was quiet, too, the next morning, agreeing to everything that was suggested and saying it didn't make any difference, when you consulted her about anything. Sara insisted that the doctor kept her under opiates so constantly that except for those first few hours she didn't realize her husband was dead. Sara was indignant with the doctor but he, Jim, always thought the man acted for the best. God knows they all had their hands full during the next two days.

Mr. Camp died on Tuesday and was buried on Thursday. When they got back from the funeral the afternoon papers were at the house with the news of the Countsville National's closing. They had known for weeks that it was going to happen, but somehow having the news made public was different. It affected Joe badly. Up to that time he had been the strong, silent business man, keeping a stiff upper lip, particularly before the women, but after the bank closed he didn't even try to keep up a front.

One evening a few days after the funeral he and Helen asked Jim to come over to their house, at six o'clock, without Sara. They had given word to the servants that they were not at home to anybody and were sitting there waiting for Jim. They had it all thought out. Joe had inherited some money from his grandmother, old Mrs. Fortescue, two or three years ago. He and Helen had decided that they were going to take that money and go abroad to live. Joe had a friend in Italy who wanted to rent them his villa. Cables had been going back and forth for days. They had the whole thing mapped out before Jim got there.

He stared at them non-plussed by the suddenness of their decision. "What are you going to do about the plant?" he asked.

"It'll be in the hands of a receiver inside of a month," Joe said. "You know that as well as I do."

Jim held his hands up in a gesture of fending them off. "You haven't got a drink?"

"Alfred's making martinis," Helen said; "or would you rather have whiskey?"

"Whiskey," Jim told her. He waited until he had his drink before he answered Joe.

"Yes, I guess they'll take the property over but you could more than likely get appointed as manager. That's the way those things usually work."

"I don't want to be manager," Joe said. "I wouldn't live through this year again for fifty businesses. I . . . My God, man . . ." His voice rose the way it did when he got excited.

Helen interrupted sharply. "He doesn't want to have anything to do with it, Jim. It would just be pouring water down a hole. We have enough money to live on if we get out now. But if Joe puts any money into the business we're sunk. . . . We won't help any of the rest of you by staying. We'll just ruin ourselves. . . . My God, when I think what Joe's been through this year. . . ."

"It's been a tough year," Jim agreed. "Still," he grinned weakly, "business is business. It'll take a year, anyhow, for the receivership to go through. And we've got to think of our men. We can't just shut down overnight."

Helen got up and came towards him, still holding her glass. "We've thought of all that but—you haven't any other plans, have you?"

Jim laughed. "No," he said, "I haven't any other plans."

He paused, then added, looking at Joe, "It's to my interest, of course, to stick around."

Joe nodded. "I've been over and over it," he said wearily, "and I'm damned if I see what we could do. Even if we raised the money—and I'm not sure we could do it—well, as Helen says, it would be just like pouring water down a hole." He extinguished the stub of his cigarette, rang for another round of drinks. "You know, I wonder—sometimes I think Father must have had a slight stroke before the one that carried him off. He just hasn't been himself for the last two years. No use denying that."

Jim looked at him in amazement. "Your father was never strong for the Countsville National."

Joe began on his second martini. "Charley Cantwell got around him, the way he did everybody else." He set the glass down, so hard that the frail base cracked against the edge of an ash tray. "I'd like to get my hands on that fellow."

"There's a lot of people that'd like to," Jim said. "They're strung out from here to Louisiana. I met old Mr. Boyd this morning. He was walking down the street in the broad light of day, crying. They say everything he had was in the Countsville National, and Charley Cantwell has been attending to all his business for years."

"He ought to have had better sense than to put everything he had in one bank," Helen said, "and he ought not to have relied on any one man's judgment about his investments."

She came and sat down in a chair nearer Jim. She looked at him intently. "Joe has to get away, Jim," she said.

He had not had time to think about it before but he realized now that she must have had a pretty bad time with Joe and she had to—or at least she thought she had to—get out. He returned her gaze with a look that meant: "All right, old girl, if that's the way you feel." They were all silent for a moment, then Jim asked:

"What about Mrs. Camp?"

"She'll go with us," Helen answered promptly. "That's one of the reasons we want to start as soon as we can. The trip'll do Mother good."

Joe said that he thought so too. When they broached the matter to Mrs. Camp, she did not look at it that way. She said calmly but positively that she did not intend to leave her home. They put a good deal of pressure on her. Helen even went so far as to intimate to her that she did not have any choice in the matter: the house might have to be sold. "I don't think so," Mrs. Camp replied. "It's in my name. I am quite sure your father arranged all that. He said that he intended to provide for my security first and foremost." She surprised them then by adding: "I've expected something like this for years. Your father always told me that there was no way to make a fortune safe."

Jim, in the months that followed Joe's departure, found himself wishing that Mr. Camp had told her either more or less about business. The few things he had said to her had sunk in. She applied them as maxims. Unfortunately they didn't apply to the present situation. She tried hard but she simply couldn't understand how they could lose the business. Jim explained to her over and over again that the bonds were in technical default and that the property would inevitably be taken over by the bondholders. She listened with the blank look that always came on her face when money was mentioned. "If you'd only foreseen this," she said gently. "Father always said that you ought not to go into anything unless you could see your way through. He said there was very little luck in business."

"We couldn't foresee that the bank would fail," he told her and then added, for he thought now that they really ought to have foreseen it: "at least we didn't."

"I wish Father were here to advise you," she said. But feeling that she had been harsh she leaned over and patted Jim's hand. "I don't see how anybody could try harder than you're trying, Jim."

During the next few weeks Jim often thought that Joe had done them all a service by pulling out. The Camp Company went into receivership in February. When the new board of directors met Jim was elected manager of the reorganized plant, but Robinson, chairman of the board, told him privately that they would not have considered Joe for the job. There were more Cantwell investments than Jim had realized. It took him the better part of two months to get things straightened out so that they knew at least how much they had lost by the bank failure. It took all of Jim's time and almost all of his energy so that during those months he rarely had time even to think about his private affairs.

Mr. Camp had died in November. Sara took her mother to Florida in January and they stayed until the end of April. He and Sara had tacitly agreed to let things rock along until some indefinite date. Sara was unpredictable in some ways and in others she was absolutely dependable. She realized that in this crisis somebody must work for the family good. Jim was obviously that person. She had enough sense to let him do the job in his own way.

He was immensely grateful to her for that, but it was as if she were two persons. To one of them he was indebted and in his way devoted, but the other was identified with some catastrophe that had overtaken him and whenever he tried to think of her, his thoughts shied away.

Occasionally he pondered over the events of the last few months, trying to account for the cloud of depression that had settled on him. He told himself that Mr. Camp's death, the loss of the business, and the general confusion that had ensued were enough to upset any man. He told himself this but he knew that it was not so. The business, even under the adverse conditions, was being run now in the way he had always wanted it run and he got some satisfaction out of that. He had genuinely liked old Mr. Camp but his death was not, for Jim at least, the overwhelming calamity that it was to the others. And it was a real relief to get Joe out of the way. No, it was something else. It wasn't even the fact that he had become, that Rice Bolling and Sara had made him, a cuckold. It was the fact that he had had to go on living with Sara. He had said in those few minutes there before Mr. Camp died that he would not do it and then things had happened so fast and so appallingly that he had seemed to have no choice. He did not know now that he had ever really had any choice, but he wished that he had had time at least to consider what he ought to do. Not stopping to consider, being hurried over the decision had done something to him, had violated an integrity that up to that time he had somehow preserved. That was gone now and he was, in consequence, a different man, not, he sometimes thought fantastically, Jim Carter but some other man, a man who ought, really, to have had another name. Occasionally he tried to look at the matter from Sara's viewpoint. He realized that she had taken up with Rice mostly as a way of striking at him. He allowed for her feelings of resentment against him, her disappointment in him, but thinking the thing over he came always to the same conclusion. Infidelity in a man was not the same thing it was in a woman. "No," he told himself as he had told her that day, "It's different. That's all. It's just different."

He heard from Sara fairly often while she was in Florida, brief notes that said that she and her mother were well and described Laura's attempts to learn to swim. Then, it was towards the end of April, he got a letter from her:

". . . You have not said anything about a divorce recently. I suppose you are biding your time. I appreciate your thoughtfulness in waiting this long. I'm writing now to tell you that

I am quite ready. I am going to ask Sam to handle the affair for me. I shall name Bess Watkins as co-respondent, of course...."

The letter came to the house. He got it when he came in from work. He read it standing there in the hall, then went upstairs.

"I have not written anything about a divorce," he wrote, "because I have not been thinking about one. If you are determined to get one I will not oppose you. I think it is very foolish to drag Bess Watkins into this. She's just a poor devil who never did you any harm. I don't know why you want to persecute her." He looked at what he had written, then decided to leave out that about Bess Watkins. Sara had a mania about Bess Watkins. Anything he said in favor of Bess would only strengthen her aversion to the girl.

He got up and walked about the room, frowning, then after a little, he tore up the first letter and wrote another: "I am sorry you want to divorce me. I don't want to divorce you. Won't you wait until you come home before doing anything about it? I feel that if we could talk things over we might understand each other better." He hesitated, then added: "You know I love you." He signed himself, "Always, Jim," put the letter in an envelope and sealed it and put it in his pocket to mail.

He looked at his watch. Eight o'clock. He had promised to dine with the Allards at the Mountain Club and it had been arranged that he should come by their house and pick them up. He hurried on over. Uncle Joe, the older butler, was just about to lock the house, but he had a message from Elise. They had waited for Jim as long as they could. He was to come on over to the club and join them. Jim said all right and then he saw the afternoon paper lying on a table

214

in the hall. He had not had time to read it before he left home. He wanted to sit down and be quiet for a few minutes. He was already late for his engagement. It did not matter much now how much later he was. Frank and Elise would not wait for him. He told Joe that he believed that he would sit there and read a few minutes and asked if he couldn't have a drink.

The old Negro brought it and then tiptoed out. Jim sat there and read the paper through. When he had finished reading it he got up and got himself another drink. He finished that but still he didn't go. It was too late for one thing, and for ·another he didn't feel like seeing even Frank and Elise tonight. He sat there in the long room where the light was gradually growing dimmer and thought about his situation. Bess Watkins was in California, he had heard somebody say. He hadn't seen her since that evening at the club. He never wanted to see the little tyke again. Still, you couldn't help feeling sorry for her. It would be rather a blow to her if Sara did name her as co-respondent, and God knows what she would do in turn. There would not be much that he himself could do in such a situation. Just stand and take it as he had seen other men do. He certainly would not make any chivalrous gestures towards Bess. No, he'd be damned if he would. . . . He wondered if Sara meant what she said and decided that she did.

There was a noise at the other end of the room. Some one had entered through the door that gave on the terrace and was slowly advancing towards him. He put out his hand to the lamp beside him but before he could light it a glow sprang up at the other end of the long room.

He got to his feet, speaking with purposeful calm: "You want more light in here?"

The person—a girl in a long white cloak—was standing beside the table that held the lighted lamp. She fixed her eyes on him and began slowly to back away. As she moved she put her hand to her throat. He heard the whistle of intaken breath and then she was speaking. "Oh!" she said. "Oh!"

He thought she was going to scream. Two swift bounds brought him up to her. He began to speak hurriedly and at the same time put his hands on her shoulders in a reassuring gesture. "I'm not a burglar. Just a friend. A friend of the family."

"Oh," she said again, "you're just a friend of the family." She began to laugh.

His hands dropped from her shoulders. He stood silent until she had stopped laughing. "I'm terribly sorry," he said then, "I must have frightened you out of your wits."

She was moving away from him, towards a big chair. She put her hands up as if to unfasten her cloak and then as if it were too much trouble she let her hands drop and threw herself into the chair. "For a minute I really did think you were a burglar," she said.

He was still embarrassed. "I know it," he said. "That's why I rushed over to you so quick." He laughed awkwardly. "Asinine thing to do. Must have scared you worse than ever."

"No," she said. "No. I realized you meant to be reassuring. A burglar wouldn't act like that, would he?"

"I never knew but one," he said. "If he heard anything stirring in a house he went out of the window."

She sat up straight in the deep chair. She was fumbling in a little bag. She had stopped that disturbing laughter but the hands holding the bag were shaking. He took his cigarette case out and started towards her but she had found her own cigarettes and had lit one before he got there. She leaned

216

back, drawing on the cigarette. "I'm Letty Allard," she said. "Frank's sister. I just got here yesterday."

"My name is Carter," he said. "I was to have had dinner with them tonight but I didn't get here on time. He was about to attempt some explanation of his sitting there in the dark but the girl's indifferent "I see" checked the words on his lips. He waited a second and said, "May I get you a drink?"

"You certainly may. Do you know where things are?"

He told her that he did and went back into the dining room. When he got there he realized that he had not asked her what she wanted.

The choice, however, was limited. Frank was out of bitters, for one thing. He decided that if Scotch and soda were good enough for him they were good enough for Frank's little sister and carried a bottle of whiskey, siphon and glasses back into the living room.

The girl, leaning back in her deep chair, drawing on her cigarette, did not seem to know he was in the room till he was right beside her with her drink. She sat up then to take the glass from his hand and said, "I see you really are a friend of the family."

"That's right," he said.

He sat down in the same chair he had occupied before. There was no reason now why he should wait for Frank and Elise. He told himself that he would go home as soon as he had finished this one drink. He snapped on the lamp beside him and then wished he hadn't for the half dark was more agreeable. As the second light came on he was able to see Frank's sister more clearly. Lying back with the long evening cloak spread out about her, she looked like a huge white moth. He decided, however, that the effect was accidental. She was not enough interested in him to have arranged it. He looked at her with idle interest. She was a pretty girl, delicately slim with burnished hair. He wondered what the proper name for the color would be: in a dog you would have called it golden. It was exactly the color of a golden retriever's coat but in a woman golden hair would be lighter.

She was speaking, in a polite, bored voice: "Do you mind if I kick off my shoes?"

"Not in the least," he said cheerfully and watched her lift each slim foot to send the slipper scuttling across the room. Then because he had nothing better to do he speculated on the manners of the younger generation. A year or so ago Sara had had a first cousin coming out and they had seen a lot of the eighteen- and twenty-year-olds. They were sweet and respectful that year, the girls "Mister Jimming" you every minute. This year, nonchalance seemed to be the thing. Or maybe this girl was just tired.

"Have you been to a dance?" he asked.

She yawned. "And how!"

"Well, how?" he enquired.

"With Bob Prentwell," she said briefly.

He remembered that old Asa Prentwell had a son named Bob. Old Asa was known as the richest and stingiest man in Countsville. Bob—if he was the Prentwell kid he was thinking of—had no chin and less brains, they said. But maybe it was a different Prentwell. There were half a dozen young Prentwell fry.

There were steps in the hall. Another light came on in the hall. Frank and Elise were standing in the doorway looking at them. Elise came into the room with her springy stride which was the thing Jim most admired in her, more, even, than her sleek short black hair which at evening parties always looked as if it had been freshly oiled and glued on.

She sat down, with a yawn which she managed to change into a sigh. "Well, my children," she said, "I see you've got acquainted."

Frank came on in behind her and went over and stood behind Letty's chair. He put his hand on the top of her head. "Well, Jim," he asked, "what do you think of my little sister?"

"I think she is perfectly beautiful," Jim replied promptly.

But the girl was not paying any attention to him. She had turned around and was rubbing her head with its lovely, shining hair against Frank's extended palm. "Did you have a good time, Old Sweetie Pie?" she asked.

"Yes," Elise said. "He had a lovely time. He got off in a corner with old Mr. Richter and I had Mrs. Richter all evening."

"Good Lord," Jim said, startled. "You never asked me to have dinner with *them?*"

Frank had been dragging a chair—evidently his favorite—over to a reading lamp. He sat down heavily. "All Elise's fault," he observed. "They were going right past and she called them over."

"I didn't," Elise said. "I just called out, 'How is your daughter, Mrs. Richter?' Well, she told me all about her."

Frank offered Jim a cigar which Jim declined, then lit one himself. "How was the dance, Lets?" he asked.

"It was all right," the girl replied indifferently. "Of course I didn't see much of it."

"Why?" Frank demanded.

"I was with Bob Prentwell."

"Didn't he see that you had a good time?"

"His idea of giving you a good time is to stick right with you and if another man cuts in he cuts right back before you get half around the floor."

Frank shook his head. "Well, if he makes any passes at you," he said indulgently, "you just let me know. I'll fix him."

"He hasn't sense enough to make passes at you," she said.

"Well," Elise said briskly, "I think that sort of thing is very good for a young girl. Heavens, when I think of what I've endured in my day! There's an old man in Richmond, been leading cotillions for forty years. He always calls on the débutantes. Takes a box of chocolates and after you've had two and he's had two he wraps them up and takes them along to the next girl. . . . Once he was tearing down a wall and had to uproot a lot of ivy. His own first cousins sent over and said they wanted some for their garden. He wanted to know whether they wanted the twenty-cent kind or the fifty-cent kind. . . ."

"Bob'll be like that when he's that age," the girl said.

"He won't be an old bachelor," Elise replied. "The Cantwell girl is breaking her neck for him and so is Ellen Manners."

"They can have him," Letty said.

Jim stood up. "I'd better be getting along," he said.

A few nights later he was at the Mountain Club. There was a dinner dance that night but it was for the young crowd. He was sitting out on the veranda playing poker with some men. Through the lighted windows they could see the couples dancing by. He saw Letty Allard dancing with Bob Prentwell and was amused to think that she was suffering. After a while he got out of the game and went in where they were dancing. Letty smiled to him from across the room. He went over and asked her for a dance. They got around the floor once—she did not dance as well as Sara but well enough for a man to enjoy dancing with her—and then he saw a youth that he thought was Bob Prentwell bearing down on them, so he suggested that they go out on the veranda.

They found one of the big swings vacant and sat down. She had on a pale green dress with a lot of ruffles. It made her look like one of those old-fashioned pictures of your grandmother until you looked at her face, which was not like those of the women in those pictures.

He saw Charley going by and called to him to bring them a drink. She ordered a gin rickey, so he took one too though he did not like the club gin. They sat there a while, not talking much, just watching the dancing. That, he supposed, that very minute, was when the thing started, when he turned to her and asked her how long she was going to stay.

She said that she would be there for several weeks anyhow.

He said he was sorry Sara wasn't at home. If she were here she would enjoy giving a party for her. The girl said with mechanical politeness that it was sweet of him to think of giving her a party.

He was a little surprised to hear himself saying, "But I want to. We'll have it here at the club. And you must ask anybody you want." She said again that it was sweet of him and that he mustn't bother. "But I want to," he persisted, and he began planning the party. He would go in a few minutes and consult Elise about the date. Friday or Saturday he thought, if the Allards had nothing else on. How many people would she like?

She was silent a moment; then she said, "Let's just have us."

He was surprised. "You sure?" he asked, and then he laughed. "You don't want Bob Prentwell?"

"Let's just have us," she repeated.

Everything went off all right. Frank evidently thought it was perfectly natural that Jim should give a party in Letty's honor but Elise must have had a few ideas on the subject. Once during the evening when they were alone together for a few minutes she thanked him for helping her out with Letty. "I shouldn't think you'd need help," he returned easily. "She's a pretty girl. Must have lots of beaux." Elise's eyes were following Letty, who was dancing just then with one of the young Howes. "Yes," she said, "Letty's always had plenty of beaux." She was silent a moment, then said, "Letty's not a bit like Frank."

"How do you mean?" he asked.

She looked at him reflectively. "I don't know. I just know she isn't."

"Well," he said, "she's a lot better looking than Frank. Frank's getting too fat. You ought to make him get out more."

She flew at him then, maintaining that Frank worked like a dog and, though a big overweight, was the handsomest man in the room, not excepting himself. He laughed and spurred her on—he liked seeing Elise who was usually calm turn into a little spitfire. Then the girl came towards them across the floor, with her partner, asking if it wasn't time to go home. Elise said that it was. He told Letty that she must dance with him one more time before they left. While they were out on the floor he asked her if she would drive out into the country with him tomorrow afternoon to look at a dog he was having trained. She said that she would.

That was when the trouble, the real trouble started. After he got her out there he made love to her, of course, though he certainly hadn't had any intention of doing so. Nothing much. Just kissed her a couple of times. The devil of it was the way the girl took it. Cool as a cucumber one minute and the next gone all to pieces. He could have had her right there in the meadow if he'd wanted to. . . . Well, he wanted her, all right, and the little devil knew it.

He had avoided her after that and then one night at the Country Club she came up to him and got him to walk out by the pool with her. He told her straight out that he wasn't going to have anything to do with her. She hadn't much to say, that night, naturally, but a few nights later when they met at the Reids' she had argued the matter with him. As he lay there in bed, his lips twitched as he remembered some of the arguments she had put up. She was going, she said, to marry somebody, a man named Bill Fauntleroy if nobody else. But she liked him, Jim Carter, better than any man she had ever met. She knew that he liked her too. She had thought that she was incapable of falling in love but she was in love with him. She couldn't see why he wouldn't have an affair with her. He could trust her to take it just exactly as he would.

They were having this conversation in low tones at the end of the Reids' big gallery. She looked him in the eye as she said that. He was thinking. "That's an old gag," and then he thought: "By God, this girl means it."

He speculated about her character. In some ways she reminded him of Babe Worsham. Letty was a lady and Babe wasn't, but their attitude towards life was much the same. It was being up against it—in different ways—that had hardened them both. Letty was hard, all right, he thought, and then his brow contracted with pity as he remembered the day he drove up to take her to the train. She hadn't expected him. The shock had widened her eyes, set her lip to trembling. Her voice, even, had trembled as she told Elise good-by.

He knew as they drove off that she expected him to tell her he had come to see things her way. He had put it off for several minutes. It was one of the hardest things he had ever done in his life—like kicking a puppy that gambols out to meet you—but he got through all right, got through and put her on her train. She was all right when she left. She had even managed a bit of malice, handing him out a book of paper dolls. Her way of reminding him that he was a family man, he supposed. He sat up in bed, breathing a sigh of relief. It had been a narrow squeak. He had been about to crack up there for a few seconds. But she would never know that. . . . Somewhere downstairs a bell rang insistently. Rising bell, he thought. They kept to the good old country ways here. Somebody was knocking. He got out of bed, padded on bare feet to the door and took the pitcher of hot water from the house girl, then went over to the washstand and started shaving.

As he lathered his face he was thinking what a narrow escape he had had. Of course he wasn't out of the woods yet. Letty probably thought he had come down here to see her. Well, he hadn't. He hadn't actually thought much about her until just now when he woke up and couldn't sleep. It was Sara had sent him down here. She had got back from French Lick Thursday afternoon, two days sooner than he expected her. He met her and Laura at the train and drove them home. Old Julie took Laura off to put her to bed. Sara went in and had a bath and changed, while he sat there in that yellow room waiting for her. John brought some *daiquiris*. He had one himself and then she came in. They hadn't talked much as yet, hadn't had time to. He could see by the tight look around her mouth that it was all going to start again. He knew suddenly that he couldn't stand it. In another room, perhaps, a blue or red or green one, but not this room where she had so often sat and looked at him just that way. He stood up and until he was on his feet he didn't actually know what he was going to say. He told her that Frank Allard was driving to Kentucky at six o'clock. He had promised to go with him. He wouldn't have done it, of course, if he'd known they were coming, but as it was he felt he had to go.

She looked at him as if she, too, were already tired of all the things that would be said. She said, "All right." He knew that as soon as he was out of the house she would call up Rice Bolling. But he didn't care. He didn't care, either, about where he was going. It would have been better if he'd picked another place but he hadn't time to think. He telephoned Frank from a drugstore, telling him that he had gone stale as hell and had to get out of town. Frank was cordial as always and not too surprised. They met at the garage where Jim left his car, started out and drove sixty or seventy miles before dinner. Frank had been glad to have him along for company. It was a long drive. . . . He lathered his face and began shaving. No, he thought, everything was all right there. Frank didn't think it was strange that a man should want to get out into the country once in a while. Still, it was just as well for Frank not to get ideas into his head. Or Letty either. The little devil! She was probably thinking he'd come because he couldn't stay away. . . . The bell rang again. He finished dressing hurriedly. As he put on his coat he thought that if he had any private conversation with Letty he would tell her exactly how he had happened to come here. In her way she was sympathetic: she would understand.

CHAPTER TWENTY-ONE

$\mathbf{F}$RANK watched the two figures cross the meadow and start up the slope: Letty and Jim Carter on their way to the Indian mound that was in that corner of the field. They had been talking on the porch a few minutes before about how the Smithsonian had sent some people down ten or twelve years ago to excavate the mound. Two skeletons had been found, a man's and a woman's, with their knees bound and drawn up under their chins. Carter's face had brightened as he listened. He had said that he would like to see the mound.

Letty had turned quickly: "Want to go now?" and they had set off across the field.

Frank took out his case and lit a cigarette. For a moment his eyes followed Jim Carter's figure moving slowly along beside Letty's lighter one; then he cocked his head on one side, listening for sounds from upstairs. His father had gone up to look for a paper, an insurance premium that had to be got into the mail today. Ten minutes ago that had been and he hadn't come down yet. Perhaps he had forgotten all about the paper and was mooning around over something else. Frank left the porch, and went upstairs.

He stood on the threshold of the great room, looking about him curiously. It had been a long time since he had been at Hanging Tree, long enough, anyhow, for him to view this room, familiar to him since childhood, with the eyes of an outsider. His eyes roved over it, noting each piece of furniture. There were the two beds, the one in the north corner for summer, the one in the south corner for winter. They had seemed enormous to him when he was a child. Now he realized that they were only medium-sized, shabby four-posters. He could remember, too, that as a child he had taken it for granted that everybody changed his bed with the seasons. Elise, his wife, had shrieked with laughter when she first heard about Mr. Allard's beds. She had made a story of it that Frank was sometimes called upon to tell at parties: his father in a temper with Old Pansy because the equinox had come and gone and she had not made up his winter bed.

There was his father's great roll-top desk placed against the south window. The floor around it was littered with pieces of old iron and scraps of leather. The green blinds above the desk were always closed and the interstices between the slats were stuck full of papers that Mr. Allard wished to preserve. Elise liked to have him tell about that too. "Your father's efficiency filing cabinet," she called it.

Mr. Allard was standing in front of the blinds now, drawing out a paper. He put it back, looked at Frank and shook his head irritably. "Can't find anything since Letty got home."

"That's the trouble with your filing system," Frank said, smiling. "No way to dust it."

"No sense in dusting so much," Mr. Allard said. "Never had 'em in here cleaning in my life that I didn't lose something."

He crossed over to the mantel—he would, of course, keep his writing materials on the mantel rather than on his desk—and bending over indited in his angular handwriting an address. To the insurance company, no doubt; he was probably late with his premium. Frank, as he turned away to the window, permitted himself to speculate on his father's financial condition. He did not often do this. There had been for ten or fifteen years a tacit agreement of silence between them. He thought, with a little pain, of how it had come about, ten or fifteen years ago, when the mortgage was first put on the farm. The first time his father had not been able to meet the interest he had been beside himself. He had got on the train and come down to Countsville. The money he said must be got. He had done all he could. The question now was what could Frank do. There had been no question in his mind, it seemed, of Frank's willingness to do what he could. He, Frank, was getting up his courage to refuse when Elise, who had sat there listening through it all, suddenly spoke up. He could hear her clear, assured tones now. . . . "Father, I don't think you really understand. It's all right for you to mortgage the farm . . . but it isn't all right to ask Frank to mortgage his future . . . for something he doesn't want. . . ."

That phrase brought the old man up short. His whole expression changed. He looked at Frank, not angrily, just in surprise. "Something he doesn't want?" he repeated. There had been some more talk. Now that Elise had brought the matter out into the open, Frank felt that he wanted his father to understand his position. He had explained as well as he could how he felt. Mr. Allard had appeared to listen. Suddenly, in the midst of a sentence, he took out his watch and announced that he barely had time to make his train. Elise had considerately left Frank and his father to make the trip to the station alone. They had talked on indifferent matters, then, just as the train came in the old man faced his son, frowning a little. "I didn't know how you felt, Son, or I wouldn't have come down here." A few weeks later he wrote that he had arranged a loan that would take care of the interest. That was all that was ever said. Frank didn't even know how his father had staved off foreclosure all these years since then. He wondered how things were going with him now and concluded that he must just have gotten a new loan, made some arrangement with the bank. There was a cockiness about him this morning. Rearing, ever since breakfast, to go out and look over the place.

He was reaching up now to get his hat off the bed post. "Ready?" he asked. "Well, come on."

They went out the front way. As they approached the big gate Mr. Allard darted forward and pushed it open so that his slower-moving son could pass through. Frank, watching the agile figure, thought that his father did not move like a man of sixty-five. He did not look his age, either in face or figure. But then he did not look like anybody else on God's earth. It was not so much the keen, pointed face, weathered brick-red up to the very lids of the blue eyes. It was the clothes that he wore. That suit that he, Frank, had had made four years before by a very good tailor. He wished the fellow could see it now, and the yachting cap which Mr. Allard for some reason affected this season. He liked the feel of it, he said, and you couldn't ask more of a hat. Frank smiled, reflecting that this disregard for appearances—a kind of selflessness it was, and at the same time a vanity—was one of his father's most endearing traits. He was proud, Frank knew, of his peculiar forms of economy, boasting that in fifteen years he had not bought a suit of clothes and that his smoking cost him fifty cents a year—the fifty cents, of course, for cob pipes. He smoked the tobacco out of his own barns.

They were at the corner of the big field which was in tobacco this year. Mr. Allard began moving rapidly down the rows. Frank followed more slowly. Ever since he was a small boy he had accompanied his father on these walks over the farm, "looking at the crops" they called it. He had dropped tobacco plants and set them, too, all over the place, but it was here in this field that he had made the only crop he had ever made in his life. When he was fourteen years old. Two thousand pounds of tobacco it had come to when tobacco was high, forty cents a pound. He remembered that his father had mentioned with pride his poundage and the price he had got. Well, he himself had enjoyed spending the money. He had bought another pony, he remembered, and a gun, but it must have been then that he decided not to be a farmer. Ever after when he thought of tobacco it was not of the number of pounds you made or even of the money you got for it. It was as rows he saw it, rows and rows of green plants stretching away interminably.

He frowned, looking down at the plants around him. A good stand—as pretty a stand as ever he saw, hardly a hill without its plant—but the plants were dwarfish with shrunken stalk and poor leaf.

In the middle of the field a man was hoeing, an elderly fellow, barefooted, wearing a single garment, a pair of overalls. Mr. Allard had paused beside him. Frank went over. He heard his father's voice, cheerful with that authoritative tone which was natural to him: "Well, Bob, I reckon you'll finish chopping this out today."

The man stopped hoeing, pushed his tattered straw hat farther back on his head. "I reckon so," he said listlessly.

Mr. Allard nodded. "I was in town yesterday and got the

Paris green. You better start poisoning early in the morning. Flea bug's getting bad."

The man nodded. "Got the poison, might as well use it. But 'tain't goin to do no good. This tobacco ain't goin to make nothin, no matter how you work it."

Mr. Allard paid no attention to this remark. He squinted at the burning sun, then his gaze wandered over the horizon. "We due to get a rain now any time," he said. "You want to get this tobacco hoed over before it comes."

The man leaned on his hoe. His eyes dwelt on the same cloud, a high-piled fleecy cloud that sailed near the horizon. "The moon's in her second quarter, all right," he said, "but she keeps herself rared back. Ain't no room for rain in that moon."

Allard looked impatient. "Well, you got to keep forward with your work, moon or no moon," he said and turned away, then took a few steps back towards the man. "Where's the rest of 'em?" he asked. "Thought they were all going to be out here today?"

The man had resumed his listless hoeing. "My boys had to go to town. Old Joe, he cain't stand the sun. Ote Mortimer, he was out here choppin a minute ago. But he had to go to the spring for water." He stopped hoeing and looked at Frank with some curiosity. "This your boy, Mister Ben?"

Frank smiled at the man. "What's your name?"

"Sheeler. I come from over in Stewart. This the first time I ever worked any Montgomery land. . . ." He looked at Allard. A sly smile came on his face. "Your boy, he don't follow farmin, Mister Ben?"

Allard shook his head. "Naw, he'd rather work for somebody else."

231

Sheeler cackled out suddenly. "Don't know but what he's right. Wisht I had me a job by the day. Yes, sir, I wouldn't ask nothin better than to git me a job and git my money reg'lar every evenin."

"Don't know about that," Allard said brusquely. "You ain't such a good worker, Bob. Still, you been working for yourself all your life. How'd you like to be taking orders every minute of the day?"

The man spat into the dust. "Hit depends on the marster," he said judicially. The sly look came back into his eyes. "Don't know as I'd mind it. Old Marster, he ain't been treatin us any too good, for two, three years now. Naw, you take Old Marster up one side and down the other, he does about as much harm as he does good. Look at this here drouth. . . . Ed Trivers, he's the only man hereabouts has got a good word to say for him."

Allard was walking away. Frank caught up with him. "Who's he mean by Old Marster? You?"

"He means the Lord," Allard said. He laughed shortly. "What's the matter with you, boy? Got so you can't understand plain English, living in town?"

They walked on. Frank asked his father what sort of force he had this year. Allard reflected: " 'Bout as good as you'd get, I reckon. Old Jim hasn't paid out for four years. But he's handy. Can mend anything and won't let stock suffer. There's five or six of those Sheelers. Ain't one of them worth the powder and ball it'd take to blow 'em up. . . . Ote Mortimer's the best man on the place. Honest as the day is long and leads 'em all in the field."

"Mortimer. . . ." Frank said. "Didn't they live here when I was a kid?"

"Old Joe made his first crop on this place. Ote's his youngest boy. There he comes now."

A sturdy, broad-shouldered young man was advancing across the field, carrying a bucket of water. Frank went towards him with hand outstretched. "Hello, Ote," he said.

The young giant set his bucket down. He shook the extended hand politely but there was no glint of recognition in the steady blue eyes he turned on Frank. Allard had come up behind them. "This is Mister Frank, Ote," he said.

Ote laughed out. "Mister Frank! Dog my cats! I didn't know you." He shook Frank's hand again and enquired when he was coming back to the farm.

Allard laughed. "He's done turned into a town man, Ote. Wouldn't be any 'count if we had him." He looked at Ote. There was affection in the gaze. "Ote's my right-hand man," he told his son. "Don't know how I'd get along without him."

Ote flushed over the praise, then as if to change the subject asked Allard some question. Frank stood half turned away, looking out over the field. Behind him the conversation went on. Allard was saying the same things he had said before. They must get some poison on the plants before the flea bug did any more damage. But the main thing was to get the crop hoed over, once, anyhow, before the rain came. "We due to get a rain any day now," he said. Frank knew the expression that was on his face as he said that.

"The moon's in her second quarter." Ote's voice was patient and controlled but there was a note in it that had not been in Sheeler's voice when he made the same remark. Frank realized that the young poor white man and his father had exactly the same attitude towards the drouth, a refusal to recognize it, a determination that it should not be. He

233

realized, too, something that he had never allowed himself to realize before. His father's voice when he spoke to Ote had the customary authoritative inflection that he used to all poor white people and yet he was speaking to Ote as he never nowadays spoke to Frank, as if Ote were in a way his equal. The tone he used to Frank was polite, indulgent, the tone one used to women and children. Yes, Frank thought, that was it. His father, since Frank had left the farm, thought of him as only half a man. He could not see, he was so constituted that he could not see how a man could abandon his land.

For all this land which would soon belong to the First National Bank was to have been Frank's land some day. Mr. Allard, Frank knew, had had extravagant plans about that. He had thought, when Frank was a small boy, that there wasn't enough. He had talked of buying the adjoining farm, but there had been no talk of that for years now.

Frank continued to stare out over the field. Behind him they were still talking, about what they would do tomorrow, what they would do next week, making plans, even for the housing of the crop. But there would be no crop worth housing. That thin veil of heat that shimmered over the field was drawing in closer every day. The moisture was already gone from the top soil. The plants would soon be withering on the hill, those that weren't destroyed by parasites or blackfire. ... Well, they would be talking then of what they would do next year.

CHAPTER TWENTY-TWO

Letty AND JIM walked slowly through the field that had once been an orchard. The old setter was with them. Jim's eyes were upon her as they walked. "Anybody ever hunt her?" he enquired.

Letty shook her head. "Frank used to but he hasn't been here in bird season for a long time. Daddy never takes a gun in his hand."

"Why?"

She laughed. "He's too busy."

"Well, I reckon he is busy," he said reasonably, "seeing to things. A place like this there's a lot to see to. . . . How many 'hands' does he have?"

"Two or three but we mostly have tenants. The Lightwoods, the Shutts, the Sheelers. . . . There must be three or four families on the place. I don't know one from another."

He was surprised. "Don't you even know them when you see them?"

"There's one of the Mortimers comes up to talk to Daddy sometimes, in the evenings. I know him."

They had come to the fence. In one place two wires had been pulled together and tied with a piece of sacking. He put his foot on the wires to hold them steady and offered her his hand. She stepped over and they started up the narrow lane—in dry weather it was used to drive the stock to water—which led to the Indian mound.

They walked along it side by side and came out into the mound field. Woods on one side of them, on the other rows of corn. Between the corn rows and the woods was the mound, a tumulus of earth covered with sedge grass and Queen Anne's lace.

Carter stopped and surveyed it. "They never cultivate it?" he asked.

She had sat down at the foot of a tree. "I don't believe they do," she said.

He set off walking around the mound. She looked away, over the field. She had been here once last summer, with Bill, about this time. The corn, marching in rows up to the foot of the mound, had been higher than Bill's head. This year the stalks were no higher than her own waist. "It's the drouth," she thought. "Why, of course, it's the drouth." Her eyes returned to Jim. He was coming around the other side of the mound, measuring his paces. He looked up. "Two hundred feet," he said.

He came over and stood beside her. "I wish I'd been here when they opened it up. . . . What did they find?"

"Two skeletons," she said.

"Did you see them?"

She shook her head. "I suppose so. I was too little to remember. They took them off to Washington. . . . Daddy remembers about it."

He nodded. "Ever find any arrowheads?"

"Frank used to pick them up all the time. Daddy says this place was a chipping ground."

"I suppose so," he said and walked off, his eyes bent on

the ground. A moment later he stooped and came up holding something in his hand. He stood, eyeing it. "It's not an arrowhead," he called. "Piece of some larger object. Might be part of an axe. . . ."

She looked at him without speaking. It was strange, she thought, how people changed in appearance from day to day. This morning at breakfast she had thought that he was not as handsome as she had remembered him. His face had seemed thinner, there were drawn lines about his mouth and his eyes were sunk too far back in his head. He had looked all of his thirty-seven years. But now, hatless, in the burning sun he was handsome again. Browner than he had been a few weeks ago, and his eyes as he glanced at her were intensely blue, bluer even than she remembered them to be. "And I must look like a hag," she thought. That was because she had not slept last night.

In those first few hours after Jim Carter's arrival she had thought that he had come to see her. It was a crazy thing to do, she had thought, to come with Frank, with no word, no warning. Still he had come. She had been so glad there on the porch that she could hardly control her voice when she spoke. She was afraid that Bill would notice the sudden change in her. She had feigned sleepiness, yawning and yawning until finally he got up reluctantly, saying he had better go.

"Yes, you had," she said promptly. "We all ought to go to bed." But after Bill had gone and the two old men had gone upstairs she and Frank and Jim sat on. A dark night and no stars so that you could not see anybody else's face. She wondered if it would seem strange if she and Jim sat on after Frank went up to bed. Then Frank, yawning and saying that he was tired from the long drive, had gone in to get a nightcap for the three of them.

They sat there, he at one end of the porch, she at the other. She had thought that he would leave his chair and come to her as soon as Frank was well inside the house. But they heard Frank walk heavily through the hall, heard him open the dining-room door and then the clink of glasses and tray and still the dark figure in the chair did not move. Finally he spoke:

"How far is it from here to Gloversville?"

"Ten miles," she said.

Frank was back with the drinks. "I ought to have helped you," she said.

He laughed. "Well, I had a time finding things."

They drank their whiskey and went up to bed. She showed Jim to his room, then went to her own room and undressed. But she could not sleep. She lay there in bed and thought. That interval on the porch—it had been too short to say anything, after all. Perhaps Frank had said something on the way down that had alarmed him, made him cautious. She got out of bed, went to the door and softly opened it, then got back into bed.

She lay there for hours watching the black square of the door. But there was no sound anywhere except the creakings you hear always in an old house at night. . . . Towards dawn she fell asleep. . . .

He was on top of the mound now, walking with head still bent through grass waist high. Each time he lifted his foot he swung it in a wide arc to part the grass on each side of him. Still keeping up his foolish search for arrowheads. She watched him with bright, resentful eyes.

During these last few weeks she had liked to think that he shared her feelings, that he was as interested in her as she was in him—if he would only let himself go. She had even fancied at times that he was suffering as she herself was suffering—his refusal of her that night had been vehement. Such vehemence came only from deep emotion, she had told herself. But this morning he did not look like a man who was suffering. "He's hardly given me a thought since I left," she told herself. *"If he had he wouldn't have come down here."*

She crossed her arms on her bosom, shivering a little though the day was hot. She felt that she hated him. He had no right to be carefree when she was suffering. . . . He was coming towards her, holding up another arrowhead. "I've been all over the top," he said, "and this was the only one I found. But I reckon the place was combed long ago."

"The little boys in the neighborhood come here a good deal," she said.

He sat down, a few feet away from where she was sitting. He held the two arrowheads on his open palm. With the forefinger of his other hand he traced the edges of the smaller piece. "They used flint to chip these off," he said.

She did not answer. The minutes went by. She was aware that he was looking at her, looking at her as he had not looked at her all day. She kept her head bent down. Apparently she was studying the setting of the diamond she wore on her ring finger. She turned it around on her finger; then as if suddenly aware of his scrutiny she glanced up. "It's horribly hot," she said.

He got up and came and sat down on a root of the same tree she was leaning against. She said nothing, continuing to turn the ring on her finger. His eyes, too, were on the ring.

"I suppose I ought not to have come down here this week end," he said abruptly.

"Why not?" she asked.

He laughed awkwardly. "I don't know. I just had a feeling I oughtn't to have come. At least I thought of it after I'd started. We left in such a hurry I didn't have time to think about it before."

"It was quite all right," she said indifferently. "We're delighted to have any friend of Frank's, any time. You know that."

"I've enjoyed being here," he said. "Your father—he's a fine old fellow. You know I like those old boys of the old school. Some ways he reminds me of my father."

She looked up, smiling. "That's what Bill says. Dad reminds him of his father too."

"I guess it's the generation," he said vaguely. "People born in that generation are different from us."

They were both silent. A June bug zooming across the field lit on Letty's skirt. Carter started up but she had already lifted a fold of the cloth to shake the bug off. He sank down again.

"Is Bill the fellow who was here last night?" he asked.

She nodded. "His last name is Fauntleroy. I don't suppose you caught it. I never do get people's names when I'm introduced."

"Are you going to marry him?"

"In October, I think."

There was silence again; then he asked: "Is that going to be all right?"

240

"All right?" she repeated.

"I mean are you in love with him?"

She raised her eyes to his. "I'm not sure I know what being in love is."

"I see," he said. Then he shrugged his shoulders. "A week ago you said you were in love with me."

She smiled. "I know, and you told me not to be a damn fool or words to that effect."

"That's right," he said. "Well, I'm glad you've taken my advice." She did not answer. "I'm a hell of a fellow," he said heavily, "to be giving anybody advice."

"Oh, I don't know. You gave me very good advice."

"And you took it?"

"I'm trying to."

The June bug zoomed back again. He reached up quickly, caught it, held it prisoner a moment in his hand then let it go. He slid down from the root until he was sitting beside her. He took her hand, the one that did not have the ring, in his.

"I've done a lot of thinking since I saw you," he said.

"What did you think?"

"I was thinking about you. I never knew anybody else like you."

"Not any of those other girls that were in love with you?"

He tightened his hold on her hand. "Don't tease me, Letty. My God! If you knew what it was to have to fend you off when all the time I want you so much."

"Want me so much?" she repeated in a low tone. "You never said that before."

"I oughtn't to have said it now."

"No," she said and her voice shook; "not if you didn't mean it."

"Didn't mean it?" he said. "You know I mean it."

She looked up at him steadfastly. He put his hand out, rested it on her shoulder, then slipped it down her back, inside the thin blouse. He drew her to him. He kissed her. "For God's sake," he said, "let's quit kidding each other. We knew all the time this was going to happen."

CHAPTER TWENTY-THREE

THERE WAS no rain at all during
the first two weeks of July. On the fourteenth a light rain
fell, quick, pattering drops that barely spotted the dust that
lay thick now on all the tobacco leaves. The same light rain
fell the next day and the day after that. And then there was
a week during which no rain fell at all.

The tobacco stood on the hill, making nothing. The leaves,
yellowish and covered with the innumerable perforations
of the flea bug, curved upwards towards the stalk instead of
spreading out in the generous arc of the dark tobacco leaf.
Ote, moving between the rows, looked down and realized
that tobacco which ordinarily would have been knee high at
this time of year came only to his ankle.

The heat fed on the light, dry air, waxed slowly, grew
intolerable. People moving languidly about the cabins commented on the fact that there was no longer any cool of the
day. It was as hot at seven o'clock in the morning as it would
be at noon. The fields were gradually deserted. Men cul-
tivated their crops only in the early morning or late evening.
The young folks made parties to the swimming hole and
immersed themselves in the water for half of every day; but
the older men, uncertain and awkward when released from
work, knew no way of diverting themselves. They spent
their time sleeping or sitting about on the porches, waiting

for the drouth to break. At night old and young gathered in the cabins and there was fiddling and sometimes dancing.

One evening Ote crossed the field and walked along the path beside the mock orange hedge to the Sheeler house. The women were still inside washing the dishes and putting the supper things away but Robert Sheeler and the old grandsir had come out on the porch. Claude Trivers sat with them, his banjo across his knee. He moved aside as Ote approached and made a place for him on the steps.

"Well," he said, "how you makin it?"

Ote sank down heavily beside him. "I ain't makin it," he said.

The four men sat silent, gazing off through the still air. The sun had disappeared behind the black rim of the woods a few minutes ago, but a few, luminous rays still winked on the horizon. Ote watched the last ray spend itself and fade into the gray of twilight. Immediately as if at a signal a horde of insects began a dry chirping in the woods about the house.

Robert Sheeler stirred and spoke fretfully: "I'd 'most as soon live in town. Them things start up like that ever' night, soon as the sun goes down."

The old grandsir leaned forward, his thin hand cupped over his ear. "Town? What you want to live in town for?"

Robert Sheeler shook his head. "I don't want to live in no town." His voice had risen but it died away on the last word. His dull eyes sought the eyes of the others. "It ain't no use," he said, "you can't make him hear."

Claude Trivers leaned forward and bellowed suddenly into the cupped hand. "Hit's the bugs. The dry weather bugs. They worry him with their raspin."

The old man looked at his son. "Hunh! They'll worry him worse'n that before they git done."

The Garden of Adonis

Robert Sheeler was gazing at the bright spot left on the horizon by the sinking sun. "She went down clear as a bell," he said. He repeated the words, a faint wonder in his tones. "Clear as a bell."

Claude Trivers leaned back against the post. "I had me a dream the other night," he said. "I dreamed I was sitting in a big field, only it warn't no field. It was the sky. And the Boss Man come along and he said, 'Trivers, they's water in this field if you can find it.' I gets up and I walk and walk. I hear water runnin but every time I git to it it ain't water but one of them fleecy little clouds drifts around about sundown. My little boy, Freeman, was with me and every time I git so tired I think I just have to sit down and rest he keeps hollerin, 'Pappy, ain't you found no water yit?'" He paused, looking from one face to the other. "I could hear him just as plain. '*Pappy*, ain't you found no water yit?'"

Ote laughed. "You must a been layin on your back lookin up at the sky. Been so hot over at Ed's don't none of them try to sleep in the house no more. They just take a sheet and spread it out on the ground come nightfall. May, she says it's six of one and half dozen of the other. Can't sleep in the house it's so hot and if she lays outdoors she can't sleep none on account of Ed lookin up at the sky and prayin all night."

Robert Sheeler leaned forward to knock the ashes of his pipe out against the post. He spoke judicially: "I ain't of the opinion that prayin does any good. I was livin over in Stewart County when that preacher brought down that gulley washer, prayin all day and all night. He got a lot of credit for it. Was a man come all the way from Nashville put a piece in the paper about it. But that very mornin he started prayin, Pap, he looked out he did, and he says, 'Hit'll rain before nightfall. Before nightfall,' he said just like that.

245

And rain hit did and hit's my opinion it would a rained if that preacher had stayed over in Cheatham whar he belonged."

Pap chuckled. "A ring around the moon and wind from the south. Warn't no chance of hit not rainin."

His son shook his head. "I been followin the signs, man and boy, now, for sixty-five years and I ain't never seen nobody can beat Pap at it. Might say I take what he says for gospel." His voice rose fretfully: "That's why I been so discouraged about my crop. Pap, he foretold along in January what kind of summer hit was going to be and it come along just like he said it would."

Claude Trivers had been staring straight in front of him. He leaned forward now, a smile on his ugly, loose mouth. "Maybe the Lord don't expect people to make no more crops."

"If I was Mister Ben I wouldn't put in no crops," Robert Sheeler said. "Long as the seasons was this contrary."

Ote spoke, reasonably, "Looks like a man has to put in a crop, come spring. And onct he gits it in the ground looks like he has to work it even if he don't see no way to make nothin out of it. . . ."

Claude's eyes were going from one to another. "But maybe they ain't goin to *be* no more seasons. We're used to it comin spring and time to set out a crop but it don't have to be that way." He spoke dreamily. His eyes still searched theirs. "Hit don't *have* to be that way," he repeated. "Could be so cold nothin'd grow. Could be so cold people'd all freeze to death."

Ote shuffled his feet, laughed awkwardly. "I reckon we'll have seasons," he said, "I reckon they'll last our time, the seasons."

The Garden of Adonis

When Claude had looked away he stole a curious glance at him. The Triverses were all alike, he reflected. Always studying about something. The idea, now, of the Lord freezing everybody off the earth! Claude, with his crazy notions, was no better, really, than Ed with his praying. He was laughing his wild laugh now and twanging his banjo:

"Whar'd you come from,
Whar'd you go,
Whar'd you come from,
Cotton-Eyed Joe. . . ."

Ote moved to settle himself more comfortably against the post. As he did so he realized that he was tired. His muscles were not yet freed from the rhythm of bending and chopping. He could see the place where he had put down the hoe, in the fence corner beside a clump of sumac. It was as if he were still there among the tobacco hills. Those behind him were black but those that were yet to be hoed over stretched away in a gray mist as if they came into being only with the strokes of the hoe.

"We was luckier'n some," he said, "We had our ground all ready and we had a good season to set in. I was lookin at some of Ed's tobacco yesterday and I thought to myself that ef my tobacco was that sorry lookin I wouldn't have the heart to work it. . . ."

Old Man Sheeler's high, obstinate voice rose above the music. "Far as I'm concerned the crop is laid by. I ain't goin to hoe no more."

Ote laughed roughly. "And set here on your butt and starve to death." He got to his feet. From his six feet of height he looked down on the three men contemptuously. "I aim to hoe *my* crop over onct," he said. "Come what will

I aim to hoe it over one time. I ain't never put tobacco in the barn without hoein it over onct and I ain't goin to do it now, drouth or no drouth. . . ."

He stalked into the house. There was a lamp burning in the chamber but the room was empty. He went through the little entry and the kitchen out on to the back porch. Mrs. Sheeler was sitting on the steps, her hands folded in her lap, her snuff stick protruding from one corner of her mouth. Idelle and Gracie had set the dishpan on the little shelf and were washing dishes from there. As Ote came out Gracie stepped to the edge of the porch and was about to pour the dishwater out. "Don't you do that!" Idelle cried sharply. She snatched the dishpan from Gracie's hand and then walked to the edge of the clearing and poured the water out.

Gracie stepped heavily across the floor—she was seven months gone with child—and sat down beside her mother. "I don't see no use in being as particular as that," she said.

Mrs. Sheeler removed her snuff stick from her mouth. "Idelle's right," she said. "You keep on pouring dishwater round a house, day after day, and first thing you know the place'll git to stinking."

Idelle had washed her hands in the little basin and now took a seat in one of the rockers. Ote sat down on the edge of the porch. He exchanged a few words with Mrs. Sheeler, then turned to Idelle. "Would you care to take a walk?" he asked.

Gracie spoke before Idelle could answer. "She better set right where she is. It's just as hot in them woods as it is here in the clearin."

Idelle had risen silently. She did not speak but Ote favored Gracie with a hard look. "I don't reckon it is," he said. "Stands to reason it's cooler in the woods than 'tis here on this porch."

248

Gracie did not answer but he heard her voice murmuring to Mrs. Sheeler as he and Idelle started off down the path. "It don't look like Gracie cares so much for me," he said.

"She likes you all right," Idelle said. "She just don't want me to go with no boys."

"No boys at all?"

Idelle laughed. "Gracie, she was all for gittin married but now she's got Clator she's all time sayin folks are better off single."

Ote laughed too. "Well, I don't much blame her, seeing what she got." He recalled a conversation he had heard the other day, between Mister Ben and the old nigger, Jim. Mister Ben was asking Jim if he reckoned there was any way in God's world to get any work out of Clator Lowe. "I don't reckon there is, Mister Ben," the old Negro replied. "That boy, he's just married and he's doin too much night work."

He realized that Idelle had been silent for some minutes. She often fell abruptly silent when some member of her family was mentioned, Ote knew how she felt about them—she hated her mother's and Gracie's shiftless ways as much as he did—and yet she was proud. She hated feeling that way about them. He resolved that hereafter he would be more careful; he would not even criticize Clator Lowe.

They had rounded a bend in the path and were out of sight of the house. He stopped behind the trunk of a big oak tree, drew her to him and kissed her, then stood with his big, calloused hands framing her small face. "I ain't seen you all day," he murmured. "I ain't seen you since late last night."

She was between him and the tree trunk. He could feel her slight body trembling against his. Then she moved a litle away and, flinging back her head, mocked him as she sometimes did. "Now ain't that a long time!"

"It's a heap too long," he said, but when she would have dropped down at the foot of the tree he stayed her. "Let's go on," he said, "let's go on and git in the woods where none of them can't bother us."

They walked on until they came to a mossy place under a big tree. She sat down. He flung himself down beside her. He put his arms around her and pressed his mouth on hers. She suffered his embraces for a little but when he would have pressed his advantage she drew away. He, too, drew back then. "What's the matter?" he whispered. "You liked me last night."

"This ain't last night," she said with a nervous laugh.

"I know what's the matter. You're worrying about what Gracie and them others'd think."

"I ain't worryin about Gracie or any of them," she said, "but we can't be doin that every night. You know that."

There was a nervous note in her voice that he had never heard before.

"I reckon not," he said dejectedly. Then he caught her hand and held it. "Pretty soon we goin to be together all the time," he said.

She turned her face to his and in the faint light he caught the ardent gleam of her eyes. He continued to press her hand softly. "They's goin to be a saw-mill set up down at the branch this fall," he told her.

"Is Mister Ben goin to build some houses?" she asked eagerly.

"He's goin to build one," he said; "he's goin to build one fer you and me. We was over this mornin pickin out the place to put it."

She laid her hand on his arm. "Where's it goin to be?" she asked eagerly. "Did he say where it was goin to be?"

250

"Hit's goin to be by the spring," he said. "Hit's goin to be on that rise thar by the spring. Mister Ben said if he was buildin it fer anybody else he wouldn't put it thar because some people don't think nothin of nastyin up a spring, but he said long as it was me and you he'd put it right thar handy to water."

"Mister Ben thinks a lot of you," she said.

"He told me he hoped I'd stay with him long as he lived," Ote said quietly. "More'n that he said after he was dead he wanted us to stay here and run this farm for Miss Letty. Said she was more'n likely to marry a city feller that didn't know nothin about farmin and hit'd be handy fer her to have an overseer she could depend on."

"I reckon she could depend on you," she said. "I reckon she couldn't find nobody in this whole country'd do better by her than you."

"I reckon that's so," he said matter-of-factly; then he added: "Mister Ben said he could put up two rooms and a lean-to fer a kitchen."

"That'd do well," she said. "That'd do well to start with. Ote, you reckon we could paint the house?"

"Couldn't paint it the first year," he said, "but the second year, after it's weathered, shorc we could paint it."

"Pappy says ain't nobody goin to make nothin this year," she said after a pause.

"Your pappy's an old man," he told her, "an old man and can't work much and beside that he ain't got a good force for the field. I don't want to be sayin anything against Wallace and Clator and the rest of 'em but you know as well as I do ain't e'er one of them ever done a good day's work in his life."

"Seems like they cain't take holt like you do," she murmured. "Ote, how much you reckon your share of the crop'll be?"

He was silent for a second. "I ain't countin on makin much out of the crop," he said. "The drouth has nigh about ruined our tobacco, for a fact. But I got this here new clover hay. Ain't nobody else on this place got a share in that, but Mister Ben's goin to give me a third of every pound of seed we raise."

"How much does it sell fer?"

"Hit sells fer a lot. Ain't everybody in this country knows how to raise it. Mister Chance Llewellyn, he was over here the other day, and he walked over that field of ours and he said we had the prettiest stand in the country. He did, fer a fact. It stands to reason I'll git two, three hundred dollars out of that field."

Her hand tightened on his arm. "Hit don't cost so much to set up housekeepin," she told him. "I got me a quilt already. Double wedding ring. Mammy's sister over at Palmyra made it fer me. Said she'd made one fer all the girls and now I come along she'd have to turn in and make one fer me."

"Mammy'll give us a bed," he said, "and some chairs, too, maybe. I aim to buy you a bureau, first thing we buy out of the crop."

"I saw one at Newson's on Third Street," she said; mahogany veneer he said it was and had a little chair to set in front of it so you could set down and rest when you combed your hair."

"Sometimes there's two or three of them things go together," he observed, "sometimes they come in sets."

She laughed. "We ain't goin to be botherin with no sets. We'll just buy one thing at a time, whate'er pleases us we'll buy—if we have the money to pay fer it." She laughed and looked about her, breathing tremulously. "Ain't it a pretty night!"

Ote's eyes followed hers. The new moon was up, silvering all the glade. He put his hand down on the moss and felt how cool it was. "You git in here," he said, "and you can most fergit there's such a thing as a drouth."

"But you can't fergit it in the daytime," she said. "Buck Chester he was by the house this evenin and he said they was fryin aigs on the sidewalk in Guthrie. He did, fer a fact."

"That don't mean they're doin it," Ote said shortly.

She did not answer. "What was Buck Chester doin at your house?" he asked after a pause.

"He was comin by," she said, "comin by to bring Wallace some whiskey."

Ote was relieved but he still could not let the matter drop. "I reckon he didn't hurry off," he said.

"I don't know," she returned indifferently, "I was just finishin up the dishes and I didn't see him."

"Well," Ote said, "I ain't goin to cry if I never see him. Low life, Buck Chester is, and anybody you ask 'll tell you that."

"They ain't a thing to him," she agreed.

He raised his hand from where it had lain in the moss and as he did so he felt a faint moisture clinging to his palm. Here under these big trees the dew fell as thick as if it was in an open field. These heavy dews would do a lot for the tobacco, he thought, if people'd get up early in the morning and draw them in around the plant. He had been doing that for some time and thought he saw a difference in the plants that had been worked that way. His thoughts went back to the accounting there would be in the fall. "Idelle," he said, "I don't want you to git your hopes up too high but I'm going to make me a tobacco crop, drouth or no drouth. . . ."

"You ain't give up hope of the crop?" she asked.

"No," he said, "I'm goin to hoe my tobacco out tomorrow. I'm goin to hoe it all over onct. A rain is bound to come along pretty soon and when it does I'm goin to be ready to take advantage of it."

"I reckon you will if anybody does," she said admiringly.

He put his arm around her and getting up himself drew her to her feet. "Come on," he said, "Let's walk a little deeper into the woods."

They went forward, matching their steps, his arm about her waist, his other hand clasping hers. They left the glade and took a path that branched off from the wagon road. The shadows were deeper here. The air had a faint, damp smell. They came into a grove of saplings. Cinnamon vine grew in profusion, festooning itself from tree to tree. Ote found a place where it hung low to the ground, making a natural arbor. "Come on," he said, "here's a house fer ye."

She crept in beside him, then raised herself up suddenly. "I heard somebody," she said, "I heard somebody coming down the road and that's a fact."

Ote listened a second, then got to his feet cautiously. He could see the road from here. Two figures were moving slowly along it. He watched them until they had passed on into the deeper shadows, then dropped down beside Idelle. "Who is it?" she whispered. He laughed low. "Hit's a man and a woman," he said, "but they don't want to see us no more'n we want to see them." He put his hand on her waist and forced the slim body down beside him. "Lay down here by me," he said. "This night can't last forever."

CHAPTER TWENTY-FOUR

THAT NIGHT Letty went upstairs for a few minutes after supper. The four men walked through the hall and out on to the porch. Frank and Jim dropped down on the steps. Mr. Allard and Cousin Rock sat down in their rocking chairs—an enormous split-bottomed rocker had been brought down from the attic for Cousin Rock—and resumed their interminable conversation. These conversations centered about their relationship. The two men who had spent most of their lives apart seemed to find their kinship a close bond. They liked to speculate about it, to trace the innumerable ramifications of the family connection. A few nights ago they had discovered that they had a common ancestor that neither had known the other had. The discovery seemed to afford them great pleasure. "Elias Winn, of Taylor's Grove. . . ." Cousin Rock repeated the name with satisfaction, adding, "Ben, now all my brothers and sisters are dead, I reckon you're the closest kin I've got in the world."

"I reckon so," Allard said. His thoughts too went back to the dead man. "Elias Winn had four children. Sam married a Roderick, Jane married Edmond Francis, Robert married Judith Clark. What about Margaret?"

"Married Thomas Winn," Cousin Rock said. "Born a Winn and married a Winn."

"That's right," Ben said.

Frank got up and went into the house for his tobacco. Jim shifted his position so that he could look out over the west lawn. He watched the moon, red as fresh paint, rise through the trees. The old man's phrases echoed in his mind. "Born a Winn and married a Winn. . . . Born a Carter and married a Carter. . . ." That was what Sara had cried out that day. The quarrel had seemed trivial at the time. He had tried to forget it as soon as possible. Doubtless she had too; neither of them had cut a dignified figure. But thinking it over now, that quarrel did not seem so trivial. Sara was intuitive; she had put her finger on the root of the matter. He did not despise the Camps—he was not, he thought, in a position to despise any one. But they were not his kind of people. These people here on the porch, this old bankrupt, Allard, and dissolute old Cousin Rock, were. He understood why Allard put off today what he could do tomorrow, left his machinery out in the rain, dressed as he did; he understood why old Cousin Rock, living alone on his plantation, shut himself in upper rooms to gamble with young niggers. What he couldn't understand was a man like Joe Camp who could desert his business, the business his father had founded, and rush off to Europe at a moment's notice. Still, aside from the money, Joe was not leaving much. The manufacture of babies' pants and women's fixings was not a thing to give your life to. . . .

His thoughts returned to his wife. He had sometimes wondered why Sara had fancied him in the first place. He was good-looking, he supposed, and that meant a lot to women, but he had no education—his mother was always harping on that—and no particular talents. He was not a good business man, not good enough, anyhow, to pull the

Camp business out of the hole it had been in for three years. He was not even accomplished at any sport. He was still a good shot and he had been in his time a good man with dogs. But that was a long time ago. Yet Sara, who might have had her pick in half a dozen cities, had fancied him. It must have been because of some deep insecurity in herself, an insecurity that he had never been aware of until recently. She must have felt that being a Carter was something in itself. His hand that held his pipe slipped from his knee. The pipe clattered down on to the step and then to the ground. He did not pick it up. He sat staring at the red moon. Yes, that was it. Sara had wanted him because he had the thing she didn't have and she had bought him with her money. She hadn't realized what she was doing and he himself had been too stupid to realize it but that was what had happened. He had been contemptuous of Helen because she had gone out in cold blood and lassoed Joe. But he had no right to look down on Helen. She had at least known what she was doing, while he had fooled himself. . . .

There was a light step in the hall. The screen door opened. Letty came through and sat down in the chair next to Cousin Rock. Jim held the door for her, then sat down again on the steps.

Cousin Rock said that he had read Cobbett Moore's funeral notice in this morning's paper. Allard said that Cobbett Moore was sixty-seven years old, two years older than he himself was. He leaned over and knocked his pipe out against the leg of his chair. His profile, hawklike, larger than life, was shadowed on the white pillar that upheld the porch. Jim watched it waver there, then vanish. Four days ago he, Jim Carter, had possessed Allard's daughter. It had been four days ago that they became lovers there in the meadow. Four days. He tried to think back that far but it was difficult. That first morning. . . . They had come back to the house around noon. Frank and his father had just come in from the field. Fortune was said to smile on lovers. It had smiled on them, for the next day Frank had been called to Gloversville on business. They had had the whole day to themselves. Old Allard found him a mount and Letty had her mare. They had spent the day in the Penhally woods. . . . He wondered whether he would ever again see that place where they had stopped first. A bed of dry leaves on the high ground above a spring. . . . He had had to take the horses off a little way to tether them. The mare would not stand until he had stuck a flybush made of sycamore leaves through her bridle. . . . Letty had stood beside him while he arranged it. As they turned away she was asking which day he would have to leave. But he was looking at that bed of leaves where he knew they would lie down. "For God's sake, don't talk about that yet. . . ."

Just before noon they had ridden out on the road until they came to a country store. When Letty had telephoned her father from there saying that they were lunching in Gloversville, old Allard grumbled about the horses being ridden in this heat with the stock flies already so bad. . . . They had bought some cheese and crackers at the store and then had ridden back into the woods. . . .

Frank said suddenly: *"Jim?"*

Jim jumped. "Yes?" he said.

"I was thinking . . ." Frank said. "Baker called me up this morning. He wants to go to Birmingham this week end and he wondered if I'd be back by Friday. If we left here

Thursday right after dinner we could make it by ten or eleven o'clock."

"Yes," Jim said, "if we'd spell each other on the driving."

"But I thought you weren't going to leave here till Friday," Allard protested.

"We weren't," Frank said, "till Baker got this idea of going to Birmingham."

"Why don't you tell him he can't go?" Letty asked.

Jim said hastily, "It's only two days sooner. I ought to be getting back too."

Letty was silent. "We'll make it Thursday afternoon, then," Frank said.

"When you reckon you'll come up again?" Allard asked.

"I'll be up again in October," Frank said. "Might run up for two or three days some time before that. You can't tell, though, how things will be, in my business."

Cousin Rock's chair groaned as he shifted his weight. He said: "One thing I never could understand is how a feller can go to an office, day in and day out. Now, farming or raising horses or cattle, they's something coming up all the time to keep a man interested. But Frank here, he ain't no better than a clerk, looking after other men's money. . . . It'd run *me* crazy."

"Me too," Allard said, "I've got to be interested or I can't keep going."

Frank laughed. "It's not any picnic," he said.

Jim got up from the steps and sat down near Frank. He had not heard anything the others had said. He still heard his own words: "I've got to be getting back."

"I've got to be getting back. . . ." On Friday, by midnight, if not earlier, he would be driving into Countsville. At the

Camp place Frank would let him out on the gravelled, circular drive. He would go in through the front hall, then cross to the stairs that led to his and Sara's suite. He would grasp the polished rail and mount. Halfway up there was a niche. From that niche a statue, a pagan-looking little boy who always seemed to be on the point of doing something dirty, had leered at him now for ten years. . . . Eleven. . . . Mrs. Camp had bought the statue eleven years ago. In Chicago, from a man named Crane. . . .

Letty was rising. She stood with one hand on the back of her father's chair. She had on a white dress. From here the stuff looked diaphanous but if you pinched a fold of it between thumb and finger it was as crisp as paper. Organdie she called it. She had the slimmest, softest body of any woman he'd ever known. He thought desperately: "And I never gave a damn about any one of them. . . . Till now. . . ."

Letty was walking out from behind her father's chair. She said that she thought she would go up to bed.

"Mighty early, aren't you?" Frank asked.

She yawned delicately. "I'm tired."

Frank laughed. "How did you get that way?"

She laughed too. "Doing nothing."

She was moving with her light step towards the door. Jim got up. She passed him and turned back to ask for a match. He held his lighter for her. She bent to it. When she had lit her cigarette she straightened up but not before she had thrust a small, folded paper into his cuff. Then she was gone, through the door into the hall.

He sat down. He clasped his hands on one knee and thrusting a finger inside his cuff brought the note out. He sat there, holding it concealed in his palm for a long while, until Frank said that he, too, was going to bed. He rose and accompanied Frank, leaving the old men to their talk. Frank stopped in the hall and proposed a nightcap. Jim refused on the ground that he was already sleepy. Inside his own room he unfolded the paper and read it. She was going down the back stairs, about eleven o'clock. She would be waiting there on the woods road.

CHAPTER TWENTY-FIVE

The NEXT day it looked as though it would rain. Ote took advantage of the sky's being overcast to work in the field all day. He hoped to have his crop hoed over by the end of the week. At three o'clock he stopped his steady chopping long enough to look back over the field. He calculated that he was two-thirds through. Another two or three days' work would finish the whole crop.

There was nobody else working that afternoon. Old Joe said that even with the sky clouded it was too hot for him. He had got to the point where he couldn't hoe except in the cool of the day. An hour or two in the early morning or late evening was all he was good for. The Sheelers, Ote reflected with annoyance, weren't good even for that. They had poisoned their crop but they hadn't suckered it, and as for hoeing it over, not one of them had had a hoe in his hand for weeks. It looked like they had abandoned the crop, all right. He wondered whether he would have Old Man Sheeler and his gang to feed after he married Idelle and then was ashamed of the thought. He remembered last night in the woods and began hoeing again with short, vigorous strokes. A man as happy as he was ought to be willing to work hard, day in and day out.

Somebody was coming along the path at the side of the

field. He thought at first that it was old Jim, who often took the short cut to the spring. Then he saw that it was Idelle and that she was coming towards him. He flung his hoe down and went to meet her. There was a big oak that had been left growing in that end of the field. She stopped when she came under its shade and stood there waiting for him. She had come off without a hat. Her yellow hair was tangled as if she hadn't taken time to brush it. She had an empty bucket in her hand.

She stared at him as he came up to her. "I picked up this bucket," she said, "so anybody'd think I was going to the spring for water."

He laughed. "I reckon you got a right to bring me a drink of water to the field if you feel like it," he said, and put his arm about her. But she started away. "I reckon so," she said with an hysterical laugh, "I reckon I got the right."

He looked at her. "What's the matter with you?" he asked brusquely.

"They ain't a thing the matter with me!" she cried. "They ain't a thing the matter with me!" She put her hands up to her face. Her thin body racked from side to side with her sobs.

Ote laid his hand on her shoulder. "Come on, honey," he said, "less go over by the spring."

They walked across the field, she still holding the bucket, he striding silently along beside her until they had crossed the fence and set their feet on the woods path. He put his arms around her then. "Don't cry, honey," he begged. "Come on now and tell me what it is.

She drew away from him. Her hair had fallen across her face. She pushed it aside with shaking hands. "I stood it as long as I could," she said hoarsely. "Last night, even, I didn't say anything. But it's been going for three weeks now. And this morning I got up and looked like I couldn't stand it no longer. . . ."

He stood staring at her. "Would you mind telling me what you are talking about?" he asked.

He moved towards her as he spoke. She put out her hands to repulse him. "Don't you try to come it over me!" she cried shrilly. "You know well enough what 'tis. I ain't come sick. Three weeks ago it ought to been but it ain't happened yet. . . ."

He had been fearing some nameless catastrophe. This news did not seem so alarming. He released his pent-up breath in a long sigh. "Well, you ain't long overdue, honey," he said, "no use worryin yet."

"Worryin!" she cried. "I ain't done nothin but worry—for three weeks now."

"Why didn't you tell me before?"

"I didn't want to tell you till I had to. And I kept waiting, thinking maybe 'twasn't so."

"Well, you don't know it is yet," he said.

She began to cry again. "I been awful sick in the mornings."

He was alarmed now. "For how long?"

"Ever since last Thursday. This morning was the worst. Lottie Wye, she was spending the night with us. I was scared she'd notice."

"Well, she didn't, did she?"

"Naw," she didn't. But she might, any time. Any of 'em might."

They had come to the spring. He sat down on a fallen log and made her sit beside him. "We'll git married right away," he said.

"But you said we couldn't git married till you got your crop in."

He laughed ruefully. "I say a lot ever time I open my mouth. Needs must when the devil drives."

"Way it is now," I'm scared of Pa," she said miserably. "He wouldn't think nothin of puttin me out in the big road."

"He better not try it around me," Ote said truculently.

"He wouldn't say nothin to you about it. He'd just tell me to hit the big road like he done Nelsie."

"Did he do that to Nelsie?"

"When she was sixteen years old. Ain't none of us heard anything of her from that day to this. Wallace said Tom Chester told him he seen her in a house. In Memphis. But that don't make it so."

"Naw," he agreed. "That don't make it so. All them Chesters is liars. . . . How come your pa's so strict about them kind of things? He ain't so strict any other way far I can see."

"I don't know. . . . That's the way he's always been."

Ote drew her to him, kissed her tenderly on the mouth. "Don't you worry, honey. I'll fix it."

She sighed and relaxed against his shoulder. "I was plumb distracted when I come over here," she murmured.

"Don't you worry," he said again.

She leaned her head against his shoulder. They sat there quietly. Her breathing had grown calmer. He looked down, wondering if she was asleep, and saw that her eyes were closed. The veins in her eyelids were blue against the white skin. They gave her a fragile look. He felt how slight she was in his arms and thought that she had grown thinner in the last few weeks. Poor little thing, worrying herself to death all this time when he had been so happy! He pondered what he would do. He could get up the license. He had four dollars. But that was all he had. Most summers there was a little money coming in from vegetables his mother sold out of her garden. Greens, beans, cucumbers, frying-sized chickens. She most always had something to sell every time you went to town. But this year there wasn't any garden to speak of and getting over here so late she hadn't been able to do much with her chickens. There was not a frying-sized chicken on the place as yet. . . . No, there wasn't any money. And he didn't know where he could get his hands on any, unless he went to Mister Ben. . . . If Mister Ben would only build the cabin now instead of in the fall. . . . If he would only do that. They could get married right away! . . . Unconsciously he tightened his hold on Idelle. She *had* been asleep. She opened her eyes, sat up. They both got to their feet.

"We better go back to the house," she said. Then she looked at him shyly. "Ote, we goin to git married right away?"

He bent and kissed her. "We shore are," he said. "I'm goin up to see Mister Ben now."

CHAPTER TWENTY-SIX

B<small>EN</small> A<small>LLARD</small> went in to take a nap after dinner. Before he went in he walked out on the porch and squinted up at the sky. "We're going to get it this time," he told the others and then he added warily, "A watched pot never boils. I'm going in now and take my nap. When I come out it'll be raining."

He awoke at three o'clock and got up at once and came downstairs and out on to the porch. There was no sign of rain. He went down the steps and walked out from under the shade of the trees to look up at the sky. It was as bare as the palm of a hand and burning blue. The rain had blown completely over.

He shrugged his shoulders, walked over and took his favorite place under the big sugar tree. He tilted his chair back against the tree trunk, got out his knife and began whittling. The dog crouched at his feet until the dust grew too hot for her, when she got up and found a cooler place between two arching tree roots.

Allard watched her move off and addressed her absently: "What you all time moving for? You ain't going to be any cooler there."

The dog acknowledged the remark with a languid movement of her tail, then sank down, groaning lightly. Allard reached up and pulled off a bough from the tree and resumed his whittling. From where he sat he had a good view of the south field. He looked up at it from time to time. It was in tobacco this year, the poorest tobacco on the place. Old Bob Sheeler had a force of four grown men but not one of them had done a good day's work in the field this summer. Well, they would have to hunt another home come Christmas. He didn't want them on the place another year.

At four o'clock Letty and Jim walked through the yard on their way to the hammock. The man carried a tray that had on it three tall, frosted glasses. Letty paused long enough to ask him if he wanted a julep. He shook his head. He had a theory that cooling drinks made you hotter in weather like this. "No," he said impatiently, "I'm going out to the field in a minute. Don't want to get all heated up with whiskey. *You* ain't got any business drinking this time of day."

She laughed. That was an old quarrel between them. He himself held to the old-fashioned ways. He did most of his drinking before breakfast but young people, he had noticed, were apt to be squeamish in the mornings. Yesterday morning he had suggested that Mattie might take the boys up a julep before breakfast—that had always been the custom in his father's house and his father's before him—but Letty had shuddered. "Daddy, do you want to *kill* them?"

She said now: "It's mostly ice, Daddy," and then she and the man moved on, out of the shade of the sugar tree, across the burnt grass till they came into the shade of the althea hedge. He looked after them, still whittling. He wondered where Bill Fauntleroy was. He used to be over here every afternoon and now you never saw him at all. His hands paused in their slow motions. He tilted his chair farther back against the tree, frowning. All day long something had been hovering at the back of his mind. He knew now what it was.

He had dreamed last night of his old sweetheart, Maggie Carew. It was a thing that had not happened to him for twenty or thirty years. Years ago, when he was a young man and even after he was married, he used to dream of Maggie. The dream was almost always the same. He would be in a crowd and would catch sight of her face. He would be talking to somebody and would go on and finish what he was saying, thinking that in a minute he would be with her. Her face in the dream seemed to promise that she would wait for him but when he pressed his way through the crowd she was always gone.

He frowned. He knew now why he had dreamed of Maggie. It was something that had happened last night at supper. Nothing much, and yet the little incident had made so strong an impression on him that he had found himself going back to it again and again. Letty had been talking, with unusual animation. Some note in her voice had made him look up quickly. He had been struck by her resemblance to Maggie. It was the nose and the short, curving upper lip, and there was something about the texture of the flesh. Maggie had been dead for something like twenty years—his mother had read the notice of her death to him out of a New Orleans paper—but there in that moment in the candlelight she had been alive for him. He had looked at his daughter, marvelling that any other human being should have Maggie Carew's nose and lips or that peculiarly transparent skin. . . . And then, looking at his daughter, he had forgotten all about his old love. Letty was leaning forward, talking to the visitor, Jim Carter. There was a look on her face he had never seen before, an ardent, expectant look—the look, he had said to himself suddenly, of a girl in love. He wondered why he had never seen her look like that before. She was twenty-four, old enough to have been in and out of love a dozen times. She had always had a lot of beaux—like Maggie, too, in that—but she had never made any fuss over any of them. He had taken it for granted that she was in love with young Fauntleroy. But was she? Now that he came to think of it she was always very self-contained in Fauntleroy's presence, none of the blushings, the ardors or even the coolness that had distinguished courtships in his day. But then the times, he had told himself on the few occasions he had permitted himself to speculate about his daughter's emotions—the times had changed. Young girls had different manners these days. Perhaps even their emotions were different. . . . But last night the thought had flashed across his mind that Letty might be in love with the visitor, Jim Carter. He had dismissed the idea at once. Carter was a married man. He was, besides, an honorable fellow. He might have pursued Letty elsewhere but he certainly wouldn't have come down to Hanging Tree—with Frank—to do it. Yes, he had dismissed the thought from his mind at once and yet at intervals during the evening he had kept going back to it and always with a feeling of apprehension.

The thought of suffering for one you loved was a knife in the heart. But suffering when it came was like drouth or hail or any other natural calamity. Here he was sick with the fear that Letty might have an unfortunate love affair or marry the wrong man, and yet he himself had lived through as hard an experience of that kind as one could have. He summoned up the memory of that time. It was so faded now, so overlaid with other memories that events did not stand out as clearly as they once had. It had been about this time of year, or perhaps later. There was no company in the house except Maggie and Ed Ruffin. He had announced at dinner that he was going to town to get a mower blade repaired. His mother had said she wanted to go as far as Penhally with him. He had looked for Ed to go along but Ed was shooting doves in the far pasture. They could hear as they drove away the reports of his gun. "Sukey will hate cleaning all those birds," the old lady said.

He had dropped her at Penhally and then had learned that he had forgotten the mower part that was to be repaired. He had driven back for it. There were no shots to be heard now: Ed must have come in from the field. He had stepped up on the porch and was walking through the hall. It was the rustle of skirts that made him turn to look into the half-darkened parlor. She was getting up off the sofa, arranging her clothes but Ed Ruffin, slower-witted, just lay there staring. It was Ed's face that stayed with him, the lower lip dropped in stupid surprise, the honest, bewildered eyes fastened on his.

That evening after supper she had come to him out on the lawn. She had stood there where the elm tree used to be. She had cried and talked a lot. He hardly listened. When she stopped he shook his head. "It's no use, Maggie. It's like you were dead. You are—to me."

It had been a boy's boast, perhaps. But he had made it good. From that time forward he rarely allowed his mind to dwell upon either Maggie Carew or Ed Ruffin. There had been times when the effort not to think of them had been actual physical pain. A dull ache in the head that went on night after night. Or it had been like tearing out a piece of your flesh—for he had been in love with Maggie Carew. . . . What was the name of that Roman who held his hand in the flames? . . . Scaevola. . . . He had been like Scaevola. As far as he was concerned they were gone, destroyed, might never have been. It had been in a sense his revenge upon them.

He would never have been able to take it if things had been different. But God in a way had been good to him. There was no doubt in his mind. He had caught them in the act. In the act. . . . The episode in his mind was always associated with a ribald story people told of old Major Jenkins when his wife caught him in the office with one of the Negro women. The old gentleman—a young gentleman he was then—had looked up, bewildered. "Well, Lou, I just wanted a little change. . . ."

Somebody was coming around the corner of the house: Ote Mortimer. He crossed the lawn and came over to where Ben was sitting. Ben looked up and motioned to one of the vacant chairs. But Ote remained standing.

Ben glanced at him, wondering if anything had gone wrong in the field. "Sit down, Ote," he said, "what's on your mind?"

Ote sat down. He was silent a moment, then he said: "Mister Ben, you know them cabins we was talkin about the other day?"

Ben nodded.

"Well, what about buildin one of 'em now?"

Ben shook his head. "I can't get to it till fall," he said. He was not going to say anything further but he noticed that Ote looked distressed. "I reckon you want to get married now," he said, "is that it? Well, I can't put you up a cabin till fall. I have to have Luther Owens do the work and he can't set up his sawmill till fall."

"What about gittin some other saw mill?" Ote asked.

Ben laughed. "To tell you the truth, Ote, I couldn't have the logs sawed at all if Luther didn't owe me some work. He cut some poplar out of my woods five or six years ago and ain't paid me for it yet. I told him I'd take it out on the logs if he'd set up here in September."

Ote was silent. Then he said earnestly, "Well, how about advancing me something on the crop, then?

A wry smile came on Ben's face. "Ote, you know well as I do there's goin to be mighty little crop made on this place."

"I know it," Ote said. "I know we ain't goin to make nothin this year. I've knowed it for two or three weeks now." He hesitated. "But you know what you was sayin to me the other day, that you want me to stay on here with you. Well, we may not make nothin this year but next year we're likely to hit. How about you lettin me have something on that?"

Ben looked at him kindly. "You'd be good for it, all right," he said. "Ote, if I had any money to lend I'd as soon lend it to you as any man in the county. But Ote . . ." He leaned forward and lowered his voice, "Ote, I don't want you spreading it around the place but I never have been as hard run in my life as I am this year."

"I know that," Ote said. "I knowed all along you was hard run. But Mister Ben, I got to have some money. Couldn't you get me up ten or twelve dollars?"

Ben laughed out suddenly. He pulled his cheque book out of his pocket and extended it towards Ote. "I got one dollar and forty cents in the bank," he said. "Ain't got that now, probably, because they charge for carrying the account. I couldn't have got by at all this summer but I've got accounts at two stores. What groceries I buy Hardy lets me have against the lambs and I'll settle with him in November. And there's one dry goods store in town where Miss Letty charges things. . . . I got a little credit left but I haven't got a nickel in the world except this dollar and forty cents. You're welcme to that if the First National hasn't beat you to it. . . ."

Ote had got up. He stood looking down at the little black book still extended in the other man's hand. Then he shook his head. "It wouldn't do me no good," he said. "I got to have as much as ten dollars." He paused, then added: "Much obliged, Mister Ben," and walked off towards the stable.

Allard watched him go. He wondered why Ote had such sudden and pressing need for money and hoped he hadn't got into any trouble. "I ought to have asked him," he thought, and then decided that it was better not to interfere. He had been handling tenants all his life and except in his early youth, when he himself had been too hot tempered, he had always got along well with them. He told himself that it was because he had never interfered in their affairs. "Keep 'em up to the mark and after that let 'em alone," he thought. "They don't look at things the same way we do."

CHAPTER TWENTY-SEVEN

OTE WALKED OFF down the dusty road towards the Old House. It was five o'clock. His father was rocking on the porch but his mother was not visible. She must be in the kitchen getting supper. He took a few steps on the path that led to the front, then turned and went the back way. No use talking to old Joe about it. His mother was the one who had the say. He might as well take it up with her now.

He entered the kitchen. Nora had just taken off the red and white checked cloth that covered the table when it was not in use and was setting out the cold supper of boiled cabbage and fat meat. She looked up as he came in. "You hungry tonight?" she asked.

He shook his head. She took a plate of cold biscuits out of the safe and set it on the table. "I was thinking of opening up some of my fresh jam," she said, "but no use, if you ain't hungry."

Ote sat down in one of the kitchen chairs. "I wanted to talk to you a minute, Mammy."

"Well, can't you wait till I git supper on the table?"

"It's all cold, anyhow," he said. "Why can't it wait a minute?"

She leaned against the wall, facing him. "It can," she said, "only I got to git through my work some time tonight. You ain't milked yet, have you?"

He shook his head.

"Well, why'n't you go on and do it?"

"I'll milk in a minute," he said impatiently. "Mammy, I want to git married."

"That's no news," Nora said tartly. "Everybody on the place is talking about how you done lost your mind over that Sheeler girl."

"I ain't lost my mind over her so I can't work," he said roughly. "If there's a man on this place puts in a better day's work than I do I'd like to see him."

Nora's expression changed. She looked at him affectionately. "I reckon that's right," she said. "They ain't one of 'em can hold a candle to you, and that's a fact."

He brushed the praise aside. "Mammy," he repeated, "Idelle and I been thinking we'd like to git married right away."

Nora was silent a moment then she said obstinately: "Well, I don't see how you can do it. Mister Ben ain't goin to build them new cabins till fall. And even if they was a house to rent you ain't got the money to rent it. Ain't no money come in here all summer. You know that well as I do." She put her hand up to replace a lock of straying hair. "Even last year, she said, "I had some chickens to sell and some garden sass. But this year I'm hard put to git anything to put on the table. I never seen such a season."

"It's been a bad drouth," he agreed. He looked at her, wondering if he dared make the proposal he had in mind, then decided that he might as well plunge in. "Mammy," he said, "lemme marry Idelle and bring her here."

Nora's face hardened. "I don't see how you can do that, Ote. Ain't enough here to feed three of us, let alone four. And soon hit'd be five, maybe six. . . ." She broke off, glancing at him sharply. "You ain't gone and got that girl in no trouble?"

"No," he said hastily, "she ain't in no trouble. But we want to git married soon as we can. She don't like it so well at home."

"Well, that's the best thing I ever heard said of her," Nora replied. "I passed that Mattie Sheeler on the way to Shutts' this evening and I thought to myself that even if they was a drouth she could a washed herself before she got out on the big road."

"They have to bring the water a good piece," he said.

"And don't you bring me high as ten buckets a day from this here spring?" Nora cried. "Naw, it ain't how fur you have to tote the water. Some folks'll keep clean if they ain't got but a teacup of water and some folks wont. Them Sheelers always had the name of being dirty. I don't see why with all the girls in this country you have to go and take up with one of them."

His face flushed deeply. "Well, I've done took up with her," he said and got to his feet.

Nora's face was red, too, mottled red and white. She looked at him, half in fear and half in anger; then anger triumphed. "Well, see that you don't bring her here!" she cried shrilly.

"I won't," he said and left the room.

She came after him as far as the door. She watched him stride across the yard towards the road. When he reached the road she called out almost timidly. "Ain't you goin to milk? Ote, ain't you goin to milk?"

"Naw," he called without turning around. "Naw, I ain't goin to milk. You can milk your old cows yourself. I ain't goin to milk this night."

CHAPTER TWENTY-EIGHT

He CONTINUED to stride on up the road. For the first few minutes his thoughts were all of the two cows that had come up and were standing in the cow-pen. They turned their heads as he passed. One of them lowed. It seemed strange to pass them by like that. He had missed milking his cows sometimes before, on Sunday evenings when he got in late or on holidays, but never before in his life had he deliberately neglected to attend to stock. And he, of course, was the main dependence. Old Joe's hands were so stiff with rheumatism that he couldn't get the milk out of a cow unless she let it down and one of those heifers was a little devil about holding it up. Nora, in her day, had been an expert milker but she had got too fat to squat down beside the cow. It must be fifteen years since she'd milked. Well, let her try it. Most men around here considered it women's work. Warn't hardly a man in the county would turn his hand to it but old Joe had always been one to spare the women folks and his boys had followed after him in that. But let her find out what it was to have to get along the best you could, like other women folks. . . .

He came to the branch and stepped swiftly over the three big, flat rocks that ever since he could remember had formed a rude foot-bridge there. He left the road and took the short cut through the pasture to Sheelers'. This part of the field had been sown in the new clover that they called "Lespedeza." Mister Ben had made him mix timothy with the clover seed. The timothy, growing faster than the clover, had already provided one crop of hay. If a man was to come in here with a mower he could cut another crop of hay now. . . .

He walked on more slowly. His thoughts returned to his plight. He would have to take Idelle to his mother's. There would be hell to pay for a few days but after that everything would be all right. He knew his mother. High tempered—but when you came down to it she always made the best of a situation. . . . If he could only get Idelle to see things his way. . . .

He came to the fence. He stepped over and walked along the mock orange hedge towards the Sheelers'. It was not yet dark but lights were lit in the cabin and he could see forms moving on the porch. He hoped there wasn't any company there tonight. He would have to talk to Idelle. If the house was full of people it would be hard to get her off by herself.

He approached the house. A voice came from the porch. "Howdy, Ote." Old Man Sheeler and the old grandfather were sitting side by side. Random was sprawled on the steps cutting holes in the flooring with his knife. Ote went up and sat down beside Mr. Sheeler.

Inside the house the women were moving about. He heard dishes rattling and realized suddenly that it was supper time. The same thought came to Old Man Sheeler. He twisted around in his chair to look into the lighted room. "Ote, you'll set down with us," he said politely.

"I'm obliged to you," Ote said. "Reckon I better go in and tell them to put on an extra plate?"

Robert Sheeler laughed. "Tell 'em to put the big pot in the little one," he called jovially.

"It's too late for that," Ote responded. "If it's like it is at my house you're lucky to git any pot liquor at all these days."

Robert Sheeler's moment of animation was over. He sank back in his chair. "We got snaps," he said. "That's about all we've had all summer. Snaps. I'm sick and tired of 'em."

The old grandsir, for once, had caught what was being said. He chuckled. "You got fat meat to put in 'em," he observed and sang:

"What you goin to do when the meat gives out?
Stand in the corner with your lip poked out."

Random took up the tune:

"Got no money but I will have some,
Git my money when the pay car comes. . . ."

Ote got up and went into the dog-run. As he went he reflected that every time he had been up here this summer he had found them complaining of hard times. "Wonder what they do when times are good," he thought. "Belly-ache because they ain't no better?"

The dog-run was dark but a lamp was lighted in the little dining room and in the bedroom. There was nobody in the dining room but he knew that Idelle would be coming in any minute from the kitchen, so he went in there and stood.

In a few minutes she came in, bearing the dish of snaps and bacon which would be the main part of the meal. Her eyes went to his the moment she entered but she walked around the table and set the dish down at her father's place before she spoke. "Hello," she said then and came over to where he was standing. He gave a wary glance into the kitchen, then took her into his arms. "Honey," he breathed tenderly, "honey, how you feelin?"

She lifted her head, shaking her hair back with the old free motion. But he saw that her face looked drawn and that she was paler than ordinary. "I'm feeling all right, now," she said, "but I was sick before supper."

"Did any of 'em notice?" he whispered.

She shook her head, then she, too, glanced back into the kitchen where Gracie was standing over the stove. "Come on," she said and led him across the hall. In the bedroom she stood before the mirror pretending to arrange her hair. Ote stood awkwardly beside her. He wanted to shut the door but that might arouse comment. Still he had to talk to her. He plunged in.

"I saw Mister Ben," he whispered. "They ain't a chance of him building them cabins till fall."

Her hand paused on her hair and fell limply to her side. In the mirror he saw her eyes widen with the same distressed look they had had this afternoon. She turned and faced him. "Well, he could furnish you some money, couldn't he?" she cried.

He moved closer to her, put his hand quickly over her mouth. "Shh, honey! They'll hear you out there. He cain't furnish me no money. He cain't hardly furnish himself."

He took his hand down but not before he had felt her lips draw back scornfully. "Cain't furnish himself!" she said in a sibilant whisper. "I notice Miss Letty goes around dressed up mighty fine."

"I expect Mister Frank gives her the money," Ote said. "Anyway, that ain't none of our business."

Her eyes were fixed on his. "Well, what we goin to do?" she demanded. Her voice rose again so that he closed his hand on her elbow warningly. She shook her elbow free. "I'm scared of Pa," she wailed. "I got so I can hardly stand to look at him. I'm scared."

"I'll take care of your pa," he said harshly.

"Well, what you goin to do? You keep talkin but you don't do nothin."

"We'll drive to Elkton tomorrow and git married," he said slowly.

"And what then?"

"We'll go stay with my folks till we git some other place to go."

She whirled away from him, then came to rest leaning against the footboard of the bed. She put her hands on her lips. She looked at him scornfully. "Go stay with your folks!" she cried. "And this evenin your mammy met Ma and Gracie in the road and said I was low life."

His face hardened. "She didn't," he said, "I don't believe anything of the kind."

"You can ask Gracie. Her and Ma was comin along and Miss Nora she was goin to Shutts'. They got to talkin about you and Miss Nora she said you was all right till you got to runnin with fast girls. Fast girls," she repeated, "like me."

He shook his head stubbornly. "She didn't say like you."

"Well, she meant it. Everybody knows what she thinks of me." He looked at her pleadingly. He was acutely conscious of the others out on the porch. They must have heard something of this conversation, must know at least that something unusual was going on. If she would only be quiet. If she would only not take things so hard. He went over to the bed and put his arms around her. "Honey, please don't," he begged, "I'm doin the best I can. You know I'm doin the best I can."

Her arms went up about his neck. For a moment her face,

wet with tears, was pressed against his. Then she broke away, sobbing. "I'd ruther die. I'd ruther lay down in the road and die than go live with her."

He tightened his arms about her. "It'd only be for a little while. Mister Ben'd have the cabin built in a month or so."

She shook her head. "I just wisht I was dead," she moaned. "I just wisht I was dead this minute."

He heard a step in the dining room. Gracie or Mrs. Sheeler must have come in. "Hush," he said sharply, "hush up. You better go wash your face. Supper's on the table."

The tears still on her cheeks, she went out of the room. He heard her on the back porch pouring water into the tin basin. He stood in the bedroom a few minutes longer, then went out into the dog-run.

Supper had been called. The others were going into the dining room. He joined them.

Mrs. Sheeler, coming in from the lean-to, looked at him in surprise. "Howdy, Ote. I didn't know you was here."

They were about to sit down when there was a commotion at the front door. Wallace came in with Buck Chester. Ote had not known that Buck was even in the neighborhood. He gave him a curt "Howdy, Buck," coupled with a hard stare. Gracie came in, carrying a child on her hip, and sank into the seat beside Clator. She had been standing over the stove, and her face was heavily beaded with perspiration. She had not bothered to wipe it off nor had she changed her dress, a Mother Hubbard she had been wearing the last four or five times he had been up there.

Robert Sheeler carved the fat meat into twelve portions and helped everybody liberally to snaps, then sat back. "Naw, I ain't hungry," he said in answer to questioning. "I just ain't hungry. That's all."

Ote looked at the old man, at his high forehead, his weak blue eyes, his sagging mouth. "Ain't got enough get-up even to eat," he thought. He recalled what Idelle had just said, that she feared most of all that her father would find out her condition. He recalled what she had said about her oldest sister. It didn't seem possible that Old Sheeler could have done such a thing. "Still," he concluded, "he may have had plenty of ginger in him then. Just burnt out now, that's all."

He caught Idelle's eye and fancied that she, too, was speculating about what her father would do if he found her out, for a little color had risen in her pale cheeks. He looked at her earnestly, trying to make his gaze reassuring but she met his eyes only for a second and looked away.

Buck Chester said he was going to drive to Elkton tomorrow and wanted to know if anybody wanted to go. "They's a carnival," he said. "I thought we might drive up in the cool of the evening. Git there just before the stores close and git our trading done and then we could go into some of the sideshows."

Ote shifted his gaze to Buck. "You must have plenty of money to spend, Buck," he said insolently, "aimin to take the whole family. Where'd you git so much money? Tell me. I'd like to know."

Buck laughed but he looked away quickly and tried to change the subject. He was not anxious, Ote knew, for everybody to know where he got his money. He had a still running on Mr. Adams' place. He had been raided once and Mr. Adams had promised the sheriff to put Buck off if he caught him making another run.

Mrs. Sheeler would not let the subject of the carnival drop. "Why'n't you go, Idelle?" she asked. "You and Random

could go along with Buck. Git me some more of that per-
cale and I could make the baby another dress."

"Gracie can go," Idelle said shortly.

Gracie laughed. "I ain't goin to be draggin around to no
carnival. Not in the shape I'm in."

Her husband, Clator, turned to her. "You ain't in such a
bad shape," he observed mildly. "You was a heap bigger
with Artie than you are with this one."

Gracie laughed and gave him a little push. Ote regarded
them both with disfavor. Gracie, he thought, ought not to
talk about such things before Idelle and Random, let alone
her own child. She must have read his thoughts. She was
giving him back a hard gaze. "Why'n't you go, Ote? she
asked.

"I got to work," Ote answered. "I'm hoein my crop over.
I ain't got no time to be gallivantin off to carnivals."

Gracie laughed. "You and Idelle'll have to do a lot of goin
after you git married. You don't do much now."

"Naw," Ote told her, "we don't do much goin but then
everybody ain't got as much time on they hands as Buck has.
It's a wonder to me now how Buck manages to git so much
free time. . . . How much tobacco did you put in this year,
Buck?"

Buck was sitting with his eyes decorously fixed on his plate.
He looked up and grinned across the table at Wallace. "Five
acres," he said; "two for me and three for the worms."

They were getting up from the table. Idelle made a move
to take the dishes off but Gracie good-humoredly told her to
go and sit with her beau. "I ain't got nothin to do but go
to bed when I git through," she said yawning.

They walked out on the porch. Ote waited until Idelle had

taken her place on the bench that ran along the wall. Then he sat down beside her. Mr. and Mrs. Sheeler and the old grandsir took their rocking chairs. The boys disposed themselves on the steps. Buck sat down with them and began a low-voiced conversation with Wallace.

Gracie came in a moment and took the lamp out of the dining room. The moon had not yet risen. The porch was in darkness. Ote moved a little closer to Idelle. He reached over and put his hand on her bare arm. "Less go for a walk," he whispered. She shook her head. He waited a few minutes then pressed her arm gently. "Please," he whispered. She turned her head then. *"I cain't!"* she whispered back. Her voice had the same hysterical note that it had had before supper. He was silent after that, fearing that if he persisted she might break down and cry there before them all.

On the steps the boys kept talking. Buck turned around and then, trying to draw Idelle into the conversation: "Idelle, who was that girl was visiting Lottie last summer? . . . Idelle, remember that time we all went down to Dover?"

Ote's anger grew. The Sheelers had no business to let Buck come on the place, he thought. And Buck himself ought to know better. He knew that Idelle was his, Ote's, girl. And he must know what he would do to him if he caught him fooling around her. He resolved to give Buck a good beating the next time he saw him out on the big road. "That'll learn him to stay away," he thought savagely.

On the bench beside him Idelle stirred restlessly. He wondered how she was feeling. His heart smote him for forgetting her for even a moment. Her hand was lying on the bench between them. He put his own hand over it and pressed it tenderly. But she did not respond. She turned her head towards him as if she was looking at him under cover of the dark; then she turned her head away. Suddenly she rose and walked across the floor.

"Cain't git a breath of air back there," she said and sat down on the top step with the boys.

Ote sat silent. His anger at Buck was nothing compared to the rage he now felt. "Slighted me here before 'em all," he thought, "and done it in cold blood too." He wanted to step down there and pick her up and shake her, pick her up and shake her good there before them all. He clenched his hands until his first rage had subsided. Then he rose and walked out into the middle of the floor. "Good night, all," he said in a formal tone and took his hat up and went rapidly off down the road.

CHAPTER TWENTY-NINE

Ben Allard waked just before dawn. The usual chorus of birds had begun in the trees around the house and in the cow pen two cows were lowing for their young calves. He lay listening to their plaintive calls that never rose above a certain note, and decided that it was not these sounds that had roused him. He would have waked quickly to the sound of any of his stock in distress but he was habited to their ordinary cries. No, the noise had been in the house and it was unusual, like a window put down suddenly or a door slammed.

He jumped out of bed. He rose always in the mornings with a sense of adventure. There were so many things he wanted to do and no day was ever long enough to get them all in. This morning, for instance, he wanted to walk over in the big field while it was still cool, to look at the new clover. He had not seen it for three or four days. As he dressed he kept thinking of it. He was not a man to run after new-fangled ways. To raise enough corn for his stock, enough wheat to feed the people on his place, and to grow, house and cure good, bright tobacco had been enough for him. But he had taken to this new clover like a duck to water. He had liked the idea of it when Chance Llewellyn had first told him of it. He had enjoyed preparing the ground and sowing it and had watched it grow with pleasure. Rarely indeed had he grown a crop that so delighted him. Standing out there in the field with Ote the other day he had pulled one plant out of the ground. They had both been surprised at its size and sturdiness. The tap root was enormously long and the plant itself, spreading generously, was the circumference of a good-sized dish pan. Letty, riding by with Frank and Carter, had commented on the delicacy and beauty of the pointed leaves. "It looks like a Japanese flower," she had said.

He paused in his buttoning of his shirt. All yesterday afternoon he had been thinking of his daughter. These thoughts came back to him now with double force. In this fresh morning air his mind was clearer. He saw farther than he had been able to see yesterday afternoon. He remembered things that he had noticed only unconsciously before. He was convinced now that there was something going on between her and Jim Carter.

He began walking about the room with the quick, uneven strides that in one day carried him miles over the place. He thought that he might talk to Frank, might ask him if he thought there was anything in it, and then he thought that maybe he had better speak to Letty herself first. There was no use bringing Frank in if he could help it.

He frowned. No, he wouldn't bring Frank in. Immediately after breakfast he would call Letty aside and talk to her. God knew what he would say. But he would do his duty as he saw it. As for Carter—he hoped to wouldn't have to see him again or at least have any private conversation with him. The fellow, however dishonorably he had acted, was no fool. He would have sense enough to leave as soon as he saw how things were. He would tell Letty that Carter must leave the place today.

He finished dressing and reached for his cap—he never

felt fully equipped for the day until he had his head covered
—then went out into the hall and started down the stairs.

Halfway down he stopped. He stood there, his head on a
level with the top stair, and looked back into the upper
hall. It was the square hall common to houses in that region.
Four doors opened off it and there were two windows at the
far end. The morning light coming in through the windows
illuminated the hall. When his mother was alive she had used
this upper hall for a sitting room. An old sofa had stood beneath the windows and an old-fashioned wardrobe had stood
against one wall. But Letty had taken those pieces of furniture out years ago and had replaced them with two chairs and
a small table that in summer held a vase of flowers. The hall
had always looked bare to him since then. This morning,
looking back up into it, he was suddenly aware that beneath
him the house was empty. Nobody sleeping in the wing or
in the room that had been his mother's.

He went slowly back up the stairs. He passed his own
door and walked up to Letty's. It was shut. He hesitated a second, then knocked. There was no response. He knocked
again, louder. Still there was no answer. He pushed the door
open and went inside.

The first thing that struck him was the condition of the
bed. It was neatly made, the counterpane drawn up smoothly,
the pillows neatly placed. The chairs were all in their places,
none of Letty's clothes lying across them as they usually
were in the mornings. A closet door was ajar. He walked
over to it. There was a hat box on the top shelf and below
on the floor two pairs of shoes. "How can she have taken
everything with her?" he thought, and then he remembered
that she had said she was leaving a lot of clothes in Louisville as she planned to go back there in the fall.

He stood in the middle of the floor, looking about aimlessly; then he went out into the hall. He did not knock at Carter's door. He pushed it open and entered without even a call. The bed was empty. Most of its covers were tumbled on to the floor as if the person sleeping there had risen so hastily that he had brought the covers off with him when he had got out of bed.

Allard walked out and shut the door. He went in to his own room. He took his cap off and laid it on the mantel. He leaned his elbows on the mantel and sank his chin in his hands. He was staring at a calendar Aunt Pansy had hung there. It advertised a seed store in Gloversville and bore the picture of a laughing child peeping out of a shock of wheat.

There was a noise below. He half turned his head, then faced the wall again. Below him heavy footsteps shook the old house. Aunt Pansy's voice floated up through the open door:

"Mister Ben, Mister Mortimer wants to see you."

"Coming," he called but did not stir.

There was silence, then the footsteps came again. Aunt Pansy called more imperatively: "Mister Ben, you comin?"

He went out into the hall and leaned over the bannisters. Ote Mortimer was below. He stood there, staring at the floor. Then he heard Ben's step and turned his face up.

"Mister Ben," he said. "How about cuttin that second crop of hay?"

Ben heard his own voice speaking in a controlled yet authoritative tone. "Naw, Ote, you can't do that. It'd ruin that fine clover."

Ote moved so that he stood at the very bottom of the stair well. He turned his face up. The light fell on it. Ben started as he saw the swollen face, the bloodshot, sunken eyes. "What's the matter with you, Ote?"

Ote kept his ravaged face turned up to the other. "Ain't nothin. . . . Mister Ben, I'm needin some money bad."

"I know it," Ben said, "you told me that yesterday. But you can't go ruining my clover just because you need a little money."

Ote looked down at the floor, then up again. "It's a third mine," he said; "you said a third of that clover was mine. I got a right to do what I want with my own."

Ben grasped the bannister to steady himself. He saw the field of clover as it had been two days ago, saw the timothy first, pale, grayish, and then under it the rows and rows of clover plants, sturdy, far-branching, delicately green. Rage and despair welled up in him. He leaned far over to look down at the young poor white man and with his clenched fist he made a menacing gesture. "It may be your clover," he said, "but it's my land. You try cutting that clover and you'll regret it. To the longest day you live."

CHAPTER THIRTY

O<small>TE</small> <small>LEFT</small> the hall by the back door and went out on to the porch that ran the length of the ell. The old cook was at the far end washing up the milk things. She looked up. "Did you see Mister Ben?" she asked. "Did you get him up?"

"Yes," Ote said, "I got him up."

The old Negro gave him a shrewd glance. "My coffee's just come to a boil," she said. "You want a cup?"

"I ain't a carin," Ote said.

He used the conventional formula for assent, but the words, leaving his lips, took on new meaning. "I *ain't* a carin," he thought despairingly. "I don't know what to do now. And that's a fact."

Old Pansy was back with his coffee. He drank it off at one draught, wiped his lips with the back of his hand then set the cup back on the table. "Well," he said, "I better be goin," and went off across the back yard towards the stable.

He took a hoe down from the rack and went out to the field. He chopped a few rows, with swift, expert strokes. But he could not put his mind on the work. He kept going back to the events of yesterday. He had been so angry last night that he could not sleep. He could hardly believe that Idelle could have brought herself to flout him so there before all the others. He had kept going back to that as he tossed on his bed. He could not get around it, that she who loved him so truly had done such a thing. But this morning he saw things in a different light. She was so worried in her mind that she hardly knew what she was doing. "And besides," he told himself, "maybe she didn't go to do it. She might a walked over there just to sit down by Wallace. She might not even have been thinking about Buck Chester."

He flung the hoe down, something he had never done before in his life—if there was anything that made him angry it was for people to leave their tools lying about in the field. But he felt that he couldn't wait. He must get to Idelle as soon as he could. He must ask her what she had meant. He must find out if she still loved him.

He took a short cut across the field, came out through a gap in the mock orange hedge and stepped down into the road. The dust still lay thick but the dews had been heavy last night. A mock orange that lay in the dust was coated so thick with moisture that it glittered. He kicked it aside and went on.

The grove was before him, serene in the morning light. Smoke from the Sheeler chimney drifted above the trees. Somebody, a man, was sitting on the porch but he rose and went inside just as Ote came up.

He stood at the steps and called: "Hello!"

He was sure he had heard stirrings back in the kitchen but they ceased abruptly. The house was as still as if there were nobody in it. "Hello," he called again, "hello," and added: "It's Ote Mortimer."

There were steps across the hall. He heard a murmur of voices, then after some delay old Mrs. Sheeler came out on the porch. She had her slat sunbonnet on already and she held a bunch of beets, just pulled from the garden. She stood there, holding the beets, and looked at him. "Mornin, Ote," she said at length.

He put one foot on the top step and leaned over so that his weight rested on his bent leg. "Where's Idelle?" he asked. "I'd like to speak to her a minute."

"Idelle ain't here," Mrs. Sheeler said.

He was startled. "Ain't here?" he repeated and then he remembered that there had been some talk of Lottie Wye's coming over. She must have come after he left and Idelle had gone home with her.

"Where is she?" he asked. "Did she go home with Lottie?"

Mrs. Sheeler continued to look at him. Her eyes, in the shadow of the deep sunbonnet, seemed larger and darker than usual. Light glinted in the pupils. He remembered that he had never liked the woman and that she had never liked him, from the first.

"Well, where is she?" he said impatiently.

"She went off with Buck," Mrs. Sheeler said slowly. "They didn't say where they was goin."

He brought his hand up, fist clenched. "You know, but you ain't tellin. Is that it?" he asked roughly and turned and made off down the road.

He went swiftly. As he came out of the shade of the grove he heard feet pattering behind him in the dust but he did not slow his pace. The feet pattered faster. A hand was laid on his arm. He shook it off without looking around. The boy, Random, ran out in front of him, capering a little. "I know whar they went, Ote," he cried. "I was here when they went off. They went to the court house. To git married."

Ote stood with his head lowered, glaring at the boy. "I don't believe it," he said.

The boy lifted a gleeful face. "I told him he better not git in your way. I told him you'd break ever bone in his body."

Ote raised his head. Before him the mock orange hedge stretched its dusty green, all the way to the big house. There was one break in it, where the gate was. They had gone out through that gate not an hour ago, maybe just a few minutes ago, while he was talking to Mister Ben. Here in the dust at his feet were the tracks of the car.

"What time did they say they was comin back?" he asked dully.

"Said they wouldn't be back before sundown," the boy answered. "Ote, what you goin to do to him?"

Ote raised a fumbling hand. "Go 'way, boy. I don't want to hurt you."

The boy looked at him. Suddenly he gave a queer cry, more animal than human, and darted off down the road.

Ote walked on. He came to the big house. At the back gate he paused. As his hand slowly lifted the chain off the nail he stared at the house. There was a little peak on one of the gables that he had never seen before. . . . It was fully a hundred feet from the smoke house to the back door. He would have said fifty if anybody had asked him.

Aunt Pansy came out of the house with a big pan in her hands. Her shrill cry rose on the air: "Chickee. . . . Chickee!"

Ote started as if somebody had struck him. He cut across the yard and entered the stable. It was dark in there and cool. He sat down on an up-ended barrel and sank his face in his hands. After a little he looked up. On one side of him was an old buggy and crowded in between that and the door was the mowing machine that Mister Ben had bought last summer. Above it there was a row of hooks. Gear hung on them, collars, extra hames, oddments of wire and leather. Beneath them something shone. Ote's gaze slipped down, found the iron ring on the tongue of the mower. His eyes travelled along the tongue, past the axle, past the wheels that still had some red paint on them, to the driver's seat. It was tilted back too far. Wallace Sheeler had fixed it that way last time he used it.

He looked at the machine a moment, then he rose and went ouside. He stared off across the pasture but after the half-dark of the stable everything was a blur of brownish green. He had to shade his bloodshot eyes with his hand before he could locate the mules resting in the shade of some willows. He went into the stable and pulled some ears of corn down out of the loft, then went forward across the pasture, holding the corn behind his back. As he approached the willows he let his hands swing forward with the ears of corn in them. His two mules came running. He tolled them back to the stable with the corn, flung the gear on them and hitched them to the mower.

The wheels rattled livelily as he rode out of the stable lot. He looked towards the house once but there was nobody in sight. He rode on down the lane and out into the open field. There were two acres of tobacco between him and the timothy. He drove the mower along the path at the side of the fence until he had passed the tobacco hills. At the edge of the hay field he got down off the mower. He thrust his hand in among the timothy and caught hold of one of the clover plants. He ran his hand down till he found the place just above the root where it branched. With one swift movement he jerked it out of the ground. It came out with the tap root almost whole. He held it before him for a second, then flung it from him and mounted the mower.

As he mounted he ran his eyes over the field. You could not see the clover anywhere. Before him there was only the timothy rippling in the wind. Pale green it was in most places but here and there it shaded off to brown. "Ought to been cut before this," he muttered through his clenched teeth.

He pulled on the lines and called to his team. "Giddap, you. Giddap!"

They moved forward at a smart pace. The well-oiled blade revolved easily. The hay fell to one side of him in shining swathes. He drove on to the end of the furrow, turned and started back. A figure had come in sight—a man making his way through the tobacco plants, heading for the hay field. Ote fixed his eyes on the moving, grass-covered blade and dove on. When he was halfway through the furrow he looked up. The man—it was Mister Ben—had come out on this side of the tobacco and was walking up to the edge of the hay field. As Ote came abreast of him Mister Ben put his hand up in a peremptory gesture. Ote looked him in the eyes but did not speak. He drove on, turned his mules again, and again started back. There was no sound but the clacking of the mower. But he could feel Mister Ben's eyes. They seemed to be fixed on a spot in the middle of his back. He stared in front of him but things blurred as they had blurred once before that morning. He drove on, seeing nothing but a mist of green, hearing nothing but the mower's clacking.

He came to the end of the row. He turned his mules slowly and started back. He had thought of Mister Ben as standing there where he had left him. But he had come out into the middle of the field. He stood in the very row that Ote was cutting. He wore no hat. His hands were folded across his chest. He fixed Ote with his eyes.

Ote slapped the line over the off mule's rump, so sharply that it cracked like a pistol shot. "Giddap!" he called, "Giddap!" The mules plunged forward. Ote leaped from the driver's seat and stood on the axle. "Git out of my way," he yelled furiously. "You git out of my way!"

Ben Allard moved aside but so slowly that the tip of the mower blade just missed him as it passed. The mules plunged forward. Ote braced himself with legs spread wide apart and pulled them up short. He got down off the mower. Mister Ben was coming towards him.

Ote bent and unhooked the single-tree from its ring. He held the stout oaken piece in his hand a moment, then whirled it and ran to meet Mister Ben.

Mister Ben stood there. His incrudulous eyes were fixed on Ote's face. Ote shouted at him and struck, putting all his force into the blow. Mister Ben went down upon a swathe of the new-mown hay, moved once and groaned, then was still.

Ote gazed stupidly at the bloody single-tree in his hand. He released it. It dropped into the clover. He looked at the prone figure on the ground and took a step backward. His eyes still fixed on the figure, he took another step and then he was running, slowly at first, then faster and faster, through the clover, towards the distant woods.

79
83
85
89